Zero Summer

Zero Summer

A novel

Jeremy Mark Robinson

CRESCENT MOON

CRESCENT MOON PUBLISHING
P.O. Box 393
Maidstone
Kent, ME14 5XU
United Kingdom

First published 2008.
© Jeremy Mark Robinson 2008.

Printed and bound in Great Britain.
Set in Book Antiqua, 10 on 14pt.
Designed by Radiance Graphics.

British Library Cataloguing in Publication data is available for this title

ISBN 1-86171-115-8
ISBN-13 978-1-86171-115-1

Note: The newspaper stories and extracts from magazines are from real newspaper and magazines. The information on nuclear war is accurate.

Contents

ONE

———

The Sun-Soaked Café

IT WAS ON a Summer's evening that we met.

Everything was full of light – the long, sloping light of Mid-West America. But in England. Into this golden light you walked. The seafront was deserted. Soft breezes blew in from the ocean. I had been living for days in the opulence of this water, this rich spice of water, heat, seagulls and wide-open spaces. Water washed our feet as we spoke on the sand. The sun was still hot. You were wearing a cotton Summer dress, white with green spots. I couldn't keep my eyes off you.

The day had begun with rain, I remember. Now the sky was turning lilac. In the heat of the day the beaches had been full of tourists and sun-bathers. Now it was teatime and Great Britain shuffled indoors, to eat, to flop down, to watch TV.

I was being my usual romantic self, wandering along the shore, enjoying the melancholy emptiness of the sunlit promenade. And *you* were there.

11

She stood in the satin-blue water. She was a creature of light, the low sun pouring through her. She was almost translucent. Children were playing nearby in the warm sand. A few bodies were still scattered about, sunning themselves. Music drifted from some hotel balcony. Waves hissed and recoiled. Boats slid across the horizon; enormous ferries headed for France.

Everything was throbbing with light. The brilliance was heavenly, apocalyptic. The trees, the sand, the water – all pulsated with light.

You were looking at me. I trembled, hypnotized. Already, you told me later, you were throwing yourself emotionally into the future, imagining your life with me. I wanted to kiss you, to embrace you.

You were there, right there; I couldn't believe it. I still can't believe it. I think we kissed immediately. Or perhaps we held hands first. Or did you speak?

That First Look of yours pierced me deep inside. Your astonishing eyes, made of gold and green and ochre, burst into my heart like the sun. Later, when we made a bushfire on the dunes, it was still your staring eyes that melted me.

You silver-girl, dredged up from the sea like a fish by the luminescence of the sun, dreamed-up by me in a fit of fever. I remember we kissed in a bliss of sunlight and everything was transformed into the radiance and hot breath of angels. My heart bled with the fantastic promise of a fabulous love. In light we danced inside each other. No, I'm kidding myself, it was really just an ordinary kiss (wasn't it?).

Pure passionate girl, with eyes brighter than the sun. A mermaid squirming into my life. Your love smashes all the boundaries between fear and desire. Push it out into eternity, you said. What? *Passion*.

'Let me take a photograph of your soul,' you said.

I was stunned as you fished out a battered camera and took a picture of me against a tree, in the last rays of the evening sun.

Then more kisses. Later, when we haunted the run-down fair-grounds and arcades, you were still snapping away.

We walked over to the phone box. She called it the 'rain-telephone' (I don't know why). I waited outside while she made a call.

Sun-soaked, life had become more magnetic. We sat in a twilit café. We talked. We kissed. We kissed and kissed and kissed. We talked, danced, laughed, kissed. I was utterly enchanted.

After those meetings in the *Café Twilight*, we'd saunter along the beach, shoes off, bare feet in the surf, entwined, kissing. We couldn't keep our hands or mouths off each other. The hot light of sunset bathed the world in the hues of amber, violet, indigo. Light breathed off the pavements, the sea walls, the windows, the store fronts. Cars in the distance glowed like fireflies. Neon signs shone with hot reds and golds. The giggles of girls and the hoots of boys on the prowl. Everything was soaked in the intense heat of Summer – an endless Indian Summer that seemed better than every other Summer.

Keeling over with love, with the ecstasy of skin touching skin. There was an openness to everything, to everybody, to every object.

Even the surly voyeurs and vultures, scavenging the beach with their binoculars and metal detectors, seemed happy. Soaked in love, you can believe anything is possible, even cheering up the chronically miserable.

It was passion for the moment and the moment lasted forever. Love span us out into timelessness. I still believe that.

Caught in the glare of a car headlamp her eyes shone strangely. In the blue gloom of night her skin glowed darkly, blacker than the sky. There was no nostalgia: life was unfurling itself quite naturally.

Her version of our first meeting differs from mine. She told me she had met me before, in Alienation City (London). These are her words:

'I was wandering around one of the big old museums in South Kensington on a wet Wednesday afternoon in Winter. I had the place to myself. After looking at the dinosaur bones and the cases of insects, and standing in the giant model womb with its seven-foot foetus and roaring sound effects simulating uterine life, I wandered into the Whale Hall. Tape recordings of whalesong were playing to the vast, empty space. Suspended under the dusty glass ceiling were life-size models of all kinds of whales and dolphins. It was like a massive aviary. The air was full of these gorgeous cetaceans, leaping and flying, yet all so strangely frozen, caught in a web of wires and posts. And all the time this melancholy wailing of dolphins and whales was echoing around.

'I climbed up onto the balcony around the edge of the gallery. I thought I was alone – so I was startled to see a figure at the end of the walkway. You were leaning against the railing, completely mesmerized by the astonishing sounds of the whales. In the dim light I saw a screen behind you showing slides of the underwater animals, so beautiful yet so enigmatic.

'I watched you for some time, looking at the dark blue photographs of shadows in the sea, listening to the ghostly noises, and looking up at the frozen forms of the fish all about me.

'When you turned to look at me I felt I was disturbing some secret ritual. You later told me you often stood there; it was your favourite place in the museum. I could see why.

'I wanted to have you.

'When we met by the telephone kiosk on the seafront I could see you didn't remember me. After I'd called my father we went to a dingy café. I knew we would make love that night.'

The first time we made love I remember the rain-telephone ringing in the empty call box. We walked on past it. In the purple light of dusk we made love on the sand, hidden by dunes. I remember the smell of her skin, the salty taste of her arms. Sand, sky, air, clouds, bodies, scents – all these things mingled into one.

Her mouth was so soft, eating mine like a fruit, piece by piece, lick by lick. I ached inside. The ecstasy of her touches. There was a continuous explosion of joy inside me. Beauty, power, passion and magic.

The beam of the distant lighthouse swept the bay every few seconds, the white ray gliding over the sand like a lost angel.

She told me 'Love is the most astonishing experience ever to hit planet Earth.' I remember that, at least.

Her father lived in London. She wouldn't tell me what he did exactly. I gathered he was in politics.

The first night we made love was the first night of the big riots. Six British cities had gone mad. Riots were nothing new: it was the size of the madness that was extraordinary.

Like me she was working part-time over the Summer in the seaside resort. We quit our crummy jobs instantly (she was waiting tables; I was delivering pizzas). We wanted us to spend all our time together.

Somehow we had decided to travel around the South Coast of Britain: Folkestone, Hastings, Brighton, Bournemouth, Sidmouth, Exeter. Big cities were to be avoided at all costs; we hoped to skirt them. The riots were so savage no one went out at night; a self-imposed curfew.

Cornwall was our goal. We remembered it from holidays in childhood, and wanted to return there.

The bliss of the day lingered on far into the night. The crescent of the New Moon hung behind her head as she kissed me, the silver sickle twisted in her hair. Ecstasy in seconds, with Venus so bright at twilight.

We lay under westering stars. We were going to follow the stars, to run West with them through the decayed towns of Albion

15

before the 'big firework', as the girl put it.

She picked up a peach and said 'Look at this, look at this colour, this texture.' Often she'd pick up bits of seaweed or stones, and muse over them; or she'd stare into a rockpool for hours. Through her I began to see differently. Nothing was beyond her fascination. Bananas, peaches, apples, strawberries – she loved all kinds of fruit. She loved plants – not flowers so much, but plants. She would study the broad-leaved plants on the promenade for ages, losing herself in the green shadows.

'I love Kew Gardens and the Botanical Gardens in Oxford,' she said, murmuring more to herself than me. 'Especially in the rain, in May, when everything's bursting with life. Some of the Palm Houses are so humid, so full of moisture. You sweat like mad. It's very erotic.'

When she said things like that I wanted to grab her, to squeeze her so tightly. She laughed, slipping away and running into the amusement arcades. I followed her, moving from the blue night into the green and red flashing lights of the busy, noisy arcades. They were full, as usual, of disaffected young males punching and shouting at bits of simulated reality, while skinny girls in jeans and croptops looked on, bored, smoking.

I found the girl dropping bombs over a desert. She turned and kissed me, stroking her hand against the front of my shorts. I grinned, remembering how she had knelt over me the night before, pressing me inside, her hair wild, above her a vast array of Summer stars.

Scream it all up inside me, I thought. This is bliss, this is such magnificent bliss. The velvet sky beyond her, the constellations and planets tangled in her hair.

She turned back to her video game and decimated a couple of Middle Eastern oil fields. Then she said, gleefully:

'I love destroying the world, boy!'

We took the train to Dover, after a long wait at the station. Trains were still just about running. I looked out as England slipped past the windows: the Valley of a Thousand Deaths. No, make that sixty million.

The night before we had walked through the coach park behind the fairground. Some blurred movements in one of the bus windows made us stop and look inside. A couple were rutting away at the back. A drunk snored on the luggage rack above the seats. A bland boy with bleached hair entered the bus and spoke to us: 'Want some shit?'

'No thanks,' I replied. The air smelt of 1967. But the girl pushed past me to join in. OK, I thought.

We slept in the coach. The other derelicts were still out of it when we left. I picked up a newspaper lying on one of the seats:

Dead Sheep – Saudi Arabia – A freighter hit by rockets in the Gulf on Wednesday docked here with 3,000 of its 40,000 sheep cargo burned to death.
Massachusetts – A forklift truck operator who fell into a ten-foot pile of frozen cranberries died struggling to free himself from the mountain of fruit that buried him.

Easy to imagine the fate of the forklift truck driver: one minute you're up on the gangway, minding your own business. Then you slip, try to grab the handrail, but miss, and fall into the pile of frozen fruit. You struggle and yell, but sink slowly deeper. (But where the hell were his buddies?).

The girl was asleep beside me on the train. I stroked her hair on my shoulder. She murmured. The train jolted to another stop, in the English fields somewhere between stations. We were alone in the carriage. The door burst open and in climbed a hulk in a dark green mackintosh, from the tracks below. He said hello and sat opposite us.

This has always intrigued me: why is it, when faced with a whole empty carriage, people always sit right next to you? The man introduced him as Furheil. Once I'd spoken, that was his cue to begin.

'Did you ever hear of the Geothermal Disaster?' he asked me.

I shook my head, hoping he wasn't a total loony, and unable to move because the girl seemed deeply sleep.

In a peculiar Russian accent the man went on:

'Last month a team of Russian climatologists and geologists took off in a plane bound for Uzbekisthan. They flew over Tashkent from Volgograd, into the Red and Black Deserts. I went with them as a geologist and photographer. We were investigating massive earthquake activity combined with the discovery by satellite of a new, gigantic source of geothermal energy – according to the scientists in Moscow.

'We drove out to the site. It was a great hole in the Earth. Not volcanic, not a meteorite. It had just appeared.'

Furheil looked excited. The girl had slowly woken up. The afternoon was wearing on, and the train still hadn't moved an inch.

I yawned. 'Well?'

'There was talk of plate tectonics, solar energy, oceanic chemistry, climatic curves and all that. Then we saw these very strange markings on the sides of the fissure. I wanted to get some pictures sent back to Moscow, but Marquand, our boss, threw my cameras into the abyss. "No pictures," he shouted. The truth is, they were into big business, and reckoned there was an unlimited store of energy down there.

'Anyway, the next morning we climbed a little way down the hole. Below, it was all black, just dust and a foul smell. As soon as we started to set up our instruments, we felt an enormous quake, very high on the seismometer.

'Chazan kept on about tectonic plates. "Perhaps in 250 millions years all the continents of the world will move back together, forming a New Pangæa. One island, one sea." This was all very reassuring. Marquand talked about the Tungaska meteorite. On a night in 1908 the whole of Europe had been illuminated by silver clouds, bright enough to read by.

'On the last day, we still didn't know what was down there.

Marquand took the others down again. I stayed in the truck. They'd been down about an hour when a duststorm blew up. You couldn't see a thing, just a brown blur. I kept in contact with them by radio. They were roped together, I think, about three hundred feet below the surface of the desert. Sand was pouring onto them. Marquand ordered them to climb down further. They found a cave. The rocks came crashing down, as a minor earthquake hit us. I was stuck in the truck, embedded in the sand. Chazan kept talking to me on the radio. He was scared, so he told me stupid facts to while away the time before the support team could reach us.

'"The deepest ocean trenches are 36,000 feet deep," he said. "The largest tidal wave ever was about 112 feet high." After that I heard some screams. A load of rocks had fallen and sealed off the cave. Marquand was dead, as were Lotianu and Kovachev. Chazan was in shock, choking and babbling to himself. I heard everything. He was alone in there. He found a crack and clambered out to the fissure, onto a ledge above the bottomless crevasse. He fell asleep for a while. It was now night. Then the radio came on for one last time.

'"There is a white light down here," he told me in a hoarse whisper. "Nothing but white," he said. Then nothing. The radio went dead.

'I had to wait a whole day before they dug me out of the truck. There was no sign of the others. We never found their bodies.'

Furheil went quiet. The girl got up, leaned out of the window.

'And?' she asked.

Furheil lit a cigarette. 'Well, it could have been an old nuclear device, from the days of the underground tests. Or perhaps it is the planet getting aggravated with us.'

'What do you think it was?' I asked Furheil; I was fascinated.

The train jolted, and moved off. We changed trains at Dover. In the harbour we saw the huge rusting hulls of the cross-channel ferries. This was the busiest time of year, but the ships lay lifeless in the port. The apathy on the streets was intense. Towards dusk our train braked sharply.

We looked out of the window. A bonfire had been lit on the tracks. Vandals on the embankments gawped and threw stones. A weary announcement told us to abandon the train. We stayed on it. The lights went out.

I fell asleep and woke to find the girl licking me. She squeezed my balls until I erupted in her mouth. She slid a finger inside me, caressing me back and forth. She held my wrists above my head and straddled me slowly. She kissed me, tonguing the sperm into my mouth. I gasped.

It was raining softly outside. Still rocking gently over me, she lit a cigarette and we shared it.

We slept in the train. Around midnight a thug crept through the train, disturbing us. He looked like he was going to try something. The girl told him to piss off. He hesitated, then carried on up the carriage.

The train didn't move the next morning. We saw why: a mass of rubble and trash had been dumped onto the line. A bleary-eyed railway worker in an orange coat picked at the junk. In a mound of newspapers I saw the headlines 'BOMBS BLACK OUT LIMA' and 'WORKER WINS PAYOUT FOR LOST SEX LIFE'.

There were also headlines about many hunger strikes in prisons. The girl wondered:

'You have hunger and water strikes, so can you have you a 'sex strike'? You tell the world you're not going to have sex for a month. Wow! Nobody listens. How babyish men are, acting just like little babies. Oh look Mummy, they say to the world, I'm not going to eat anymore! Big deal.'

The girl frowned. 'By the way, I'm *starving*. Have we got any more of those tinned peaches left?'

TWO

─────

The Submarine Silos

THE GIRL WAS pure mystery to me. I knew nothing about her. The childhood in Oxford, London, Germany. The many schools. The Easter trip to Italy. On one of the lakes in Tuscany in a rowing boat, when she was fourteen, a boy had touched her, sliding his fingers inside her.

She remembered a lack of affection from her father – he was the classic distant father (her mother left when she was young). She recalled the rain and the forests of Germany, roads of endless trees, and living behind the fences of military establishments. The British kids hung around in groups, not mixing with the locals. They knew more American soldiers than German citizens. They developed their own secret culture, which grew into a peculiar Britishness of ex-pats and exiles.

The girl still saw her father occasionally. She wanted so much to talk to him, but when she saw him she couldn't speak. When he was there, right in front of her, she couldn't say a word (and he wouldn't open up). I sensed she was full of yearning, but for what I didn't know.

The girl was restless. At times she couldn't keep her limbs still. She was full of tensions. She seemed incredibly mature to me, so sophisticated in her thoughts. She seemed to live at a higher level or a deeper level than me. She made me feel inadequate, yet she was so unself-conscious. She was the most spontaneous person I'd ever met. But she could be very difficult, obstinate, vicious, stupid. I hated it when she went silent, and wouldn't talk to me.

In the dingy bed and breakfast hotel on the South Coast that morning I had had a strange dream. As soon as I met the girl I began to have bizarre dreams. This one I called *'The Clown School':*

'I was walking in a Russian city. You were there beside me. So many hungry people about. We stood outside the Winter Palace and it snowed into our upturned faces. We kissed. A famous film star passed us by. We walked along the Neva. We went to the Red Square. We queued up to see Lenin.

'Remember the Clown School, Ilyich?' you murmured as we filed past the embalmed body of the messiah. Darkness outside. I had my third finger inside you. You jerked your legs open on my chest. I was amazed at the amount of wetness pouring from you. You giggled, a Moscow schoolgirl.

You met some friends and talked about ballet, theatre, music and painting. We sat on a bus. We were going to the Clown School. The passion-sun was trying to melt the snow. I had my fingers inside you again, on the tram.

At the Clown School they loved you. Clowns in white, green, red. You danced with them. I wanted you madly and dragged you in a sleigh to a distant snowbound log cabin, deep in the snowscape between Kazan and Saransk. We had a bed, a sofa, a fridge, even a record player. Our appartment overlooked the river. We stayed there all Winter. We heard wolves howling.'

I woke up. You were staring at me.

A white pane of glass behind you made me think we were still in Russia, still in my dream.

'Come on,' you said. 'We're going to the dockyard today.'

Huge ships lay rotting in the slipways of the disused dockyard like dinosaurs, their hulls covered in mud, barnacles and debris. In an office we passed a radio spoke: "The streets of London are full of litter, whole streets. The East End is twenty feet under refuse."

Somewhere offshore, out of sight, a cargo ship was trying to make radio contact. The docks were deserted; a helicopter buzzed overhead.

In the empty café we found a sulky man who sold us some bitter coffee and stale bread rolls. You read the *Daily Bullshit* while I stole some oranges from the counter when the man left us.

New Line in Burglary – Burglars ran up a 30,000 dollar phone bill after breaking into an empty house.
Boy dies on roof of train – A youth was found dying on the roof of a train after horrified passengers saw streams of blood pouring down the windows.

In Elizabethan times these slipways and docks rang to the sound of a nation constructing a naval fleet to arm itself against the Spanish and the Dutch. Now the place was as desolate as a planet in *Star Trek*. The passion-soaked girl was wearing only a long yellow T-shirt and trainers.

Words cannot capture the hot magnetism of those glory days. Two fishes out of water, drunk on each other's love, we roved the landscape like maniacs, feeding off society as it dislocated itself. In our lovescape *everything* was transformed. Get on with the detonation, I thought.

In the bushes insects buzzed; cicadas kept up a constant din. The whole insect life of Britain had been transformed after years of global warming, not to mention plants and crops.

It was scorching noon. The place was beautiful in its desuetude. The colossal wooden hangars had the outlines of boats

23

drawn on the floor. The run-down workrooms were full of dust drifting languidly in the sunlight. Amongst this bright isolation the girl stripped off her T-shirt and lay on a towel. I left her sunning herself to walk further along the coast, next to the estuary.

Here was nothing but waste ground. In the silence I moved across the rubble into the hangars. They were cool and perfectly dry. At the far end was a massive wall of glass, the group of rectilinear panes looking like some mid-20th century abstract painting. Stepping over railway lines and heaps of smashed machines and cardboard boxes, I made my way further into the giant halls of construction.

Then I saw the submarine silos.

The wet docks sloped downwards into the estuary. They were dammed up. In the middle of the last one lay one of the most extraordinary structures I'd ever seen: a huge submarine shaped like a whale. Constructed out of bits of old ships, trucks, cranes and numerous irregular sheets of rusting metal, it looked like something out of Leonardo da Vinci's wilder notebooks. I studied it carefully. Yes, there definitely were fins, a tail and a great mouth. The whole thing must have been forty feet long.

I walked back up the hangar. I noticed a ramshackle caravan to one side. As I got closer I saw a figure inside, hunched over a pair of binoculars. He had his hand inside his trousers. Photos from scientific and pornographic magazines were pinned to the wall behind him.

As I backed away I stumbled. The man turned to glare at me. He started shouting. Gradually I managed to calm him down a little.

'I've seen your sub,' I said.

He froze. He stopped spitting and hissing.

'My whale? What do you know about whales?' He shuffled out of the caravan, peering at me suspiciously. He was a decrepit old thing, in his sixties, with a wrinkled, sneering face that had known decades of loneliness.

I told him what little I knew – about the peace organizations, about saving the whales and returning them to the deep waters. The girl walked up, attracted by the shouts. The man looked warily at her. He had been looking at her through his binoculars as she sunbathed nude.

'It's bin difficult findin' out information on whales,' he muttered, 'wiv the libraries all closed down.'

He was trying to build a whale, he explained. He loved submarines. 'When they go down, when they go down,' he kept repeating to himself.

'Will you show it to us?' asked the girl.

The man looked at her as if she were an alien. He probably hadn't been that close to a young woman for months. He nodded. We followed him to the dank silo. He was ecstatic at having an audience for his machine. Men need their mirrors, the girl said afterwards.

We climbed down the ladder into the dock. On the other side of the iron dam I heard the water of the incoming tide lapping gently. The girl kept close to me.

The man stalked across the wooden boards around the machine, muttering to himself, grinning, patting the metal whale.

'I'm launching her tomorrer,' he said, 'wiv Dave an' Fred.'

We left him as dusk fell; he was still fiddling with his whale-boat. I promised to return, to see the launch. The girl wanted to press on, to the West. The man was a creep, she said. A weirdo.

Sure, I said, but what an idea! I had to see this wild machine float. We sat on the quay for a long time, listening to the police sirens far away, over the estuary, and watching the plumes of black smoke rising from the tower blocks.

That night I dreamt of the man, Trenchard, working below the geosync line.

In the morning we sidled into the dockyard under thin cloud. The whale-machine wasn't quite ready. Trenchard was buzzing with incoherent enthusiasm. Dave and Fred, his grizzled buddies, sat on some oil drums, smoking roll-ups, watching the old man's obsessive behaviour. Knee-deep in mud, Trenchard was painting eyes and teeth on the head of his whale.

'What d'you fink?' he asked us.

I smiled. 'Great.'

The girl watched as I helped Trenchard fix up his beloved metallic monster. He was very thorough, like all psychotics. It had to be just right, just perfect. I wondered if he had fantasized about the girl last night. Every time she said something his head jerked up like a dog's on a leash. After an hour we slipped away for some food.

'What a jerk. That wreck! It's never going to float! Ishtar, at least my pictures should be good.'

The girl had been taking lots of photographs. But she never printed them. Instead she sent them away – to London, I think, to her father. She laughed, kissed me. She was delicate as a star, delicious as an angel. I put my hand under her T-shirt and caressed her nipples.

We ate in a seedy snack bar in one of the side streets leading off the dockyard.

Trenchard's ambition was to catch a whale. The girl was laughing.

'He wants to capture a whale so's he can drag it up the silo and take measurements – that's what he told you, isn't it?' The girl shook her head, giggling as she bit into a sandwich.

Back at the dockyard there was no sign of Trenchard in the caravan, or around the silo. The dock itself was full of water and mud; the gates were half-open – just enough room for the whale machine to squeeze through. Fred and Dave were clearing away some trash. They waved.

'Hey, Fred. What happened? Did it float? Has he gone?'

'Yep. He's gone. 'Bout half hour ago,' Fred grunted, and spat out some tobacco. 'The thing floated, yeah. And it sunk too. It went under away over there, beyond the lighthouse.'

Dave pointed past the tide gate to the open sea beyond the estuary. 'You won't see him again.'

THREE

The Fairground

BREATHLESS NIGHTS DOWN by the ocean, looking for a place to contain us and our lust. As the nights got shorter towards High Summer they began to tingle with electricity. Hordes of people about. One last grasp for pleasure before the Final Countdown. The town was charged-up and ready to burn. Everyone was out, down at the beach, milling around.

Hot, happy and ignited by this sudden inrush of faces and smells, we dived into the fray. The whole place was buzzing. The arcades were full of hundreds of kids pumping money into machines, faces glowing red in the neon. The cacophony of hisses, clicks and whirrs from the video games was glorious.

The fairgrounds of Britain still held their olde worlde charm. Carnival time on the Ghost Trains, Big Wheels, Waltzers and Dodge 'Ems. Candyfloss stuck to our lips. The smell of toffee apples and waffles seduced our senses. A sugar rush. I was dazzled by the multi-coloured lights. The energy of the sun had burnt into them. They whirled and flashed crazily. The funfair was full of every type of subculture: hippies, punks, rockabillies, soulboys, mods, teds, heavy metal freaks, New Age travellers, ravers, rappers. At the top of the Big Wheel you could see the deep blue ocean beyond the glow of the lights.

Kissing and squeezing each other on the Waltzers we felt like little kids. Girls screamed, while the boys tried to look cool sitting on the wooden fences. The romance of the sideshows, the arcades, the stalls and the rides swallowed me whole. The swirl of noise and light was intoxicating. On the bumper cars we were drenched in ancient rock 'n' roll hits: *All Shook Up, Papa's Got a Brand New Bag, Locomotion, Rave On, Voodoo Chile, Tiger Feet.* All life seemed to be twistin' 'n' jivin' 'n' walkin' 'n' dancin'. I didn't want to leave.

Behind the fairground we made love viciously. She started by licking my ears and neck. I squirmed. She rubbed her mound on my thigh. Reaching round her, I felt her wetness, pulling her buttocks apart and pressing a thumb inside her. She gasped when I brushed her clitoris and pushed harder on my thigh. Her mouth was bigger than the ocean, sucking me in. Shuddering in orgasm, she grasped me tightly. I pulsed in her fist, suddenly, coming over her belly and fingers. She laughed. We heard screams and shouts from the fairground. Then police sirens. Someone crashed through the bushes near us, yelling.

A riot was on. The clans were clashing on the seafront. The more organized gangs were chanting and saluting. I remembered once seeing a group of skinheads nazi-saluting on the statue of Eros in Piccadilly, at the heart of the British Empire. The promenade was a mass of blue police lights. A water-cannon started spraying the crowd. Thugs lashed out with bottles, knives, baseball bats and one or two axes. The subcultures seemed to group together: the New Agers, hippies and ravers were pitted against the hip-hoppers, heavy rockers, chavs and skins.

We were about to leave when someone from the surging crowd called out to the girl. It was Kaspar, a black friend of the girl's in his mid-twenties. He wore a leather jacket sprayed with political slogans, and plenty of studs and piercings. He was very excited.

'Two pigs are dead,' he told us, 'an' I know who did it.'

I saw the headline: TWO POLICE DEAD IN BRIGHTON RIOT.

'You'd better watch it, Kaspar,' said the girl. 'It's two weeks before the Attack, and this is the time the security services will be rounding up all political 'subversives', 'dissidents' and 'extremists', like after 9/11. Special Branch might be booting down your door when you get back to your squat.'

Kaspar swore, laughed, and lurched back into the rioting throng. The girl told me he was some kind of radical activist. He had started up a political pirate radio station in London. He liked to 'kick heads' as he called it.

'His mob probably killed those two policemen,' the girl added. 'Asshole cop killers. He's wired on amphetamines at the moment. I went out with him once when I was fifteen. He used to call for me on roller skates and take me to a junkyard where he could grope me in private.'

The violence of the riot exhilarated us. We couldn't sleep. I felt hot and itchy, as if I had a fever. We drank bottles of water. We stank of sex. The girl lay over me for ages, moving back and forth slowly over my mouth. We lay within earshot of the sea, under our one blanket, the sound of the waves muffled by her smooth thighs.

Sometimes we'd just lie for hours, hardly moving. I was hypnotized. Never have I been so soaked in another person, so amazingly drenched in someone else. With a little smile she'd pull off her T-shirt and rub her breasts over my chest, smiling. Inside, I'd be aching over something fabulous.

We'd spend hours just kissing softly. Tongues licking, or just teeth, or just lips. Her mouth was so delicious, with full lips and a hot tongue. It was like making love to an angel, there on the beach. Strollers on the sidewalk would see only a couple lying together, not really moving. We'd be oblivious, in ecstasy. We lay in a soporific state, an exquisite torpor, a delicious languor. The rhythm of the sea became the rhythm of our love-making. The night, the stars, the sea, her body, the funfair, the revellers, the rioters – all this fused together.

I looked at her: she lay back, eyes closed, gasping quietly, her thighs spread so wide. She was so open and hot and wet. She was the most beautiful soul. For a long, long, slow time we kissed, while I stroked her clitoris, her head cradled under my other arm. I knelt down and licked her, dipping my tongue deeper between her labia on each pass from ass to clitoris. She was so sensitive along her perineum.

I loved to lick my tongue very gently along the shaft of her clit, along the edge of the tiny hood, up the stem, and back down to the divine sphere. Her favourite was soft, wet and wide splays of me tongue across the width of her clit, in gentle circles.

'Oh babe,' she murmured.

Her smell engulfed me. She gripped my head, pulling me deep inside her, and then deeper again. We lavished, ravished, languished in the deliquescence of bliss.

Sometimes we were so absolutely passionate I thought the rocks around us would ignite. Every touch hurt. We were *astonishing*.

Sometimes I couldn't move I was so entranced. We had passionate passion-passion. The girl was voluptuous, so succulent. The near-quarter moon rose over an ocean tinged with the gleam of archangels. She kicked me for a six when she kissed me. I was knocked flat when she came out with phrases like:

'Only you can make every tiny part of me feel such a degree of pain, joy, warmth, melancholy, exhaustion, love.'

Or, when waking up after an afternoon's drowse, I'd find a note saying:

I'm wearing my short skirt and T-shirt. I'm very sleepy and you could make me come very quickly. I wish you would.

Such gorgeous words would make me hot and hard, tingling

for the moment when she'd return from the stores or the toilets. She'd flip up her shirt, and press a nipple into my mouth.

The girl would devastate me when she murmured things like 'No one else on this planet can have such an effect on me.' Or: 'I'm wearing your shirt today. It's nice to feel something of yours close to me.'

These words burnt into me like the noonday sun.

'Even when I'm hurting you I'm loving you.' Why did everything she say sound right, so authentic?

A note under a half-drunk bottle of red wine:

I want you now, this instant! Please, please let me hold you when I see you. I want to love you forever. I'm sorry about our stupid argument. Sometimes I can't express myself.

But I thought she was the most eloquent being I'd met.

'I want to hold you gently and to kiss you so softly. It makes me ache,' she said.

She wrote to me:

You want to know what I'd do with you? I'd lie with you under a silver sky, surrounded by treasures – stars, candles, birds, fish, mermaids, witches, in a magic circle. Then I'd bring you so close and love you until I'd be lost in you and you in me. I would show you EVERYTHING.

I want you to let go with me. Oh yes! You hypnotize me, fill me, lull me, caress me inside so I lose all boundaries. I spill over and flow all over you. I drown you and fill you up. I am expanding. I can feel my wings stretching out, touching new places.

Jesus, that sun. You fucker, spilling oil all over me, rubbing juice into my belly, me straining and shaking with such rapture. Christ, you mad girl, thrashing around on top of me, you're so wet, so painful, you ridiculous girl, with your shining dark eyes and body made in heaven. I held your elbows, blood racing, pounding you, coming in floods, like the sun, the rain, you rain-drenched sweet-wet girl. Whirl your hurricane arms above me, block out the starlight and the stormlight, you've got the afterglow of the sun between your legs. Swim over me, in me, fill me with melon seeds and wine, your arms a crucifix of passion, your legs gripped in mine, so lustful, so beyond-words, you astonish me.

The sound of the sea was the accompaniment to our journey. If we couldn't hear it we got anxious. The sound of the ocean is one of those primal sounds – like the wind in the trees, or a baby crying. You can't resist such sounds. They speak to the deepest part of you.

On our way to Southampton we stopped in a small roadside bar. We had been hitching but were now walking. Over a ham sandwich we watched a lunchtime TV programme on channel 8 or 24, I forget which. There was news of fuel and food shortages; some petrol stations had been 'frozen'. Certain official groups (like doctors, police) were given priority. Shell, BP, Mobil, Texaco and Esso were trying to enforce their emergency policy. But the official word hadn't come from the government yet.

An oil pipeline had been sabotaged between Wymondham and Thetford. The screen showed thousands of gallons of crude oil gushing out – all those billions of petro-dollars.

People were fleeing the South-East for Wales and the West Country – images of traffic jams, and stationary cars that couldn't get any more petrol. Cars were pushed off the road, while others were set alight by vandals.

Russian ships were circling gas platforms in the North Sea. Troops were building up on the NATO borders in Europe. Schools and colleges were closing, some of their premises being requisitioned for the emergency services.

The newscast ended with an odd item. A journalist called Julia Smith was telling how she had been pestered on the telephone by a strange man. Eventually the caller was traced to a derelict Fleet Street newspaper office. Julia went there, and met Izimbard Rahn, the day before he committed suicide.

Izimbard Rahn was an old press baron, an archetypal press lord – the cigars, the fat balding head, the expensive suits, the extravagances and the many rumours surrounding his private life – divorces, affairs, prostitutes, under-age sex, homosexuality, frauds, drugs, the usual smut. He ran the *Daily Planet* newspaper, from the ancient offices in Fleet Street (he'd moved the operation back from the Docklands area). His multi-channel television empire spread over four continents. Julia Smith's newspaper, *Daily Trash*, was in search of some good stories.

'Everything's been done, been written, been published,' said Smith on TV. 'But then I started getting these strange phone calls.' There were some shots of Smith's apartment next – on the eighth floor of a bland 1980s block. 'A man kept ringing me, bugging me, just like in those old American TV thrillers. He said, and these are his exact words: "I've got the secrets of psychosis". He said exactly that.'

Cut to shots of Smith on the streets of old London town. She got the call traced to Fleet Street. Sensing a story, she decided to visit the place alone. As she walked up the old Art Deco building with its big globe in the entrance hall, she thought of the man's words: "I've got the infinity of desire in me".

'I kept thinking as I climbed the stairs of the headlines for tomorrow: MANIAC CARVES UP JOURNALIST. I knew I was being stupid.'

The old *Daily Planet* headquarters were empty, it seemed. Smith used to work there. She recalled the days when they used to discuss gossip, current affairs, sex, money, cars, celebrities. Those were the days when news had to be 'sexy' to get printed at all.

'You wouldn't believe the things that were said in those old 1930s newspaper buildings. Such cruel words, such venom,' Smith said. The TV showed shots of the building, the desolate interior, the peeling posters. Smith remembered the old names of the newspaper world: Dick Johnson, Ross Rockwell, Ed Gardner, Robin Spears, Izimbard Rahn.

'I knew he'd be up on the top floor, the executive floor,' said Smith. The TV camera showed us the room. It was completely covered in newspapers. There were newspapers on the floor, the walls, the ceiling, stuck on with glue.

'In the middle of all this,' said Smith on the soundtrack, 'sat an old man. I couldn't see much in the light of the candles. I remember his cold eyes gleaming. I knew he couldn't harm me. I knew what he wanted – to talk.'

Smith was repulsed by this decrepid creature sitting in the middle of the vast newspaper-covered room.

'Hello, Julia,' said the freak. She switched on her tape recorder. The voice-over intercut Smith's tape with her commentary.

'That's it,' the man said softly, 'get it all *down*.'

'He sounded like a serpent,' said Julia.

'I used to be in newspapers,' said Rahn. 'Ah yes, I used to deliver the goods every night. The empire of the journalist takes in the whole world, doesn't it, Julia?' He went on babbling for some time. 'Lies on top of more lies! Such mediation, eh, Julia?' And so on.

Smith was getting ready to run. 'Just one picture, sir, for the records?' she asked him. He nodded. She took a very bright flash photograph. Cut on the TV to the picture: it was extraordinary – that forlorn fat figure in the middle of all those ancient, yellowed newspapers.

After the picture the telephone rang. Rahn picked it up and snarled some obscenity into it. Then he said to Smith:

'Look at all these great stories around us, Julia. So many stories, so much print! I was Lord of it all, for a while. Power, that's what it's all about. So much *kultur* – reach for your gun, Julia.'

Rahn was decaying psychically before her very eyes. He shuffled on his knees to find a story.

Stockholm – A naked man drifting on a latrine door was rescued from a lake in Sweden. He was stranded on a small island when his boat drifted away. So he unhitched the latrine door and took off his clothes to keep them dry during an unsuccessful attempt to pursue his boat.

Rahn laughed manically. 'I like that one a lot.'

'Goodbye,' whispered Smith, and ran.

The communications landscape was dead, she said. Forget the internet, style, spin, marketing, computers, satellites, the digital realm. It was dead long before the war. The headline the next day ran PRESS BARON RAHN SUICIDE. Smith got her story after all.

We left the sandwich bar. 'What a strange story,' the girl said after a while. 'I think I've met Julia Smith. She was a friend of my father's.'

The girl kept amazing me. 'What does your father do?' I asked. He seemed to know everybody.

'You wouldn't want to know. You wouldn't like it.'

Half-an-hour later I said something stupid about her and she flew at me:

'You may mock my naïvety and ignorance but I have experienced things you'll never experience. I feel stronger through you. I enjoy you. Don't underestimate me, boy; I've got more than you think.'

At times like these I realized she had an extraordinary rage inside her. Certainly more powerful than any atomic bomb. Her every movement entranced me. She confused me, abused and delighted me. If we suffocated each other, fine. We loved the intensity. For now, it was glorious.

FOUR

The Travelling Circus

WE RAN INTO the travelling circus on our way out of Southampton. We'd hitched a lift with a bigoted remnant from previous wars, a seventy-two year-old grump in tweeds. He had a lot to say about the present world conflict. He was bitter. He was one of those car drivers who hate everything in front of them, behind them, and on every side. He moaned at the slow traffic ahead, caused by the circus convoy. He probably played Wing Commander Smythe to his wife's W.A.A.F. at home. A neat little bungalow on a peaceful suburban estate; perfectly mown lawn; tins arranged label-out in the cupboard.

I looked at the familiar countryside between Southampton and Bournemouth. I knew the area quite well, from childhood. I thought of my mother on the other side of Winchester, living in that tiny house on Salisbury Plain.

'Bloody gypsies,' hissed the man as we slowed to make way for the circus. Traffic was at a standstill. We got out and walked up the convoy, past trucks, wagons, horses, winnebagos and caravans. It began to move, slowly, at a horse's pace. I was amazed the horses had enough food with the shortages (there had been rumours of stables being raided for horsemeat).

'Southampton was a flop,' said one of the trapeze artists who climbed down from a truck to walk beside us while he smoked. 'No one was interested in having a good time.'

Toni was a boozy entertainer in his late forties who told us about France. 'I was in Provence last year. It was marvellous. I've been to Russia with the Circus. They love it there.' He told us about the storm at Avignon, during the Festival. 'The animals went mad.'

His wife, leaning out of the truck window, chimed in. 'It'll never be like the old days, like Moscow. Things were grander then. One of the monkeys died, last night.'

She talked about some of her friends in the truck beside her: Frau G, a fortune-teller; a lion-tamer from Rome; two Cockney clowns.

After two miles, a man on stilts strode up the caravan of dreams, informing everyone that they had reached their campsite. It was then I saw someone I knew.

'Christine!' I was amazed to see her there. She was doing a story for the local newspaper in Southampton.

'Isn't this great?' she grinned, 'this big Circus, full of colour and life, while the country collapses.' She was clearly enjoying herself. Toni twigged that we were travelling.

'Stay with us at the camp,' he said.

So we stayed the night with the Circus. The encampment was an eye-opener: dwarfs, magicians, clowns, jugglers, animals and dancers wandered about. Hundreds of kids were playing in between the vehicles. It was a city in miniature. The fires blazed, lighting up the fir trees. It was a cold, cloudy night, and we were glad to hunker down by the fires.

'We had a lot of abuse in Southampton,' said Toni. 'We had gangs coming to the Circus to jeer – calling us Jews, German bastards, you know.'

We knew. 'Part of the tent was set on fire,' he said. 'The world crisis brings out the worst in people, as well as the best. It's like the Second World War all over again.'

It was very dark when we left the fires and circles of downcast faces to find the back of the truck Toni had kindly leant us. The girl shivered under the blankets. The sky was already lightening.

The girl wanted to know who Christine was. I told her I had gone out with her, once, in London.

'I don't want to know. You don't want to know about Kaspar and me, my boyfriends, or my father. So I don't want to know. We haven't got any time left. Dad says things are going to get a lot worse.'

The girl continued very quietly. 'We don't need the past, old lovers, old cultures. It's all such shit. Did you hear what Christine said?'

'No. Tell me.'

'She's been reading a report by an educational psychologist on Europe's schools. One child is dying every week from parental injuries, while governments are saying that humanity could be wiped out by teaching children about homosexuality! Can you believe it? More like a couple of thousand megatons of nuclear warheads. Teachers call calming down their classes 'policing'. The one sure way the report found to silence a class was to switch on the TV. Even then kids would come out with lines such as: "I'd rather wank than be in your class, Miss."'

'But that's normal,' I protested. 'It's always been like that, kids have always been vicious, hated everything.'

'Yes. But heroin-spiked milk, knives, guns, chains? The whole armoury of the immature, military-minded male? Kids are being turned into smackheads. If not by heroin, then by the latest run of *The Alienation Game* on TV, or some trashy soap opera or reality TV.

'The daughter of Peter Naughton, the Canadian scientist who discovered the latest killer disease, HRK, which works quicker than cancer or AIDS, has died of it. Germany is rioting after the assassination of the nazi leader Cenni.'

I was drifting off to sleep. A loud, blood-curdling scream woke me from deep sleep.

'What was that?'

I peered out of the back door of the truck, and saw only the dim shadow of the pine trees beyond the encampment.

The girl rolled over and said '*Icanthus.*'

What was that scream about, I wondered?

'*Icanthus,*' she murmured again, in her sleep.

When she was half-awake, she told me it was a word from her dream. Did she really mean the word *ichthys*, the Fish-God? No, she muttered, *icanthus*. She drifted off. I watched her sleeping for some time before drifting off again.

I over-slept. When I woke the girl was gone. The Circus camp was in a gloomy mood; pale, sleepy figures lurched about. A woman had been murdered with a hammer in the New Forest at about four o'clock in the morning. Toni's wife said it was the racist thugs who did it, the ones who had the Circus in Southampton. A note had been found with the body – something about Jews and gypsies.

The girl arrived with Toni. He'd driven her to a nearby post office.

'I've got a message here from my father. Like us he likes collecting news stories. Look at these.' She handed me a page of print, unsigned.

Shark bite – Texas – A shark bit off a 16-year-old's girl's arm as her father tried to fend it off.

Sharp rise in suicide among men – Suicide is increasing among men in Europe and decreasing among women. Suicide now accounts for about 15,000 deaths a year (in France). It is the most common cause of death, after accidents.

Suicide Trip – Cologne – A West German computer programmer committed suicide yesterday after killing his wife, his pregnant daughter and her three-year-old son. Early evening he drove to his mother's house and killed her in the cellar. Police later found his mother-in-law in the car's trunk.

Etna deaths – Sicily – Gas and rocks killed ten thousand yester-day. Pundits claim the eruption was nuclear-triggered.
Jerusalem – Israeli soldiers have permanently sealed off the Old City in Jerusalem.
Lima – Terrorists crucified three government officials last night in a prolonged orgy of destruction.

'We should have sliced off the Phallus of Patriarchal Capitalism at its powerbase instead of taking pot-shots at the rim,' pronounced the girl. I laughed.

'Let's go. We've got to keep moving,' she said.

We offered our goodbyes to Toni and his wife. Christine had driven back to Southampton the night before.

'Pity she went; we could've used her car,' mused the girl.

That day we walked through the winding backroads of the New Forest. No horses, ponies or sheep, usually everywhere in the New Forest, to be seen at all. We were relieved to be free of other people at last, free to think about ourselves.

The girl pulled out a banana and peeled it.

'Where'd you get that from?' I asked her.

She smiled. 'Oh, you know. I have my ways.'

It was nice to watch her eat the fruit. She knew she was arousing me. She laughed as she bit into it.

We turned off the main road to Burley in the late afternoon sun. Down a narrow lane we saw a crashed car, a silver Rolls Royce. We approached it cautiously.

Inside were two people. A chauffeur complete with dark blue uniform and cap, and a young woman, wearing an elegant Gucci top and, oddly, a black rubber skirt. Both of them were dead. But the interior of the car was full of masses of paintings. The doors were wide open. The car had not slewed into a tree, it was just pulled over on the wayside, in front of a gate.

I couldn't work out how they had died. I was more astonished to see the paintings. The girl gasped.

'There's a Monet here. And a Turner. And a Raphael, a Titian, a Memling. And they're all sodding original!'

She took out a penknife and started to cut the canvases from the frames. I looked at the dead woman, lying on the back seat, her legs apart. There was no blood, or sign of wounds, or a struggle. They could have poisoned themselves.

Suddenly I froze. A truck was approaching from the other end of the lane. We scrabbled out of the vehicle and ran into the trees. We hid in some dusty bracken and watched an army truck pull up beside the Rolls. A couple of soldiers studied the interior of the car, muttered something into a radio, scanned the area, then left. We waited ten minutes then crept out.

'Get the keys,' the girl hissed. 'We'll steal the car.' The girl started to search for the keys. They weren't in the ignition.

'Search the woman for them,' the girl insisted. But I couldn't face touching the corpse.

'Damn it,' grumbled the girl. 'They're coming back.'

We scurried into the forest again, and watched. Two trucks rolled up, and took away the car. No ambulance. No police.

Later we went over the scene, hidden in the gloom of some pines.

'Haven't you see a dead body before?' the girl taunted me. I said I hadn't.

'Well, what are we going to do with these?' She pointed to the paintings she'd managed to take, which lay in a heap on the pine needles. 'A few years ago we could've sold these and never had to work again. But they're useless to us now, really useless. We can't eat them, or burn them.'

She mused. Perhaps we could bury them, I suggested, like pirates or gangsters, and come back in a couple of decades. It was a good idea.

'I'd like to keep the Turner,' I said. I rolled it up. It was too big to carry. In the end we sent them to the girl's father.

'Dad'll get these paintings sent to the Arts Bunker at Blænau Ffestiniog in North Wales. The artworks from the British Museum, the Tate and the National Gallery were dumped there last week, he told me. Imagine it! A priceless Rembrandt or Egyptian statue has its own bunker with steel doors and concrete, while most of the population can't even afford the stuff needed for their own makeshift Two-Week Nuclear Family Bargain Basement Lifetime Guarantee Fall-out Shelter!'

FIVE

_____

Ocean Boulevard

WHEN THE TRAVELLING CIRCUS reached Bournemouth it clashed with a right-wing demonstration. The Circus had planned to set up on the seafront, near the Square. Half-an-hour later the neo-fascists stalked through the Winter Gardens towards the Pier. Two helicopters droned overhead. The police moved in with shields, batons and water-guns. In the heat everyone was glad of the cool water. Cops on horses yelled through megaphones. The ice-cream and hamburger stalls were smashed. The girl and I ran up West Cliff. Police vans trundled in as people were arrested. Sirens wailed. We heard gunshots. Louder screams as a petrol bomb was thrown into the arcades.

It was the hottest day imaginable. Digital signs told us it was 38 degrees. The passion-sun was drenching the planet in extra bouts of light and heat. It was shining through the hole in the ozone layer, frying us voluptuously. We were stripped to swim-suits.

So this was Bournemouth, land of evergreen hedgerows, lace curtains, landladies, rows of hotels and crusty, retired civil servants. At Branksome Dene Chine we slipped into the sea. It was glorious. Two silver fish, we swam out a long way, beyond the end of the Pier. We ignored the three oil rigs spoiling the skyline and drifted on the warm currents curving in from the South-West.

From Boscombe to Sandbanks the five-mile crescent of the beach was nearly empty. The heat was too much, and there was the riot to enjoy. We heard a distant roar as the crowd discovered some new form of torture or entertainment. More gunshots.

Then five RAF jets screamed overhead. It was stunning to witness their low flight from the water.

I tipped over in surprise as the girl swam between my legs. Was she turning into a dolphin? My mouth was full of water. She was turning over and over in the water, her brown form rippling below me. When she broke the surface she looked transfigured, smiling like a dolphin. The glare off the waves was making me dizzy.

We headed back for the shore. Every surface, every tree, every face was ringing with light. The sand was as hot as radium. We fell onto our towels, gasping, exhausted.

This place was Atlantis Revisited. The landscape shimmered in the blinding heat. As the sun dipped to the West, faces began to shine with a new bronze veneer. Hot, hot, hot. All the way from the Town Hall to the empty cinemas, from the freeways to the Piers, the heat trembled on every surface in this most delicious of all Zero Summers.

And you, fantastic dream-girl, gliding along so sinuously in your short skirt, turning to me in the crowd, opening your hot mouth. Crushed up against you, I press fingers against your pussy. Your tongue flicks out, you flash brilliant teeth in the blue night air. Having you naked under your skirt maddens me. I touch you until I can't stop.

'Later, boy, later,' you grin.

Everyone was out, cruising the streets, stepping around the mounds of trash, past the boarded-up shops, the burnt-out chainstores. The area around the Pier, where the Circus had been that day, was a mass of junk, as if Bournemouth had been stricken by a gigantic tidal wave, which had receded invisibly, when no one was looking. The people wandering the streets certainly looked like bizarre sea creatures left behind. They were all 'looking for something'.

Many people were converging on an open-air concert that was still going ahead despite the mayhem earlier. Spotlights played on the sky. We heard the crash of guitars and the hiss of synthesizers.

At nine we walked to the chain ferry at Sandbanks, rusted up but still running across the mouth of Poole harbour. We had to wait while a huge battleship slid past the big white hotels in the darkness. It was an enormous black shadow, a silhouette punctuated by gun-emplacements and missiles.

'Dad says two weeks. That's all we've got.' The girl was morose.

We watched the red lights on the navy ship fade. On the far side of the harbour, we stumbled into a telephone box, half buried in the sand.

'I want to call my father,' said the girl quietly.

I sat on the sand outside. Afterwards the girl told me what her father had said:

'He said "Can you hear the screams of billions people dying of boredom? You can hear these screams slowed-down as if on tape, to form television programmes. Slowed-down cries of apathy that become audience-reactions, hosts' jokes and the rehearsed laughter of chat-show guests. Life has been turned into a sit-com of mind-numbing banality. And the public is sitting back and accepting this war as if it's another television war, one you can watch from your armchair, like a video or DVD or computer game. What they don't realize is that this war is going to churn up their lives in unimaginable, unfilmable horror."

45

The girl turned to me. 'Do you think my father is over-reacting?'

I didn't know what to say at first. This wasn't how most dads I knew spoke.

'I don't know. Life's always been crazy. I read today in a newspaper that a man in hospital choked on his wife's get-well gift: a jelly sweet. He died.'

We were walking along a very dark lane near Studland Bay .

'OK,' replied the girl. But we're going to show that our love is more powerful than a nuclear holocaust.'

People say "I feel nuclear about him" meaning they're lusting after someone, I thought. Breaking-up in romance is called fall-out. Making love is the meltdown.

Fine. It is the ultimate fusion: the intimate, gentle darkness of two people in love and the exterior, public brightness and horror of a nuclear attack. The two kinds of pain were becoming synonymous. Love and war; sex and the holocaust; orgasms and bombs.

As we lay side by side under banks of brilliant stars on the Dorsetshire hills overlooking the ocean the girl continued to think aloud:

'We won't sink into a dreary long-term cynicism. I couldn't spend the rest of my life with you – with anyone. This war'll finish off all of that stuff. That's why it's good, and clean, and terribly tragic.'

She rolled onto me, beginning to press herself into me, softly.

'Ishtar you're beautiful,' she murmured: 'You make me so wet.'

She rolled onto her side and lifted her thigh over me, enclosing me in her heat. I yelped with lust when she took me into her mouth. Her lips felt softer than strawberries. I squeezed the incredible curves of her bottom as I licked her wet slit. She moaned with passion around my cock. Her clit was big as an egg, and smooth as polished marble.

It was impossible to stop rocking my hips to and fro, pushing deeper into her mouth. I exploded inside her, and she came just after me, groaning around my penis as I dabbed my tongue on her clitoris with tiny flicks, making her convulse violently.

She threw back the blanket and straddled me. Moving back, she took me inside her.

Open-mouthed, open-legged, open-hearted, we made love lusciously. I squeezed her soft breasts, pushing them up high. She rocked her hips back and forth in a frenzy. She leaned down to kiss me, dribbling semen into my mouth.

I slipped out of her, she was so creamy. She held me tight, chokingly tight. She writhed, reeled and writhed. She smelt of heaven. I kept kissing her, giving her love-bites on her neck, arms, breasts. She was hungry, so hungry for the deep experience, for the depth of passionate love-making. She gorged on me voraciously. She rubbed her clit over my penis, her nails digging into my chest. She pressed her fingers into her cunt.

I held her tightly as she began to orgasm. Her hot, full mouth came down on mine. It was delicious. Her hips kept bucking up and down. She couldn't stop orgasming. She kept gyrating over me, murmuring, gasping, panting so loud. She was so strong, so high, so beautiful. I loved to touch the swell of the flesh around her hipbone – it drove me mad.

It was a hypnotism of love-making. It went on for hours. The stars wheeled above her head. I was in love with this dream-girl, this Goddess of a human being who could make the stars shiver in their slots.

'I love to suck cocks,' the girl said once, grinning up at me as she swallowed me whole yet again. 'I can suck cocks for hours,' she added. 'Hours and hours.'

Coming in her mouth was an incredible experience. Sometimes she liked to yank my cock out at the last moment, laughing as the sperm flew over her face.

We never discussed contraception. We wanted to be inside each other, and that was it. Sometimes she'd say, 'I want to feel you inside me', or 'I want to feel you close'. So we never bothered with condoms. She could've been pregnant a thousand times.

In the morning we made love again. I was rock hard. She slipped her thighs over mine. I pushed in deeply. We both felt sore. Bodies interlocked, we were still half-asleep, tangled in the blankets. The girl rolled her torso around in small circles of desire. I came very quickly and stayed firm inside her. We gyrated for a long time, her head buried under my arm. We hardly moved. She kept squeezing me with her inner strength.

Then, after an age, when I moved only slightly, to lick her neck, she came very suddenly, very loudly. I kissed her softly. I loved to kiss her at orgasm, to feel the breath of her hot and gasping.

I looked up. A man was watching us from a distance, from the other side of a low stone wall. The girl cried out 'Hey!' or something like that, and he scuttled away.

Later I watched her, from way off, doing tai chi on the cliff path, sweeping her limbs around slowly, as if underwater. She was into yoga, too – I remember she wanted me inside her while she was doing the lotus position. Uncomfortable.

'But it might mean extra enlightenment,' she giggled.

We spent the rest of the day walking along the coastal path. Past Anvil Point, with its lighthouse and crashing waves, further West, along the top of the cliffs. We could have been the only people on the planet. We didn't see another human being for hours and hours.

'I love to listen to you,' I said. 'To hear your flights of fantasy. You make me smile inside.'

'Where shall we go?' she said. 'I don't care where we end up.'

We saw the usual detritus of the holiday season: remains of camp fires, piles of litter, as well as more unusual sights: a cluster of pills and bottles beside ten oil drums. Nearby was a heap of porn magazines. The owner of this junk must have had a good time. The girl picked up a magazine.

'Listen to this:

EXTRASUCK The ultimate sex machine. It looks like a vibrator. It tingles. It expands and contracts. And then – at the perfect moment – it starts to suck. What an Experience!

MADAME ORGASM Guaranteed to heat up even the most frigid.

PENIS STRETCH An amazing device that you can wear while you walk, work or sleep...

'And here's the ultimate in male-made alienation, the sex-doll:

RUBBER LADY A quality blow-up plastic doll with hair – always willing, always available. Matching pubic hairs! Air-powered mouth and lips! Human-size pressurized vagina! There is even a fully realistic anus, and Rubber Lady will not complain if you should want to experiment with her! She opens her legs at the touch of your fingers! She has everything!

The girl walked ahead of me, warming to the theme of pornography.

'Rape, gang rape, bored housewives, teen virgins, trans-sexuals, TVs, gonzo, a million kinds of torture. It's scary. Those sex dolls, with their mock mouths and vaginas, battery-powered ejaculations. Isn't that the most dispiriting invention of the bruised male psyche?

'*THRUSTER VIBRATOR, SEXUS STIMULATOR, MONSTER MULTI-SPEED...* It's creepy. These telephone sex-lines: *SWALLOW HARD!. NYMPHO IN NYLONS. WET AND WILLING. PICK A HOLE!. BIG TITS WIDE PUSSY. 945-ANAL. LET ME SLIDE IT IN. SHOWER GIRL. BEND OVER, TAKE THAT. I NEED TEN INCHES. LESBIAN HOUSEWIVES ORGY. FUCK MY ASS.*

'Think of all those pre-recorded tapes whirring slowly in empty office-blocks, all those frustrated white collar workers ringing up secretly from the office in their lunch hour. Someone somewhere is making billions of dollars. You wouldn't think the pornography industry is bigger than the movie and the pop industries combined, would you?

'Then there's the classifieds, the Lonely Hearts:

Man 2 Man – On your own and gay? Ring now and listen to people like you wanting to meet people like you.
Male, slim 30, seeks females, one or more, for sexy mutual fun. Unshockable.
Attractive newly wed, 18-year-old, looks younger, AC/DC, anything kinky, needs more than husband can provide. Would love gang bangs.
Lesbian 28, short bleached hair, enjoys gay scene, into soul, funk, seeks friends.
Hi I'm Divina, I'm seeking Dom Bi females or couples to use me and my husband.

'Millions of people all around the world, stuck in nowhere apartment blocks and quiet suburban housing estates, all yearning, yearning. This skin mag's got photos of people's genitals in their Lonely Hearts adverts. Colour snapshots taken with the curtains drawn, after dark. Sex reduced to rape, the anguished cry of the motherless male, unable to deeply connect with another human being. "Keith the rapist can make you fall in love by gently removing your panties. Anywhere..." Psychotic reductionism, all of it, from Plato to Freud.'

The girl said she felt hollow and nauseous. I remembered stumbling into a room of young men watching a porno video at Christie's house in North London. It was a sunny day, but the curtains were closed. The guys sat in a row on the couch glued to a limp penis being twiddled against a woman's buttocks. The whole thing was carried off by the sound, the over-dubbed woman's gasping. The lengths men will go for release. The 'love-motels' where people go for 'drive-in sex', the anonymous encounters in the dimly-lit cabins.

My feelings for the girl were deepening by the second. She was astonishing. We sat on some rocks in the fields above the sea, eating cheese out of a packet, watching an army truck clear away the bodies of some sheep they'd just hit. The girl was still carrying on with her polemic:

'*Love*. It's the most amazing four-letter word in the language! There are so many lies to be hacked to death, about orgasm, orgasm-failure, the nature of sex, about the erotic, emotional capabilities of women. The number of sexually-unsatisfied women throughout history must be billions. But a revolution needs more than a few feeble government leaflets to make it work. Advanced capitalism is rape on the biggest scale yet – from personal violence to global war.'

The wind was blowing up around St Aldhelm's Head. The cloudscapes were beautiful: pyramids of velvet purple clouds obscuring a smoking scarlet sky. I wanted to say something meaningful, but the girl was hot: she was cooking.

'I want to live in a world where people don't say, glibly: "The village was napalmed in five minutes"; where the computers are not spelling 'raw' backwards; where womb-magic flows instead of this computer ice-age freezing up everything; where the television, the hand gun, and the nuclear missile do not exist or are even thought of.'

Below us the waves were surging up against the limestone cliffs, sending up mist which fell over us from time to time. We were far away now from the race-riots erupting in South Africa, Indonesia and Israel. There was a mass of movement on the railways of Britain between depots. The road lobbies reported increased traffic out of London to the West. The Russian government was activating its civil defence procedures.

'They're getting ready for the Big One,' said the girl. 'And Dad says the useless 'Protect and Survive' government guidance will be inserted in the pages of all tomorrow's national daily newspapers.'

We couldn't see the missile silos or convoys of trucks. We were out of reach of the media networks. Society was collapsing around us but we took our love and played it against death and

51

disaster. We lived in the unreality of an epoch determined to annihilate itself. There were mass-executions of rebellious workers in Thailand and China but we were kissing even more passionately. The painful, tragic, tiring, stupid, horrific, numbing world was coming to an end, but we were going to burn like angels in the midst of the conflagration.

The sun broke through the clouds. We sat in a pool of sunlight, spotlighted as the first people to walk the Earth, a new Adam and Eve. The girl picked up a fossil from the stony path.

'Excellent. I love fossils.' She studied it closely and smiled.

She put it in her bag. She had quite a collection in there (fossils, shells, stones, leaves, seeds).

The New Stone Age was just around the corner. The bombing would begin in a couple of weeks.

A ship hove into view on the horizon, plying very swiftly for the Atlantic beyond the South Coast.

'That's the aircraft carrier HMS *Hermes*,' said the girl. I looked at her in amazement. Did she know about everything?

Even from that distance, we could make out the gun turrets, the rows of planes on the deck, the radar and telecommunications masts. It was soon a tiny speck of grey.

'That ship'll be bombed out of the water in the first exchange of missiles, along with the 90,000-ton nuclear-powered *Enterprise* class super aircraft carriers, and the *Kiev* Class with its SS-N-12 surface-to-surface missiles.'

The waves slammed into the cliffs, the wind blew, the clouds drifted over the sun: we'd been sitting there on the cliff for ages. The girl grabbed my hand.

'Come on,' she said. 'We've got to get witchcrafting.'

SIX

The Rain-Telephone Box

SEAFOOD FOR ANGELS. We bypassed Weymouth – plumes of foul-smelling smoke obscured the promenade – and headed for the mediæval village of Abbotsbury, where we found a shop that was well-stocked. It was delicious to wolf down a tin of new potatoes, of peaches. We even had cream, real West Country clotted cream. It was weeks-old, but as long as it wasn't full of maggots or fungus, we'd eat anything.

We sat outside the tropical Abbotsbury Gardens, with the peacocks screeching in their melancholy fashion on the walls behind us. Nobody was visiting the gardens now; the peacocks had the sunlit, overgrown paths to themselves.

Further along the coast we moved deeper into Thomas Hardy Country. But there were no Gabriel Oaks about, no Tess d'Urbervilles, and no cows, goats or sheep. With its short grass and softly-rounded hills, Dorset looked like some primæval landscape of the Jurassic period. There wasn't a single soul to be seen for miles each way along the Dorset coast.

I felt a deep erotic yearning in that lonely, windswept landscape. The hissing of the grass, the sea down below with its tiny white breakers, the swooping seagulls – and the fact that England behind us was falling apart – all this made me feel very erotic. The girl embodied the landscape for me – she was eroticism personified.

Earlier she had stood above me, after we'd eaten, and I had looked up her smooth legs to see the redness inside her, whorls and folds, receding into darkness. The vision reminded me of being in a church, looking up from the nave to the underside of the spire. The church and the woman – two kinds of womb. One juicy and crimson, the other dusty and grey. Out of one comes life-giving liquid and childbirth, out of the other dust and cold drops of rain. I know which one I'd rather be sitting under.

The girl looked at me sidelong. 'Did you fuck Christine?'

I was taken back for a moment. 'Uhh, no. Well…'

'Did you?'

'Not really. Shit, I thought you didn't want to know about exes.'

'Tell me, boy.' She folded her arms and looked at me darkly.

'Uhh… We made love but… but we didn't fuck, like that,' I added lamely.

The girl smiled slyly. 'How,' she murmured, 'did you do it then?'

'Do we have to get into this?' I turned away.

'Yes,' the girl insisted.

'Well… I, uhh… we, uhh… you know.'

'No. What?'

'We… fooled around, you know. We were just kids.'

'Did you make her come?' the girl asked with that incisive suddenness.

I thought for a moment. 'Yes, I did.'

'Show me how.'

'What?'

'Show me how you did it with Christine.'

I look at the girl; she was grinning evilly. She loved to tease me.

I knelt between her thighs and dipped my head under her skirt. The girl groaned as I kissed her hairy pubis.

'Like this,' I whispered as I dabbed my tongue over her bud. I inhaled her tangy aroma; she was already slick with honey. She bucked her hips upwards, urgently. I had her coming in moments, one orgasm followed by another.

'Like that,' I whispered when she'd finished trembling.

The planet span around the sun some more, then the girl said 'Look.'

She pointed to the sea. Five or six cars were window-deep in the surf. Then, as we watched, another car sped down a track, climbed onto the steep bank of shingle of Chesil Beach, and crashed down into the water on the far side. It seemed like a new form of joyriding, to see how far into the ocean you could land your stolen vehicle. But the kid had not waded out of the sunken machine. Perhaps he couldn't open the door.

Another car raced down to the beach, carrying a couple of boys and a girl, who ran down the stones to help. The car had been dragged further out. The current was fierce at Chesil Beach. In a matter of moments, the car had gone under. Hard to imagine the panic of the person inside, trying to get the windows open against the weight of water.

An army truck rolled up later. But I didn't want to hang around while they tried to find a coast guard boat. We moved on.

'I don't think the driver meant to get out,' the girl mused. We both knew that, and we both knew we wouldn't rush down to the shore to the rescue.

It was clouding over again. A storm was forecast. The heat at noon had been as dense as water – it was difficult to move or breathe in it. This was heat from the Sahara, hot and spicy.

Pressure was high. I could feel my blood boiling. We tipped the last of our water down our parched throats.

'I feel faint,' I murmured. Then I saw the telephone box, a red speck on the top of a low hill above the beach. We fell asleep on the grass in its shadow.

At dusk we woke to the first roll of thunder. The girl tried to make a call but got nothing but static and the soft hiss of abandoned technology. Inside the box the girl found a Tarot card stuck to the wall. It was 'The World', which meant big changes. The girl told me about the Tarot spread Frau G had done for her at the travelling circus. The Moon, the Devil and the High Priestess had featured prominently. No sign of The Lovers. I was The Fool (of course).

'When Frau G did a reading for the present world situation,' the girl recalled, 'it was dead accurate: The World, The Wheel of Fortune, and Death, which is just what we ordered when we popped out of the womb, right?'

Right. The first crack of thunder was so loud and so close we thought the Apocalypse had started, and ducked as if from flying debris. The sky darkened to a sombre yellow-grey. Below us, the sea was being whipped up to a frenzy by the South-westerly wind. The hillside car park was deserted. There was not a soul in sight. Soon the hills, which stretched North towards Stonehenge and Glastonbury, were alive with flashes. So many flashes! The whole landscape was lit up for a few, blinding moments, then the darkness rushed in again. Titanic energy was being released here. The planet turned malefic and radiant.

'This is fantastic,' I yelled to the girl above the roar of the wind. I loved this great crashing splendour. It was really breath-taking, this bewitching phenomenon. Our eyes were shocked by each flash. Two or three storms were converging on us. We clung to each other outside the telephone box, delighting in these magnesium-blue and powder-white flashes. The waves were frozen for a moment in their fury. This was pure power, and it was terrifying and exhilarating. The thunder was so loud, it left us gasping. A glorious sorcery gripped the world as black devils and bright angels fought in the heavens. Then came the rain.

The whole ocean lifted up over the hills and drenched us, flattened us. We flew into the phone box, standing amongst our blankets and bags. The rain lashed the glass mercilessly.

'This thing's a great lightning-conductor,' said the girl as another explosion fizzed perilously close. She pulled wet hair our of her eyes.

'You're supposed to crouch on the Earth, so it bypasses your heart,' I said. But we were not going out there, into that boiling mess.

The colours turned from livid crimson to dim grey as the sun fell out of the sky. This was a Romantic poet's dream: all nature exploding into light and colour. We shivered and changed into our only dry clothes. The rain would not stop. It poured on and on. Outside was all carnage, inside was pure passion.

I felt the girl's hand on me, soft and mesmerizing as an angel's wing. She slid her hand into my shorts. I gasped. We kissed, her mouth was as hot and wet as the storm outside. She ground herself against me. I pulled her bottom tightly to me. We gyrated into each other. I slipped her cotton skirt down, knelt, and slid my thumb gently back and forth over her pussy lips. She moaned softly. She smelt of the ocean, salty and tangy. She clamped her thighs around my jaw, rocking her hips backwards and forwards over my thumb and tongue. I loved the way her hands explored my head, like someone blind. I pulled on her asscheeks hard.

'I want you inside me, I want to feel you come inside me,' she moaned. She pulled on my T-shirt, but I wouldn't move my face from her crotch. 'Come on,' she implored. 'Fuck me now.'

I peeled her swollen labia apart farther, burying my tongue deeper, my thumb sliding ever further into her sweet womb.

The rain gushed down outside, and her juice drenched me inside the telephone box. I listened to her rapturous cries, those so-familiar soft moans ('ah ah ah ah ah'). Her erect clit was

57

enormous. She undulated above me, orgasming.

'I'm coming, I'm coming, coming, coming, coming,' she gasped.

She bucked wildly, grinding herself onto me. I reached down and rubbed myself swiftly to orgasm, coming over her legs and the floor. She laughed madly. I kept licking her. She went mad, jerking back and forth like crazy, her belly convulsing, her buttocks clenched. The storm came inside us, swept into the phone box, into us, and washed us away.

I found myself lying on the grass outside. I had slipped and fallen. I had dreamt of hideous monsters on stilts, stalking across the countryside, out of the eye of the storm. It was only spitting rain now. I wiped the water from my eyes. The girl was looking at me from the door of the kiosk, smiling. The sky was lurid grey. It was early morning. The storm, and the night, were finally over. I felt exhausted, freezing cold, and stiff with cramp.

'Let's get out of this bloody phone box,' said the girl. She threw the bags out. We hadn't walked more than ten paces before the telephone rang. The noise was startling.

The girl snatched up the receiver. 'Dad?' The line was silent. Then it crackled and a voice said: 'The Black President is dead.' Just that. Nothing more. Obviously a cross-line: Africa to White-hall perhaps? Later we heard of the assassination of an African president.

We were very hungry and very thirsty. I started seeing things more sharply: hunger heightened my perception. Our lips were dry. The girl's idea was to keep moving.

'We're in motion, we've got energy. Nature loves that.'

Then she pointed to the beach – an abandoned car was wheel-deep in the water, a red Mini. We ran down a track and clattered over the stones. I hung back while the girl examined the car; I'd seen enough corpses already. The keys were there, and fuel in the tank. It started up. The girl climbed in.

'Probably another suicide,' she said. 'There's probably a body down there wearing brogues and a tweed jacket, leaving a distraught wife somewhere.'

Who cared, I thought, about the owner of the car? Who cared if he had a recently-married daughter and shares in a plastics company? Who cared if he was going to leave his wife, and had been having an affair with a lawyer? We had the car, that was all that mattered.

There is a stretch of coastal road, from Abbotsbury to Bridport, that is thoroughly exhilarating. We flew along it, all the way to Lyme Regis. We were in the little seaside town by seven in the morning. It was empty. Many shops had smashed-in windows; only some of them were boarded up. Glass and trash were strewn across the street, as well as a burnt-out truck.

On the high street the girl told me to stop. She leapt out onto the pavement before I'd stopped and pulled something from a store window… a wedding dress. She held it against her.

'I'd like you to fuck me in this,' she said, grinning.

Higher up the street she dived into a grocer's shop and came out with a carrier bag of goodies. I knew she was planning something. We raced North through dark country lanes to the secret spaces of Marshwood Vale. We parked the car then walked deep into the trees.

'First we're going to get drunk,' she said, 'then you're going to give me half-an-hour to prepare myself.'

We broke open a bottle of wine and a small bottle of gin.

I staggered back later from the car to find four candles flapping in the breeze. It was very dark under the old oak trees of ancient England. The breeze ruffled the leaves. A solitary bird trilled a complex pattern of notes, never once repeating itself.

The girl stepped into the clearing, wearing the wedding dress. She was a mass of lace and taffeta, a vision of frothing layers of white and cream. Her hair was piled up and she had made her face over in pink lipstick and thick black kohl. She looked like an archangel on heat. The lust literally burned from her eyes.

She smiled, took my arm and we stood in front of the altar – a tree stump. Then the perverse service began.

'Dearly beloved,' she began, addressing an imaginary congregation, 'we are gathered here in the light of Ishtar to fuse together this woman and this… 'Man'.

'Do you, Lory,' she continued, 'take this wreck to be your unlawfully be-bedded house-bound?'

The girl shrieked 'NO!'

Then turning to me:

'Do you, Fin, take this delicious, powerful, witchcrafting Woman to be your unlawful rebel? To hold, cherish, and nourish with the blood of a thousand virgins until you both shall die in Hell's many holocausts?'

The girl nudged me, grinning.

I shouted 'NO!'

Strange as it may seem, this was the first time she'd uttered her name. Now I knew it: Lory (but not her surname). Somehow, we did without names.

The girl continued in an unearthly monotone: 'To create and to make bold, till death do you rend asunder and the heavens below turn to blood orange. Put the ring on her finger.'

She took the middle finger of my left hand and bit it.

'We pronounce you woman and slave, man and knife, and let no ghoul pull them asunder, in the sight of the Goddess, so help me Isis.'

She then turned to me, with her eyes shining and her body trembling:

'Now you may fuck the bride.'

She grabbed me. Wild flowers were crushed between us. She smelt heavenly. The oaks rustled above us. A gust blew out the candles. She ripped off my shirt and shorts. We swayed together, moving about the glade, half-drunk and full of lust. I felt big with life. She was expanding me. At first, we were dancing to an invisible jazz band playing a slow smooch. But the girl wanted to fuck.

Her mouth was hotter than a furnace. She was so wet already; Ishtar she was *so wet*. She was a witch, shrieking with laughter as she straddled me, climbing up my body. She threw her arms around my shoulders, leaning down to suck on my neck like a vampiress.

Now we were making love really deeply. We were in a frenzy, utterly beyond everything. I held her firm buttocks and pressed upwards; she reached down and guided my cock inside her, groaning loudly in my ear. She bent down and snatched up the wine bottle, giggling as we nearly toppled. We both took a deep swig. We worked up to a tremendous pitch of fever and emotion. We orgasmed together in a fury of fervent fucking. It was tumultuous sex, sex beyond everything, orgasming into one, so hot and sweet.

We fell onto the grass, laughing, laughing, laughing. I poured some wine into her mouth. The wedding dress was stained with crimson. I drew it off her, gently. She watched dreamily as I set it alight. I didn't think about what I was doing, I just did it. We watched it burn and slithered over each other, wet with wine, blood, juice and sperm. The girl laughed.

'That's the only way to get married – by fucking the system from the foundations upwards.'

As night fell we sat in the car with the doors open, talking. 'Do you remember the balloon-boy?' I asked her.

We had met the balloon-boy in Brighton – he was standing in the middle of a bunch of gas-filled balloons. Nothing happened, he just stood there. I was amazed by his silence, his repose, his aura ('I was a balloon-boy once'). All the holiday makers bustled around him, but he remained so calm.

'Make me a fire. I'm fucking starving. Make me an omelette.'

While we busied ourselves with collecting firewood the girl was talking in her polemical fashion again:

'We've got to turn the failures of our fathers and mothers into successes.'

'But doesn't every generation say that?' I replied. 'Until they *become* their fathers and mothers.'

The girl laughed sardonically.

As she spoke I remembered the radio in the car. We switched it on when the fire was going. Shocktroops were moving into cities all over the world. While the locals read love-comics, the heavies were arming themselves with every weapon imaginable.

'These news reports are brought to you by the world service of Radio Moscow... Radio Sofia... Radio Jerusalem... Radio Death... Radio War...'

I panned the airwaves and heard the anti-nuke chant:

'One-two-three-four, we don't wanna nuclear war. Five-six-seven-eight, we don't wanna radiate.'

Statues were being torn down; the political arena had been smashed, the United Nations was powerless – there were so many targets for mass-hatred, so many chances for acts of extreme violence and terror. With just a few atomic hits the major cities of the world would be in turmoil. All those computerized businesses would fail, the world markets would collapse.

There were many reports of rallies and sabotages in dear old Britain. People were not going to 'stay put', as the government wanted. The food shortages were getting worse. The Buffer Depots had been raided and their stocks of flour, sugar, margarine, biscuits and sweets had been ransacked. Many people were already dying, of neglect, disease, starvation. There were tales of lost children wandering the streets of Leeds, Glasgow, Manchester, London. The asylums were forgotten about. The hospitals were over-full or closed. A gang had broken into a German zoo and slaughtered most of the animals.

The only people benefiting from all this horror were the media professionals. Gleefully they filled their news broadcasts with the escalation of world violence. Every news item was 'sexy', had the maximum amount of personal pain and political significance.

Sixteen prison wardens are stabbed to death in Jakarta? Great, great, stick it near the top of the show. But wait – here's the latest on the gay riots in San Francisco – good pictures with this. And don't forget we open the programme with the latest Mombasa crucifixions – close-ups and all.

The world was being turned into a sick horror flick. The video vultures were present at every eruption of carnage. A new delight in death pervaded the airwaves. Television had become necrophiliac: *film it, film it, it's big audiences.* All of life can be pornographic. Realistic hard core. The ultimate snuff movie.

One radio station was playing old Frank Sinatra and Nat King Cole songs in an effort to blanket over the violence. Another station was all public information and repeated recorded messages on how to 'Protect and Survive'. Another featured a list of closed roads. Then we found a station broadcasting invocations to God: 'Lord, help us now and in the hour of our need.'

But we did find a fascinating late night news show which dramatized current stories. The corpse of a young woman had been found tied to a buoy off the Canadian coast. The girl and I listened to this reconstruction pieced together from her diary and friends:

'MJ first head the songs of the whales in her bedroom after making love to her boyfriend, Kaspar. The haunting noises from the ocean's depths hypnotized her. She became obsessed by whales. Her bedroom was strewn with books, posters and models of whales. She became a whale-addict, joining every association, every club. After a few months she won the first prize in a competition: to visit a whale sanctuary in West Canada, on Vancouver Island.

'She went swimming with a pod (herd) of whales. She wrote: "Excited beyond words to be in the cold water with the whales."

'She camped out with 'Booz', the owner of the whale sanctuary. They recorded the whales' songs by dropping mics from the cliffs into the water. MJ was stunned to hear the whales singing below her, in the sea. She learnt about lives and habits of

63

whales, their breeding and feeding, courting and eating.

'They went out again, in two inflatable boats. MJ rode with Booz. They followed a group of whales with radio tags all day.'

The next part of the radio programme was all conjecture:

'A squall blew up. The storm came out of nowhere. They got blown off course. Out of the black depths a gigantic shape rose. It was a blue whale, the leviathan of old. Booz was stunned. With one flick of its tail-fluke the blue whale flipped the two boats over.

'In the confusion MJ was separated from the others. First she felt the shattering cold. She was wearing a wet-suit, but it didn't help much. She tried swimming but the current was too strong. When the storm disappeared, there was no one in sight. She wasn't sure which direction land lay. She was thrown about on the swell.

For a while she drifted in shock. Below her was a thousand or more feet of water. She knew no help would reach her before she died. It grew dark. Nothing but black waves and black sky surrounded her. Ever since a child she had been fascinated by the 200-ton sea creatures, never thinking one might kill her (albeit indirectly).

'She hallucinated. She imagined a fleet of whales moving up through three thousand feet of water towards her. She yearned for a dolphin to save her, to carry her back to the coast.

'The night was utterly black. No stars. All her energies were spent on keeping afloat, but she was exhausted. Sometimes she found herself sinking and would kick to the surface violently, gasping. She kept slipping back under. This would be the way she would die, she thought: just one more ducking under, with no return to the surface.

'Then she saw a small buoy, a dim form in the formless dimness. It was very close. She managed to reach it. But she didn't have the strength to climb on top of it. She simply couldn't do it. She held on to it, though, gladly. She tied herself, umbilically, to the buoy. She drifted off into a semi-sleep. A roar awoke her: it was a jet, screaming from Russia to America on the first airstrikes.

'She woke again to find herself sinking into black water. She felt something brush against her side. Shocked, she kicked to the surface. It was a whale.

'Gulping savagely, she watched the whale circle her, breaching and diving. If it was a male, she wanted it to make love to her, to take her into another world. If it was a female whale, she ached to be mothered. In profound loneliness she watched the whale swimming round and round. She spoke to it. She thought that it sang back an answer. In the sky she now saw a thousand moons.

'Eventually, she could hold on no longer. She fell into the water. Immediately, the whale swam up and pushed her to the night air. This went on for some time, the girl sinking and the whale keeping her afloat, until MJ drowned. She was found two days later, still tied to the buoy.'

I switched off the radio. The silence of the night rushed in; the girl was utterly still and quiet beside me.

'What's up?' I asked. She threw her cigarette into the dark forest.

'MJ's boyfriend – it was Kaspar. Remember him? We met him in Brighton.'

I said I didn't think it was the same person. If it was, then the girl was linked with MJ, the drowned whale-addict. The girl believed in deep connections between lovers. She had been Kaspar's lover, once, and he had gone out with MJ, so the girl and MJ were enmeshed together. I thought it highly unlikely that the anarchist activist we met in Brighton was the same one, but the girl wanted to believe it. I sensed she was contemplating the way MJ died, in the deep ocean at night, tied to a buoy.

I went to hug the girl but she shrugged me off.

'Don't touch me. I can't bear it. Not now.'

She slammed the door and strode into the trees. I switched off the interior light, and fell asleep in a few minutes across the lowered front seats.

The girl came back an hour later, waking me with a start.

'You'd better hold me now,' she ordered, climbing in beside me. Sleepily, I hugged her.

SEVEN

———

The Stone Circle

EVERYTHING ABOUT YOU amazed me. You were the passion-girl and you completely astonished me. When you moved into the sunshine and said 'True learning is in experience,' you left me dumb, I couldn't answer you. You yearned for a child but hated to wait for it. You never asked me about my background, my life, my parents. You were always at the centre.

We lived by spiralling around your menstrual cycle, you, passion-woman. You were *so powerful* during menstruation, and sex during the blood-time was the best. Just about everything about you fascinated me.

You stood in front of the sun and said 'Love me.'

You looked so beautiful, like Ishtar, Venus or Aphrodite. You took off your T-shirt and put on a floppy hat. You stunned me, made me dumb. You stretched your brown arms to the sky. You stripped me and we walked along the dusty track naked, in the brilliant sunlight. You felt wonderful. You told me we only had a few days left, before the holocaust.

It *was* good to be alive, with you. We moved across the scrubland, the marshland, the moorland. I loved it when you sweetly sang nonsense songs. Your voice and nothing else in that emptiness, near the ocean, somewhere between Dorset and Devon. We passed the time, walking, singing songs from the cradle or the bordello. You sang:

Lying upon the right side is proper to Kings,
Upon the left to Sages.
To sleep supine is the position of the Saints
But flat on the belly is the way to the Devil.

I wondered why, and you told me. When you lie flat you are defenceless. And buggery is always associated with the Devil – and then there is the Black Kiss of occultism, the obscene kiss, on the Devil's ass.

Where did you get all this stuff from, about Black Kisses and esoteric practices? I never knew who you were, really. You are pure mystery.

We sang and danced, kicking up the dust. She grabbed me and murmured 'Gimme a smooch.' So we smooched, we kissed.

A jet, bristling with rockets, screamed overhead, curving out to sea. We waved.

The girl led me by my penis off the road, into the bushes. We felt very relaxed. She could make me orgasm in seconds, or she could spool it out for hours. In the full-blown sunlight we caressed each other gently. She pulled on some stockings she'd found. Her thighs felt deliciously smooth. She held my prick and rubbed it between her legs. She was already soaking and peeled open. She jerked the foreskin back hard and looked down.

'How ridiculous,' she said, 'this phallus. What a fuss about nothing.'

I laughed, staring intently into her eyes. 'Yeah, but not mine, honey.'

She bent swiftly and took me into her mouth. My legs shook as she sucked me hard. I pulled her up.

I grasped her hips, bent my knees and slid inside her, all in one, as deep as forever. Her eyes opened wide. She grinned, climbing up me. We nearly toppled. I didn't fancy falling – we were surrounded by prickly gorse bushes, standing on a tiny patch of grass. She opened her mouth wide and wriggled her tongue magically between my lips. I kitten-licked her neck as she jerked her hips frantically up and down. The orgasm was swift, overtaking us both. We staggered, and fell.

'Ouch!' the girl squealed and leapt up. I was still shuddering, strewn across a spiky bush. We stood up shakily and clutched each other again; we could never have enough of each other.

She squeezed my balls softly. She was so wet. I could put two, three, four fingers inside her when she opened her thighs. I stroked her clit in circles, my palm on her belly, until she started to quiver feverishly. Eyes tightly closed, she held my shoulders and trembled. She orgasmed again. I embraced her tightly.

We heard a truck approaching and ducked down. A small convoy of army trucks thundered by, then it was quiet once more. It was time to move, the girl in just her long yellow T-shirt, and me in my faded shorts.

'I would like to be a fairy tale princess,' she said after a while as we walked, eating some chewing gum. 'But only if princes and knights were as they should be. Unfortunately, men would rather watch football, drink beer and talk about laptop computers and cars and share prices. That's not exaggeration, that's accuracy.'

She continued after a while: 'I feel *hungry*, and men don't satisfy my hunger. The more I eat, the hungrier I get, in a way. Men's emotions seem to stop short – of real depth. In sex they never really let go – they always have to be watchful and aware. Why can't they just feel it – so powerful, so overwhelming?'

She grasped me tightly around the waist. Her eyes glowed.

'Fill me up, boy!' Her hands were restless – all over me.

'Come on,' she gasped, 'come run with me like wolves – right over the Edge.'

Our night in Exeter was extraordinary. Around the Cathedral and in the high street were hordes of people. Broken glass and refuse was crunched underfoot. Kids were screaming and sirens were wailing. We turned a corner to see a mass of young people bouncing up and down in the darkness, lit by strobes hung from broken street lamps. Someone had set up some speakers to create a mobile sound system. The reggae and hip-hop music echoed around the streets. Drugs and drink were being consumed in vast quantities.

Around another corner we saw lights flashing in a graveyard. As we drew up some shadowy figures ran off. Two graves had been opened. I remember the look of the black, wet soil lit by sodium lamps. There were some spiders crawling over the coffin.

We bumped into a derelict wearing a battered yellow sandwich board. One side read: "The End Of The World Is Nigh". The other panel said: "Bert's Caff, 156 Sherborne Street." The tramp ponced a couple of cigarettes off us.

Every so often we heard the sound of smashing glass and hoots as another shop was looted. Torches flickered along the dark streets. All the streets lights were off.

We managed to buy some half-rotten fruit from a store lit by two gas lamps. I noticed a rifle next to the counter as I paid the edgy Korean store owner who eyed us as if we were going to knife him. The shop had no tinned food left – in fact, very little worth having, apart from some needle and thread, plant seeds, and ancient cosmetics. People had been panic buying and hoarding for weeks.

We walked past a supermarket, once a gleaming house of plenty, a beacon of twenty-four hour consumerism. By the light of a broken strip light that flickered eerily we saw empty shelves, and a body lying face-down between the check-outs. It was naked from the waist down.

When we heard gunshots we started to run, on unspoken cue, back to the car. The music from the sound system thudded in the cold night air. We caught a glimpse of revellers silhouetted against fifteen foot bonfires in the street, dancing wildly like mænads. Two people lurched out into the road, waving their arms and trying to stop the car. A vehicle with gas was a precious commodity these days. We swerved and managed to miss them.

We drove out of the city but got helplessly lost down winding lanes. The whole countryside was dark; there wasn't a single light in a window or a street lamp to be seen anywhere.

We pulled over to study the map. We had the shock of our lives when we heard thumping on the roof of the car. Someone was trying to get in, battering at the windows and bellowing. (Luckily, the girl insisted we travel with the doors locked.) I caught a glimpse of a man's bruised face as we raced away. We were both shaken up mightily by this attack, now suddenly vulnerable in the Mini, which had been our little sanctuary for a day or so.

Then the car ran out of petrol as we struggled up one of the many steep inclines of Dartmoor, somewhere outside Moretonhampstead. We slept in it until morning then moved on. The girl wasn't happy about staying in the car, after the scary incident with the maniac. I figured we'd still be safer in the locked car. But the girl had me reverse the Mini into a field and behind a wall. By that time, it was after two, and we were too tired to do anything else.

In the clear sunlight of a new day we forgot all about the horrors of Exeter. In the lush, peaceful fields of Dartmoor, the rioting and looting of the night before seemed a hallucination. Soon the heat made us feel beautiful again. We expanded. We made love feverishly. Nearby some electricity cables were seeping their man-made energy into the Earth; they had snapped loose from the major power lines which covered the whole of Albion.

Last night in Exeter we'd seen television pictures of motorways full of abandoned cars, coaches and trucks, just ditched on the sides of roads, some with their doors open, as if the occupants had left in a hurry. It was an eerie, desolate sight, those

71

heaps of metal lying about – especially strange because a day or so earlier we'd seen TV news images of vast traffic jams populated by angry motorists, families with belongings piled high on the roofs. And now, rows of deserted vehicles, some with their windscreens smashed, and some on fire.

We came upon an abandoned roadblock a while later, with nothing left of it except plumes of black smoke smelling of rubber and plastic. If we saw legs sticking out from under piles of smouldering debris, like the Wicked Witch of the West, we swiftly moved on. By now these sights were becoming all too familiar, losing their power over us.

But the countryside was so quiet now – without the harsh sounds of cars and trucks, that constant background of 21st century life in the West. Also there seemed to be fewer birds singing (but insects proliferated). Perhaps all the birds had flown away? For sure the landscape didn't sound the same anymore. Everything was out of sync, as if the clocks had been put forward too many hours, to adjust for this abrupt change from British Summer Time to Zero Summer Time.

The mass demonstrations and protests in the major cities of the world were also a thing of the past now: demonstrations, peaceful or riotous, were way down on the list of priorities of most people. Food, water and survival had taken over. We looked back on the global music concerts to 'Stop the War' with nostalgic affection, those days when a few chart acts and older, reformed rock bands got together to do their bit for the peace cause.

Now we were aiming for the ocean again, for the mouth of the River Tamar, our entry into Cornwall. After we'd eaten, and drunk some exquisitely refreshing Dartmoor stream water, I fell asleep for a while in the heat. When I woke the girl had gone but she'd left one of her letters behind:

'I have bruises, aches and longings – on my breasts, my thighs, my mind. I feel good. You make me believe in myself, that I am all the things I want to be. I walk in the bright sunshine and you leave me

breathless and so excited. I am full of you. I want to touch you, to taste you, to bury you inside me, to take all of you and feel your energy, your power. Just thinking this makes me ache and open for you.'

I reeled as I read this. It was unreal, this passion. I never believed it could happen. There had been nothing for so long, just emptiness, and then this – like being filled up by a flood, a mythical, body-breaking flood. When she came back from nowhere I hugged her hard, so hard we were both breathless.

'I watched you while you slept,' she said. 'You looked so helpless. Look–' she pulled out a tub of dairy cream she had bought '–taste this.'

She scooped out some cream and pressed it into my mouth. It was pure magic, pure Cornwall, the essence of the dream country.

'Tonight we cross the Tamar, into the Duchy,' she said, smiling softly. In the empty, grassy landscape, under an eggshell blue sky, we embraced.

She made me convulse. As we kissed her body began to roar. Then I saw them – the jet fighters coming from the North, swooping very low, so low, over the tors of Dartmoor. The noise became unbearable. Instinctively, we crouched on the grass, as if we were the target. The aircraft seemed to be aiming straight for us, but they screamed overhead and disappeared within seconds. We watched the low trajectories of the aircraft, stunned by their sudden appearance.

Then another sound: the distant roar of army trucks. We had nowhere to hide on the open moorland. They approached slowly, four of them, and began to slow down.

A black American soldier in his late twenties leaned out of a window and asked us where we were going. He took in the girl with a faint smile (she wore a grubby T-shirt and short skirt only – she was usually barefoot, and never wore a bra). The girl told him about the stone ring. He offered us a ride. It was hot, and we had long ways to go in the heat, so, warily, we climbed in.

'We're ordered to pick up any stray people,' the man told us. The girl asked him if we were under arrest. 'Sort of,' replied the soldier, winking at me and laughing. 'You've got to stay at home.'

'Bollocks to the 'stay-put' policy,' said the girl. 'My father knew it was dreck when he wrote it.'

The guy laughed, and winked at me.

We motored down a section of the A30 (codenamed 'Cat' in military jargon), until we were traversing Bodmin Moor. We hit a road block outside a military zone. The American soldier explained about us two civilians briefly. The guard hesitated.

When the girl got down from the truck to talk to him, he soon waved us through. I didn't think much about that at first – I thought the girl was spinning him one of her crazy lines. She had the ability to talk to anyone, to be comfortable in any social situation. But thinking about it later, I wondered if she'd found another way of slipping past guards. Offering drugs, perhaps, or sexual favours? I allowed myself a little jealousy – the girl was phenomenally desirable. And why she singled out me, I had no idea.

After an hour of slow driving down winding narrow lanes, we halted in front of three abandoned cars.

'Get them out of our way,' barked the soldier who got out of the truck behind us. Orders were relayed and five soldiers leapt out of the back of the truck and pushed the cars into the ditch. There was a corpse in one of them, and a soldier painted a big cross on the windows with whitewash. They left the body for another unit to deal with.

'We've got to keep the Essential Service Routes clear,' explained the driver. 'Sometimes we can't shift 'em, so we radio for an M2 tank to squash 'em flat. Or we get Charlie here to blow the junk off the road –he's dead accurate with his Dragon ATGW.'

We drove through the downlands, past abandoned stone houses and lonely limestone tors. Soon we were at the stone ring. The American troops had set up a camp right on top of it. They called it a 'monitoring base' and had planted their communic-ations gear right in the centre of the circle. A few soldiers lazed about on the fallen stones. They offered us coffee and marijuana.

Dusk fell slowly. We hung about the encampment, somehow reluctant to press on just yet. The girl took some pictures of the huts and radio dishes silhouetted against the purple sky.

The American soldiers were intrigued by us, and our voyage to Cornwall. They were bored. The girl sold them some heroin. I watched amazed as she made the deal calmly. She told me she'd got it in London.

'The old and the new,' she said. 'The secular camp on top of the old pagan ring.' She was talking to Harry, the friendliest of the soldiers.

She added: 'You can't keep us here forever, can you?'

He smiled. 'It's the dream of every American I know to drive across the States – preferably in an opentop car with a case of bourbon in the trunk. I suppose you're doing the same, walking across England.'

He passed around a joint. The girl smoked; I didn't.

'We're having a party tonight. Wanna party?' he asked, eyeing up the girl. He wished I were someplace else all of a sudden, I could see.

'We have a party pretty much every night,' another soldier said, grinning and taking another slug of beer.

It was a lonely spot, there on the hill, at the stone ring, surrounded by the endless moor on every side. When it was fully night the soldiers turned on the music. It was odd hearing old hits echoing about the empty hills (James Brown, the Doors, the Beach Boys, Prince). The girl danced with Harry and Punch, a giant black soldier, under a sky of bright stars.

I sat in the communications tent and listened to the radio reports coming in ("Radio Sierra, request new report, over."). The radio operator logged every communication meticulously in sullen silence.

Harry tottered in with a bottle of Bourbon and thumped me on the shoulder.

'Lory's a real *heart*,' he said, mysteriously. So he hadn't managed to jump her, then, I thought.

I wanted to get out of there. The girl was all for staying. She was getting on very well with the soldiers. Ten or so were dancing drunkenly in the stone circle. In my paranoia (my way of describing my sexual envy), I sensed a nasty scene in the air – gang rape, perhaps. They could easily kill me and take the girl. We were miles from anywhere.

A cluster of low-flying aircraft saved us. The camp of doped-up soldiers woke up and sprang into life. In the uproar we slipped away. These fruitbats were not American or Russian planes. Harry had told us the war was not like the Cold War, between the USA and the USSR.

'It involves everybody, so you don't trust no one.'

We heard him barking orders as we ran down the hill. I turned but only saw the flashlights flickering madly. We were free. I held onto the girl's slippery form. She grinned and pulled something from her bag to show me. It was a gun.

As we walked along under the canopy of stars, I asked the girl why she had a gun.

'Things are getting worse. We may need it.'

'But why? I thought we were trying to get away from all that nonsense – men and guns and technology and nuclear missiles.'

'Don't be so stupid. We'll probably need it, before the end. Society is falling apart, becoming de-centralized. The whole place is splitting up into little self-sufficient communities. It's not dog-eat-dog but dog-kill-dog – and quickly, before the other one gets in the first shot.

'There's no fuel. Horses will be back (if they're not all eaten), and bicycles. How much will be left when the bombs strike? How much will still be needed? Will we still require trucks, computer games, skyscrapers? I don't think so. There are twenty foot piles of trash in all the cities. The shopping arcades are empty – of food, goods and people. The roads are deserted.

'I knew some people who lived in the country who used to

hide from the milkman when he delivered, because the sight of another human being terrified them. They used to cower under tables so that no one could see them when they called. It's like that everywhere now. Refugee camps are being built out of colleges, community centres and schools. The government's taken control of the airlines, ferries, haulage, fuel, energy. Ex-pats can't get back to Blighty. So we can walk naked on the roads, and fuck madly, and nobody notices, because no one's *there* anymore.

'Time is spooling out, transforming. The sky above is big and timeless. There is silence – listen, boy: utter, utter silence. Completely beautiful. Just wind, and hardly any birds. How shocking now is an articulated truck going by, when you haven't' seen another human for weeks.

'We are playing the chaos game. We're changing chaos into love. This national breakdown will leave a far deeper and longer-lasting wound than World War Two did. It's Hell on Earth and it's here to stay. The Inferno. Dante lacerated.'

I listened quietly while the girl spoke. We walked hip to hip, in sync, glued to each other. I was getting tired, and wanted to find somewhere to spend the rest of the short Midsummer night.

'We are travelling from entropy to ecstasy. We are going to have ecstasy in this hideous entropy. We are fighting entropy with ecstasy.

'Everything we used to take for granted has been demo-lished: electricity, gas, water, sewage, supplies, milk, heating, air-conditioning, lighting, travel, telephones, food, radio, news-papers, television, internet, computers. It's all gone, up the spout, up the creek.'

She fell quiet for a while.

'Will it always be like this?' I wanted to know.

She whistled low. 'Oh yes. For about fifty to a hundred years, at least. Dad says so. He says –'

'– What does your father know about all this?' I asked her, suddenly angry, bitterly resenting her eternal recourse to her father.

'He's partly responsible for all this –'

'What? How come? *Day says, Dad says* – is he the President of Federal Europe?'

'Close. He's – He's the Pr–. Oh, stop pushing me. Stop going on at me about him. Kiss me.'

She turned to me and kissed me voraciously, eating me whole. When we broke apart we looked at each other for a long time. I stifled a yawn.

Then she smiled. 'I think I can hear singing.'

Yes, it sounded like... like a group of people singing. We were on the outskirts of a village. As we approached it along a lane we both saw a shooting star.

'That was a shooting star,' I said. 'Not a jet, a satellite, a missile.'

'You're such a stupid, romantic fool,' she laughed. 'It's just a fleck of dust entering the atmosphere.'

The singing seemed to be coming from a small church in a lane leading off the village square with its drained duck pond. We crept up to the windows.

Nothing could have prepared us for the scene we saw inside. It was straight out of every junk horror film ever made. A group of people in white stood in the pews. In front of the altar knelt six naked people, in three couples. A wizened man in his late sixties wearing stag's horns and a black gown presided over the congregation. The dingy Victorian interior was lit by candles. The words to the song included *Mother Earth, stars, wicca, life, love*.

The girl started to giggle.

'Oh shit, a witches' coven. Except they've got it all terribly wrong! Look at the man impersonating Old Nick!'

I was fascinated. By day these people might have been accountants, farmers, storekeepers. By night they were mad.

'I guess they'll be ritual buggery after this,' I said.

'I don't care as long as children aren't involved,' she replied. 'What a bunch of idiots. Napalm's too good for them.'

'There's still something sinister about a bunch of shop

assistants and nightclub owners who dress up and play witches in the local Anglican church, isn't there?' I wondered.

'There is if they do it right, if they go all the way.'

The girl had wandered around the corner of the building. She found a moped, clearly belonging to the mock-Satanists inside. The key was still in it. They thought no one would be bothering them at two in the morning in an isolated village, after curfew.

The girl wheeled it away and started it up. The noise sounded deafening in the night. The singing had stopped. The girl revved up the motor. I looked round the corner. The door of the little church had opened. A figure stood against the candlelight and shouted 'Oi!'

I leapt on the back of the moped. We sped off, the man running after us a little way; he tripped on his gown and stumbled, cursing.

We slept in a hollow behind a coppice of silver birch trees. I woke up when it was still dark, and chilly. The girl was sleeping softly. Her face was inches from mine. I could hardly see her. I pulled the blankets closer around us. It took me ages to get back to sleep, but I was in heaven, listening to the girl gently breathing, smelling her, feeling her hot breath, and feeling glorious simply because I was *with her*.

We rolled into a deserted boatyard at seven a.m. The far shore was a smudge of blue mist. Seagulls wheeled above. The tide inched silently across wet mud.

'We can't row across there,' said the girl. 'And the bridge will be patrolled. We must find a motor boat. I can't do anything today. I feel like a slug. I'm going to stay under my large, wet rock today.'

'What?'

'I'm a pretty slug, though.'

'You are.'

The girl turned to me and slid her hands under my clothes,

stroking my belly.

'Be my Tristan, be my Arthur, my Lancelot, my knight – get me across this water. Use your magic, boy. Move!'

She taunted me until I eventually left her and walked along the track behind rows of warehouses covered with enormous graffiti – swastikas, 'fuck yous', and the usual tags. Two men were throwing crates into a small craft. I asked them for a lift over the Sound. They looked at me suspiciously, squinting eyes sizing me up. For a moment I thought they might kill me for the clothes on my back. I offered them two packs of cigarettes and a fifty. They grudgingly accepted. In their boxes were tinned food, cosmetics, and medicine.

Half-an-hour later we were over the water, standing on the miracle soil of Cornwall. I lay down and kissed the Earth. It was sacred to me. The girl watched me, smoking.

'All you men want to do is to cock up your toes. Give juice for jelly.'

She was talking nonsense, it seemed to me. I looked up at her. She smiled softly. I was aroused in an instant, pressing myself into the ground.

'Make me into a Goddess,' she whispered.

I kissed her feet. I kissed the ground she walked upon. She seldom wore shoes. Shoes were for cities, with their carpets of broken glass. I licked her toes. She gasped softly.

At last we were in the land of monoliths and barrows, beaches and stone circles, the Celtic wonderland, the enchanted, pagan queendom of Cornwall. I romanced the place until it became mythical for me.

'"Give juice for jelly." What are you talking about?' I asked a little while later.

'Oh, it's just a word for orgasm Dad used to use.'

The girl baffled me. I never knew how she felt, how her mind worked, how she thought through things. In Southampton I remember she came out with this, in between ravenous bites into a hamburger:

'Everybody's had everybody, and everybody loves themselves.'

She grinned.

EIGHT

The Aquarium

IT WAS IN Liskeard, Lostwithiel, or Looe that we found the decimated sex shop. I forget which town: the days were melting into one another. It was a familiar sight: the door on its hinges, smashed-in, but the the dingy interior had a creepy atmosphere, with its racks of pornographic magazines and books, the sex aids under the counter, the DVDs stacked up to the ceiling. Outside the streets were utterly silent. It was a ghost town.

I stood by the door while the girl rooted around inside. It looked like someone had set off a grenade in there. The girl started showing me pictures.

'Look at this one. It's quite repulsive.'

She showed me two women entangled with a video camera; women writhing atop hairy male bodies; women with dildoes, chains, leather; women with animals.

I was amazed when the girl started to rub herself through her skirt. I knew she was nude underneath. I watched her dumb-founded.

I glanced outside, down the street. Nobody to be seen. I don't know, but I was nervous (I was also absolutely starving). I could see the wet stain on the girl's skirt when she turned to pick up some more magazines. It never took much to get her creamy.

'Come on, let's go. Take some stuff if you want. Let's go,' I said, picking up our bags.

But the girl wanted to stay. She started to read out a facts page from a skin mag: 'When you are anally penetrated, does your orgasm feel different? Men speak of anal orgasm, of general orgasm impossible to fix at any one location.'

The girl laughed. 'I want to feel what it's like, I want to know what it's like,' she kept repeating.

What? I wondered. I'd already made love to her in the ass many times. WHy was it different now?

'Come on,' I hissed.

But she wanted to make love, right there, in the middle of the smashed up sex shop, in amongst the debris of pornography.

'No no no no,' I said.

She reached over the counter and found some petroleum jelly. She undid my shorts and smoothed the jelly over my hard cock. I convulsed. I was always aroused by her touches. I felt sick. She turned, leant on the counter and flipped her skirt up over her back. I couldn't move but I couldn't resist her.

'Screw me,' she whispered. 'Screw my ass.'

So I did, easing gently inside her, opening her asshole with my thumbs. She writhed frantically, moaning.

'I want to attack patriarchy from the foundations upwards,' she told me in a strange, slurred voice. ' I want to go down to the powerbase. In my ass, in my ass. Fuck my ass good… Fuck me good. Fuck my ass.'

As I moved deeper inside her she told me she wanted every experience imaginable.

She groaned, 'It hurts, it hurts.'

I pulled out of her slowly – I didn't want to hurt her – but she yanked me back in by my balls. She wriggled around, bucking

83

her ass at me frenziedly. Her buttocks slapped on my belly as I thrust harder.

She went on tiptoes, dished her back and ground her bottom round and round. I was balls-deep inside her. She felt so hot and tight inside. I kept my eyes fixed on my cock sliding deep into her butt. She was panting loudly. I gripped the curves around her hipbones firmly.

She bent right over, still holding onto the counter, her head hanging down, her body shaking and trembling. Her smooth back blushed pink as we approached the end. When she pressed her palm over her clit she started to orgasm loudly, her ass clenching around me so tightly.

She was still gasping when we heard a noise from the back of the shop. I was still rammed inside her, hard as a bone. A teenage boy stopped, frozen, in the doorway. It seemed as if he worked there. He was horrified at what he saw. The girl laughed like a maniac. The kid's hand went to his crotch involuntarily. Then he ran. We got out of the sex shop in a rush and ran down the street.

'I wanted to be buggered by pornography,' said the girl later.

I couldn't think of anything to say to that.

She continued to muse: 'Imagine that kid growing up in the sex shop, surrounded by all that junk.'

It was only a week since we had met on the seafront. Already she had astounded me completely. It seemed as if the energy of the war was pumping through us. It seemed as if we had been together for centuries. Not for us the old ways of Western romance, the letters, the courtship, the meetings, the walks, the contracts and plans and wedding services. We did all of that in the moment we looked at each other, on the beach. Instead of spending weeks or months apart, appraising each other's suitability from a distance, dropping hints, sending notes, we had made love deliriously, and instantaneously.

'But even without this war and breakdown speeding

everything up madly,' the girl said, 'I'd still want to fuck you instantly. It's all there for us in that First Look. We are bypassing all of conventional romance: going to the cinema, theatre, restaurant, pub. All of that stuff constrains real wildness. Instead, we've got orgasms in moments.'

It sounded like rhetoric but it wasn't mere words with her. She was for real, all of her. I remember the girl said once, out of the blue, when we were talking about the war:

'I've slept with most of my friends.'

She meant men, but also women. Then she said: 'You're about the only person I feel happy about touching in public. I think about sex a lot. It's very important to me.'

As we walked West, in the blinding heat, along the edge of a field of dried, cracked soil, somewhere between Lostwithiel and St Austell, she said:

'We've got love-magic and it's special and I want to try all kinds of loving. When we separate, that's the real test. This is the great love-affair that haunts you for ages afterwards. I know because everyone talks about it. I'm glad the war's raging. It'll end everything prematurely; it'll stop the rot.'

And that mad moment in the sex shop, what was that all about? I wondered.

She said she was experimenting, seeing how far she could go. 'I want to do everything with you, try anything. I want to do all the wild things.'

We made love again, and again. Her body was hot and squashy and firm, like a fruit. We squished together, entwined.

'You're an angel,' I said, clumsily.

'No,' she laughed. 'No.'

'Then you're half-demon, half-angel,' I replied.

'No,' she said. 'No, I'm not.'

She jacked her legs out wide, so wide. She went wild, really wild.

'How do you like to fuck me?' she murmured. 'From behind, on top, the side, reverse cowgirl, horse and mare, snake fashion, whale fashion?'

She laughed, gripping my hands, holding them over her head, her body bent double. Then she moved her ankles back over her ears, so I could ram incredibly deep inside her. I could feel every ridge of her cunt.

She gasped like a bird. Her face was open, breathing me in, her eyes slitted. I sucked her nipples hard. She held my head, softly. I pressed inside her, going six strokes shallow then one deep, and grasped her hips. She felt juicy all over, and so wet.

At the last moment, I pulled out of her, firing a rope of come over her breasts and face. She laughed, smearing it into her skin and licking it off. Then she kissed with engorged lips.

She was whispering to me all the time – about fish, and their tiny, open mouths.

'Take me to the fish,' she said.

She meant the Aquarium, nearby. She seemed to know the whole of Cornwall. It was a sacred map, in her heart.

'Come on then, mermaid,' I said after we'd orgasmed together in a teeth-rattling, bone-shaking, nerve-shredding bliss.

The Aquarium was open. It was painted black inside and was run by a man called George Logue. He tottered about on a walking stick and called us 'gents and ladies'. He prodded the fish into action with his stick. The place tasted salty and smelt musty. The fish were magnificent and the girl lingered over them for ages. I was amazed that the place was still open.

George showed us eels from the Sargasso Sea, plaice, herring and guppies. He smoked a pipe and gesticulated with it as he told us stories of his days at sea. He spoke of that wonderful feeling of solitude and space, of not seeing anybody for days on end. Three months he went without seeing anyone, once.

'I love their mouths,' said the girl softly. Her face was pressed up against the glass. George prodded the fish and a crab crawled out from underneath them. All the sea creatures lived on top of each other, all messed in together. I liked to listen to the man, the king of his bubbling tanks.

While he sat in his tiny ticket-office eating sandwiches we chatted. I noticed a headline in his newspaper: 'FINAL TALKS FAIL'. Below that, a story about Korea moving into China using napalm.

'I've got a snake, if you'd like to see it,' said George.

The girl stirred violently. She hated snakes, couldn't even bear to hear the word mentioned. She loved plants, feathers, fans, fishes, jewellery, all kinds of exotic things, but not, never, snakes.

'No thanks. Goodbye,' she said, and left.

George shrugged. I followed the girl down the street, towards the riverbank, thinking about another story in the newspaper: a young suicide; gun in a garage; girlfriend had an abortion; the youth had just passed his exams.

The television stations, when they were broadcasting at all, spoke now of computer banks crashing; traffic and street signals failed; factories, hospitals and office blocks all dead and dark. The cities were sinking into darkness.

I thought of the desolate fairgrounds and arcades; the blank neons; the rows of lifeless TVs in shop windows (no one bothered to loot them, because broadcasts had ceased); the trains dead on the tracks; the stations empty. I thought of the deserted subway stations; all those vast, labyrinthine underground passages of tile and concrete that used to echo to the sound of sleazy jazz saxophones and buskers playing Bob Dylan and Tina Turner songs on acoustic guitars.

I thought of the streets full of trash, the boarded-up windows. I hadn't realized there was so much shit in the world. And I don't mean just the people, I mean the countless objects of everyday life.

Libraries had had all their shelves up-ended, and burnt. One newspaper told of trains full of corpses. There were also rumours of mass graves, huge pits dug to house the disease-ridden and the murdered people. There were rumours too of prisons being cleared of inmates by killing and burning. Cars had become tombs, the last resting-places of many a cook, waitress, mechanic, or analyst. We had seen mounds and makeshift crosses beside some roads.

Electricity was a major target of Britain's enemies, the girl told me. Already power was severely disrupted. A priority service was in operation – to hospitals, rescue services, Sub-Regional civil defence headquarters, etc. Temporary prisons had been created in old Army camps. The Royal Navy had taken over all shipping. Industries were collapsing rapidly as people stayed at home, building shelters, stockpiling supplies, or evacuating to remote regions. The Emergency Feeding Stations were overloaded with people demanding food. Looters were being shot.

I felt no sorrow for those smashed technological cities and towns. All those mirrored skyscrapers collapsing, all those utterly bland towns: Basingstoke, Maidstone, Leeds, Croydon, Milton Keynes, Guildford, Birmingham. It only needed one service industry to fail – electricity – and everything went with it: water, gas, dairies, food, transport, the media, hospitals, education. (Education was probably the last thing on anyone's mind at the moment).

We camped under the beech trees on the riverbank. The girl stripped and plunged into the water. I washed our clothes. It was excellent to drift on the outgoing tide, swaying under the leaves of the overhanging trees, listening to the fevered twilight songs of the birds. It was like being in a jungle. The sky turned through purple and rose to a deep azure.

We rolled about on the grass, laughing. It was glorious to be alive. Slow orgasms, slow touches, slow-motion loving. Then the slow glide into sleep, disturbed occasionally by shouts from the village.

I woke up aching all over from the tree roots and cold, hard ground beneath me. A chilly breeze was blowing up the estuary.

The girl murmured beside me, her long hair plastered over her red cheeks. I tucked the blanket around her, gulped down the dregs of the wine, pissed, stretched and went for a stroll.

The sea was rushing in, lifting up the boats (nothing, not even a global nuclear holocaust, could stop the tide). The sun, already high, gleamed behind high, thin clouds.

But my heart sank as I approached the Aquarium. The windows were broken. I called out through the open doorway.

George appeared, looking pale and haggard. His lips trembled and he was bruised badly on his face and arms. He told me what had happened: about two in the night he'd heard some shouts and went down from his bungalow to investigate.

A bunch of punks had smashed their way into the Aquarium. All the tanks had been broken, there was water everywhere, and most of the fish were dead, or gone.

'They told me they wanted the fish for food. They said the shops were empty and they were hungry. I tried to fight them but they beat me. The police wouldn't answer my call. I've had these vandals in here before. Usually they buzz off when I approach them. This time there were too many of them.'

I saw the ringent forms of the fish on the floor, like so many dead angels fallen out of a glass-walled heaven.

George heaved an old, rusty shotgun from under the counter of his ticket office.

'Next time I'll be ready for them.'

I helped him clear up. Outside four spotty thugs lazed about on a fence, grinning vapidly. They called out to me; I hurried back to the girl. She was all for leaving, so we skirted the village and made for the coast, following the river.

She told me about her morning's dream as we walked in an overgrown lane, the nettles and grass higher than our heads:

'I lived in an ice rink, between Stockholm and Acapulco. A black boy kept wanting me. I said there was enough to go round of me for everybody. He took me to Rio to watch the Carnival. He touched me and

my body felt like it was being blown up, like a rubber bed. I wore my hair in a bun. We took a chair-lift over the snowy valleys and Swiss chalets. I thought I was pregnant. In a kitchen a group of women were working a bacon slicer, putting a whole pig through it. They locked me in a brilliant white room. The heaters didn't work. Zurich Radio told me I was in a mental institution.

'Later we crossed the border in a political convoy, bound for Moscow. We escaped. You hammered someone's head off who'd attacked us, the piercing scream cut out suddenly. We made it to Poland, or it could have been Salzburg. We ate sauerkraut and coffee in a suburban café. A spray of bullets outside the Town Hall. Then we limped down to the Steppes, behind the Ringstrasse, into the Dorfeplatz. We waited for a train in the grey slush, fighting through a crowd of panicking schoolgirls.

'The Mongol machine moved off, and the Food Train rolled in. The hordes pulled down statues. A church organ played Mozart. Sandbags everywhere. We were hounded by Alsatians and wolves. I rubbed grease into your hands, to stave off the chill. Jews with revolvers and icy smiles played cards. The train stopped. In Kiev we holed up in an oyster hotel. We made love.'

'What do you make of that?' the girl asked me.

'I think you have very strange dreams. You scare me –'

'How can I scare you? You're *male*,' the girl snapped, her mood switching in an instant.

I couldn't answer her. I never can, when she speaks like that. She is a wolf, running through snowbound forests, and no one can catch her.

Then she talked about George and his Aquarium:

'Men love violence but hate the consequences… George said Cornwall was a continent, with rivers, mountains and many countries. I was here many times as a child. George didn't remember me. I stole one of his fish once, and threw it in the river, to set it free.'

We passed a solitary gas station with a blurred face at the

window. Outside were big hand-painted NO PETROL signs.

'Get something to eat. I'm starved,' the girl said. But the face disappeared when I approached, and didn't answer when I knocked and finally beat on the door.

We dived into the trees and fields again (after spotting an Army truck at the top of the hillside ahead).

I climbed one of the electricity pylons halfway up and saw the ocean.

We had some cake George had given us, that was all. I could hear her stomach rumbling. She slid her hand into my shorts, and rubbed me to hardness within seconds.

'Roll over,' she murmured. I lay face-down in the long grass, watching a cabbage white butterfly flutter by.

She pulled my shorts down slowly and started licking my buttocks. She gave me the obscene kiss, the Devil's kiss, on the anus. Her tongue in my ass drove me wild.

Then she straddled me, lying flat on my back and pressing her body over me; her skin seared my sunburn. Her hair fell around my face. I bent round to kiss her.

She ground her hot wet gash up and back, up and back. The sap was flowing from her like a flood. I reached behind and stroked her pubic hair and wide-open slit. I circled her engorged clitoris softly. She rocked her hips back and forth. I loved it when she kneaded my buttocks and shoulders.

I pressed myself into the grass, undulating. She reached in her bag and pulled out a long black dildo. My eyes went wide and I laughed.

'No way!'

She pushed the tip inside me, gently. I gasped. It hurt madly, it felt huge.

'It's too fucking dry,' I moaned.

The girl giggled. She spat on her fingers and pressed them inside me.

'Come on come on come on,' she gasped, pushing the dildo in deeper, making me cry out. The trees above rustled, the ground swelled beneath me, the air throbbed and I pulsed into the soil, coming violently.

The girl lay flat over me, writhing and gasping like a landed fish. She was pressing her mound on my hip rhythmically, and her breasts into my back. Her hot breath on my neck.

'Kneel over me,' I whispered. 'I want to suck you.'

But she wanted to fuck.

She seemed to be in a faint. I felt ecstatic – sore and opened out and beautiful. Then we began to wrestle like angels, our lust becoming mystical and extreme.

She fucked me really hard, with amazing wildness. She was so aroused, so hot and wet with palpitating sex. She terrified me. She smelt strange, bitter, pungent. Extraordinary intensity. We were filled up with the heat of archangels. Utter passion, utter bliss, fucking like idiots in the sunlight. She enfolded me, cascaded around me. She bit me, gave me suckmarks all over, dug her nails into me. A crucifixion of love.

The whole world fused with us. The trees above, the electricity poles looming like ogres, the breeze tantalizing and hot.

She made me come with the dildo rammed in deep, her fingers pressing on my balls. I pulsed into the grass, then shifted suddenly, still hard, and entered her deeply from the side. She cried out in surprise, but loved it. She held her toes, spreading her legs so wide and high, her ankles up around her ears. I hooked my shoulder under her knee, to press in ever deeper. I shifted on top of her, to pull her bottom onto my knees, so I could ram even deeper. She loved it like that. When she came she clawed me, bit me, went utterly wild and wild and wild.

Afterwards we were sore as pigs, hot, sweaty, sticky. I felt castrated, the girl felt derailed. We wolfed down the last of the cake, and the girl lit one of our last cigarettes to celebrate.

'You thought it was the Devil buggering you then, didn't you?' she murmured, stroking my face as she sat looking down at me.

I smiled.
The sun was shining right into my eyes.

NINE

The Garden Maze

THE FURTHER WE travelled West, the more the landscapes looked like something out of a dream – one of the girl's dreams. I hadn't been in Cornwall since childhood, but it never looked like this. In a creek we found a dry boat park. Someone had opened the sluice gates and let all the water out. Boats lay stranded in the mud, painted in a garish, funfair colours: red and blue, orange and green. A sign advertized boat rides by the hour. The remains of a fire, broken glass, feathers and three lengths of blue rope lay next to it, marking the spot of some obscure night ritual. Oddly-shaped houses were hidden in the trees. It was eerily silent. There was something really haunting about these deserted spaces, these leisure parks and boat yards, the kids' playgrounds and picnic spots. In the shingle lay the litter of a family meal. I picked up a wrapper:

'Animal and vegetable fat. Maltose Syrup, Modified Starch, Diphosphates, Sodium Bicarbonate, Malic Acid, Potassium Sorbate, Sodium Alginate, Dextrose, Sugar.'

But everywhere was so empty, as if there'd been a complete and sudden evacuation, or an instantaneous plague. Perhaps we were the only people left on Earth? No, there were a couple of kids catching crabs on the rocks. A pile of the creatures lay next to their trainers.

Roseland, Zone Point, Marazion, Mullion Cove, Wolf Rock, Black Head – the magic names of Cornwall. And our favourite: the Lizard.

The girl called me over. She'd dragged a rowing boat down to the water's edge. We climbed in and set sail. For a while we marvelled at the saturated colours, the deep blues of the water, the vibrant yellows of the flowers.

'I've always wanted to have the world to myself,' I said.

The girl dipped her hand in the sea. I rowed and watched the beautiful cloudscapes while the girl followed a giant aircraft moving high up in the empyrean. We could hear the roar and rumble of the plane for ages, echoing around the estuary.

We floated dreamily along the shore until we were startled by a very loud explosion. A plume of black smoke rose into the sky beyond the trees. We rowed on. The girl rummaged around in her bag. She fished out the camera and threw it overboard.

'We won't be needing that anymore. No time to print or send the images.'

'What about your pictures?' I wondered. 'They would be amazing.'

She shrugged, then she threw more stuff into the sea: the dildo, cosmetics, a notebook, some empty plastic bottles, jewellery. She then pulled out a vibrator.

'Oh, I'd forgotten about this. I got it from the sex shop.'

She pulled her skirt up and spread her thighs. I kept rowing and watched her pull a tampon out and flick it into the sea. She switched on the vibrator and played it over her clitoris. She closed her eyes and sank into an erotic reverie.

The buzzing noise made me want to laugh. It seemed as loud as an express train in that morning sea-silence. I didn't need to look around to see if anybody was looking; we were totally alone.

After a few minutes she started to talk, still with her eyes shut.

'I used to use the shower-head to do this, in my father's house. I used to lie for hours in the bath, covered in bubbles, coming and coming. It's delicious.'

She kept rotating the vibrator on her swollen clit. 'Kaspar liked to do it in front of mirrors. He liked to see himself inside me, and liked me to watch myself. Strange boy.'

I looked round – we were drifting too far from the shore, out to sea. As I turned the boat around, we heard a deafening explosion. Again a mass of black smoke boiled behind the tree tops.

'Who's doing that?' I wondered.

'I know who that is,' smiled the girl. She pushed her belly forward and arched her back. She began to gasp, quietly. Her torso tightened as she orgasmed. I loved to watch the familiar rippling of her belly, the jerk of her thighs, her nipples hard points under the T-shirt.

When we landed the girl leapt out of the boat and strode into the trees. I pulled the boat onto the stones and followed her.

She was far ahead of me – in every way.

When I caught up with her she was talking to a bizarre looking youth, dressed in black leather. His right eye had been punched in, and swelled up so much he couldn't see out of it. His hands were covered in bruises. No doubt there were wounds all the way up his arms from too many needles. He looked rake-thin.

It was Kaspar, the political fanatic we'd met in Brighton. The girl was very excited to see him.

'I knew it was you,' she said, hanging onto his arm. He grinned and squeezed her. This was the freak the girl had been fantasizing about just now in the rowing boat. She was still creamy from the thoughts of him.

He was the cause of the explosions. He had been blowing up

cars. Why? For kicks, I guessed. But then he explained:

'I'm terrified of stationary cars. They just stand there. I think they're going to explode, because they always do in American movies and cop shows.'

He had a few cans of petrol with him, and some explosives. His hands were covered in oil. He took us along a dusty track to the burning remains of the car he'd just blown up. The wind shifted and we caught the smoke head-on. Coughing, we moved away. He was certainly playing the chaos game well. He was like a kid living out his fantasies. But then, so were we.

'Come on, I'll take you to my place.'

He dived into the trees. I didn't want to go. The girl yanked my arm and dragged me along. After a few minutes we came to a huge modern house, an architect's wildest dream, all crazy angles and blocky, over-hanging concrete.

Kaspar had smashed in a window. The occupants – like everyone – were elsewhere. It was astonishing to walk back into luxury, to see the full drinks cabinet, the fluffy rugs, the smoked glass coffee tables, the open plan rooms, the pine furniture. Pop Art prints on the walls. A huge fish tank, but all the fish dead. Book shelves full of religious works. An immaculate kitchen, but bereft of decent food. No water in the taps. Kaspar glugged at a bottle of vodka.

'I've been here for five days,' he told us, 'to escape from everything. I got tipped off about this place by a mate.'

He'd been sleeping on the gigantic red sofa. Was he scared of bedrooms? A couple of needles lay on a table. He told us many of his fellow 'activists' had been arrested and put in a transit camp near Guildford.

'Will you stay here? I've got to go out – I need some more gear –' He pointed to the needles.

'Sure,' said the girl. 'You go, Kaspar. We'll hang out.'

I had no intention of waiting. But the girl scoured the cupboards for food, then lay on the bed upstairs. I felt uneasy. I didn't like the look of the place. I wandered into the den, dominated by a pool table and a pinball machine, and found some old newspapers:

Cities in fear as addicts turn to crime – Drug addicts have unleashed a rising wave of muggings on British cities this year in a desperate bid to pay for their craving.
Sheltering for peace – Five hundred police yesterday raided a village where drugs and sex were for sale in the grounds of a stately home.
Blows to the head of chopped wife – Susan Brown received 10 blows to the face and head before her body was cut up and scattered across London.

I switched on the television. It was amazing to see the unreality of television after so long without it. I hadn't missed a thing. But it was all still here, all the banality and the violence. Only one station was broadcasting, and it was all news interspersed with emergency flashes. TV as a nanny, an auntie.

I found that it was all true – the mass graves, the trains full of corpses, the inner city riots, the burning houses. Packs of wild dogs were roaming the streets of Britain. The refuse in the larger towns was unmanageable now. The stench was intolerable. Fires blazed.

Pictures from around the world showed similar states of destruction: Seoul, Sao Paolo, Chicago, Bangkok, Sydney, Johannesburg, Osaka, Moscow, Madrid. Images of London by night revealed darkness speckled with bonfires. Churches were also burning. All kinds of raids were going on, everywhere.

A bulldozer had piled up mounds of earth around Stonehenge and the hippies were digging themselves in deep: it was a stone age bunker. The same thing had happened at Avebury, Cerne Abbas, Callanish, the Rollright Stones, Tintagel and Glastonbury Tor, all the mystical centres of Britain. The images of naked hippies dancing on top of the hanging stones lightened the mood for a moment.

A couple of adverts followed this broadcast: for fall-out shelters ('equipped with the latest security systems!'), then a list of emergency telephone numbers. An advert for a website that logged the global death toll: www.death.com. Then a blank screen. Then the whole thing repeated – exactly the same news, the same adverts and warnings.

I turned the TV off. As I knelt down something caught my eye: a DVD entitled *The Nuclear Requiem,* handwritten in green ink. Curious, I set it running.

A face appeared on the screen, the face of a haggard, battered woman. But what struck me was her surroundings: she had been filmed in the lounge of the house we were in: the same prints on the wall, the same free-standing staircase. Clearly this American woman was some colleague of whoever's house it was. She was relating a bizarre story which had started in a delicatessen on 59th Street in New York last month:

'It was May or June, and it was snowing. I remember that. Can you believe it, snow in New York in June –?'

Here the woman looked quizzically at someone off camera.

'– Tommy, my producer, came in and we talked about doing a piece on the spiritual feelings of America. I thought it was a waste of time, but he was persistent. I agreed to do it.

'I knew what he wanted: big evangelical stuff, to placate the network's backers and shareholders. And I wanted to get out of New York, to get away from the people we'd met on the streets doing a vox pop; the people who told me "if I had a gun I'd blow you creeps away." The whole of New York teeters perpetually on the edge of a nervous breakdown.

'Well, Mark Hata had heard of a crazy messiah figure somewhere upstate, in the Catskills. America is full of would-be messiahs, as you know, Tony: Joseph Smith, Thomas Lake Harris, Huntsman T. Mason, Martin Luther King, J.F. Kennedy, Charles Manson, and now Josh Williams.

'The crucifixions in Kenya were getting more frequent, so the timing was good. We had some good stuff on the revivalist rituals, the Mormons, Christian Scientists, Ranters, Jumpers and snake-handling cults. Biblical hysteria was spreading like wildfire with the war. We'd already done a powerful piece on the Indian Holi-Day, complete with film of the turtles that clear away the partially burnt bodies.

'All of our material is sensationalized by Tommy and his network, but we don't care: it pays. You'd show some guy carrying around a twelve foot wooden cross from state to state and they'd put hideous music over it, get Dick Meyers to voice it, and turn it into trash.

'Once we did a piece on what people would do in the last minutes before The Bomb. Nearly all the men said they'd screw anybody in sight, but the station blanded that out. Instead we got repentant sinners praising the Lawd Gawd in a Louisiana chapel. We knew the network suits would make anything we did vapid. You can't tell Americans about panpsychism or the psycho-pompous or olonism, the MBAs told us. It's too scary.

'Anyway, I was meeting Mark at the airport. As I came out of my apartment building this guy came up to me and asked if I was Emma Daniel, and am I doing something on religion in America? Yeah, I told him, now take a walk. He grabbed my arm and wouldn't let me go. He was quick. I yelled, but a woman hollering in Manhattan doesn't attract any attention. He forced me inside a car at the kerb. There were three guys in their twenties in the car, including a Puerto Rican with rancid breath. They filled me with a load of shit about 'how their voice should be heard too'. These were Josh Williams' buddies.

'After God knows how long and how far – it was dark – we pulled up at a farm. Children ran about; a radio played Gospel music; the place stank of pigs, goats, chickens, sewage.

'I was introduced to Josh Williams in his battered stetson and dungarees – a relic in his late fifties from the Civil War, it seemed, a gnarled remnant of the frontier days. He told me about the commune, his plans for a cult surrounding Joshua Irving Williams and his Indoctrination Plan for the Twenty-First Century. It involved sinless open marriage and the brainwashing of children, among other things.

'I told him I ought to be getting back to town, but he wanted to make sure the network got the right coverage. The man, with his beard, red eyes and slurred post-stroke speech, was clearly mad. His sons were too. The ceremonies came later.

'Williams put on a flowing white gown. With outspread arms he began a sermon to a congregation of farmers and their families: "Blessed be the people, blessed be the harvests," and so on. The crowd murmured at appropriate points. Candles flickered, the incense stank. The barn seemed packed with all sorts of folk – many of whom would have stayed home watching *Oprah* or *Letterman* a few months ago, before the religious hysteria created by the war.

'The white-clad maniac spouted his baloney: "And the Earth shall break apart in fire! Only those who have taken the Oath shall be free!" I felt sick of this mumbo-jumbo.

'Then the floor was cleared. Occult signs were patterned with salt on the boards. Rugs were placed in the centre of the barn. Williams started annointing a group of couples looking glum in their tatty dungarees. Everyone was high on drugs. The lovers lay down, nervously undressing each other. Williams kept intoning madly, keeping up a stream of holy platitudes. Then the ritual copulations began. The floor was soon a mass of writhing loins.

'Williams glowed as he surveyed the orgy, muttering: "No emissions, no emissions." Ejaculations were not allowed (neither was alcohol – but hallucinogens were fine). I felt like laughing, but couldn't. A youth with stains on his jeans was led away, embarrassed.

'I was feeling drowsy; I think the drinks may have been spiked. Smoke wreathed the room. It was difficult to see anything clearly. The night ended in a stupor.

'The next day the farmers came to pay Josh Williams for his blessings.

'"Even spirituality has its price," Williams told me, slyly, looking at me sidelong.

'It was all pretentious vapour, a load of unholy smoke. "When will the cameras arrive?" he kept asking me.

'How men need their mirrors, I thought grimly.

'I was shown around the commune. Families lived on top of each other in squalor. Obscure Oriental deities were stuck on the walls.

'The kids' speech betrayed the over-use of LSD-25, and brain-washing, year-in, year-out. "Father's always right," they said, like zombies.

'Williams gave meditation lessons: "Let your self go until you reach the *muga*," and so on. There was frenetic dancing, and moaning and thrashing around on dirty carpets. Mass regression. The farm was a workshop of battered psychoses.

'Then the television crew rolled up (late as usual). I was relieved to see them, even Robin Konigsberg, the idiot producer, who wrecked my Iraq story when he re-cut it for the six. I felt a little sorry for Williams the messiah as they exposed his hoax.

'Back at the network, Tommy was excited. "Great, great," he told me on the telephone. It was a good story. We broadcast it that very evening. Then the police moved in and cleaned up.'

The DVD suddenly ended with a screen of white noise. I turned off the TV and looked for the girl. She wasn't in the huge orange bed, where I expected to find her. I looked out of the floor-to-ceiling lounge window.

She was outside, sitting in the centre of a grass maze. She was crouched in the lotus position. I half-expected to see her douse her T-shirt in petrol and set fire to herself, like a protesting anti-war Zen monk.

When I went outside she wasn't humming a *mantra* but was gobbling a tin of cold beans. She looked up at me and grinned.

TEN

The Open-Air Cinema

SOMEWHERE BETWEEN MEVAGISSEY and Falmouth – near St Mawes perhaps – we stumbled across an open-air cinema. It overlooked the sea. An old film was being screened on the tattered sheet: *The Night of the Iguana*. Or perhaps it was, aptly, *Intolerance*. We sat on some rocks and watched the flickering images. About ten people sat about near us. The projectionist looked like a Quaker.

The girl pulled out some sheets of paper. It was another message from her father. God knows how he sent it to her. She began to read quietly:

"Arms escalation, ground shock, detonation, air burst, broken arrows, ground zero, maximum yield, deterrence, the sanctuary theory, overkill, overpressure, time-sensitive targets, stealth, fratricide, launch-under-attack, single-shot kill probability, first strike, AEW, CIWS, HEAT, SOSUS, MAW, WPO, NATO, ICBM, SS-20, Pershing II, BGM-1099 – the wonders of nukespeak and nuclear theology."

'My father loves all this techno-talk,' the girl explained.

I looked over at her serious, frowning profile. She flicked her hair away from her ears, licked her lips and continued:

"Minuteman III, Mark 12A warhead, 375kt yield. Tu22 M/26 Backfire medium-range aircraft, Mach 2.5 speed, 7,927kg weapons payload, 3,000km combat range.'

"B52H strategic bomber, range 16,000km, payload 70,000 pounds. SS-N-18 Mode 3 submarine-launched ballistic missile, 7 MIRV, range 6,500km, total yield over 150 megatons.'

"1,000,000 dollars per minute spent on arms (1982 figures). Over 100,000,000 people work in the military forces worldwide or in back-up services. Arms are second only to oil as money-making enterprises. There are 30,000-plus tactical and inter-mediate-range nuclear weapons and 20,000 strategic weapons. One Lance battlefield missile can deliver six Hiroshimas. A submarine costs 1.5 billion dollars."

As the girl read out this list of horrors I watched the big close-ups of Lillian Gish and the vast long shots of Belshazzar's Feast in D.W. Griffith's epic silent movie. There was no soundtrack: just the sea, swishing up and down nearby.

'I thought the nuclear stockpiles had been dismantled, decommissioned, or something,' I said.

'Since the highpoint of nuclear paranoia, in the Cold War, sure,' the girl answered, 'when there were 60,000-plus warheads in the 70s and 80s. But don't be so naïve, cute boy: the leaders *said* they were dismantling bombs, but were they really? They were not. These things cost a *fuck of lot* of money.'

I went to touch her hand, but she shifted away from me. She was engrossed in her father's letter:

"Maximum capability is about one strategic warhead hitting a target every twenty seconds. Let's take a one megaton air-burst scenario over a small city. At ground zero, all buildings would be destroyed. Winds of 1,000 mph. All combustible stuff would ignite. Flesh would melt. People would die in the suffocation from the firestorm. From two to five miles away, most buildings would be flattened. Winds of 130 mph. Clothing would ignite. Radiation sickness is inevitable.'

"At three miles away you'd feel a flash of light; then intense heat which chars to the bone (full-thickness burns); fifteen seconds later the windows would be blown in by the blast wave; and you'd be thrown around by the wind.'

"Most people would be permanently blinded by the light. Fall-out is second-stage radiation, contaminating water, the food chain, everything. Everywhere would be a 'Z Zone', a fall-out zone."

On the screen at the drive-in, the St Bartholomew's Day Massacre, Christ on the Road to Calvary, the 'Mountain-girl' in Babylon and the innocent husband's execution merged together in Griffith's masterpiece. It was all the more powerful for being silent.

The bald projectionist put on the last reel. Nobody said anything; they seemed to be listening to the girl reading aloud, over the sound of the motor of the protector.

"Nuclear reactors will be hit with ground-bursts: the fall-out from the cores will be deadly," the girl continued. "Not just cities but airfields, communications centres, military stores and camps will also be targets.'

"A list of targets in the United Kingdom would include: submarines and bases; stockpiles; strategic command centres (Hawthorn, Whitehall, High Wycombe, etc); communications links (including British Telecom centres, cel phone towers, and the microwave tower network); the very low frequency radio stations at Rugby and Criggon, used for talking to submerged submarines; missile and long range radar centres (such as Clee Hill, Fylingdales and Bishopcourt); air defence missile and inter-ceptor bases; nuclear production sites (such as Burghfield, Aldermaston, Sellafield and Cardiff); power stations; nuclear power stations (such as Dungeness, Douunreay, Wylfa and Heysham); the chemical industries; oil and gas terminals and ports; troop concentrations (Salisbury, Aldershot, Colchester, etc);

fuel depots; ammunition stocks; ports; government administration centres; and finally the major urban and industrial centres: London, Manchester, Birmingham, Leeds, Bradford, Sheffield, Southampton, Bristol, Glasgow, Dundee, Newcastle, Huddersfield, Hull, Portsmouth, Swansea, Leicester, Coventry, Liverpool, Cardiff, Nottingham, Derby and so on.

"If birds are killed insects might devastate crops. Fires fanned by the winds will destroy much woodland. The 'Square Leg' operation of 1980 estimated 100 US military targets in Britain, including Upper Heyford, Boscombe Down, Greenham Common, Burtonwood, etc, as well as Birmingham, Sheffield, Liverpool, Swansea, Glasgow, etc. A million dead, three million injured. Or 35 million surviving, depending on which survey you read.

"Switzerland says it has shelter space for 90% of its population. They'll be hiding in freeway tunnels. The advice is to dig a hole and hide in it. Or turn a room into a fall-out sanctuary, for two weeks.

"The US will try to disperse their aircraft around the country, and many airfields will be hit. Towns such as Oxford, Cheltenham, Carlisle, Chester and Birmingham will have airburst attacks – the idea being to kill as many people as possible. Places such as Liverpool, St Mawgan, Coningsbury, Bracknell and Farnborough will receive ground bursts to knock out machinery, ports, industries, ships and buildings. Places like Felixstowe and Canvey Island will have ten times more bombers attacking them than, say, Swindon or Manchester.

"Don't forget chemical, biological and radiological warfare. Get yourself some NBC-protective clothing. For example, the nerve agent GB incapacitates quickly; if inhaled death follows in a few minutes.

"The 'H-hour' approacheth.

"London and Glasgow are already flooded from underwater explosions. The emergency flood gates in many subway train stations haven't prevented the fatal flooding of the secret underground communications centre beneath London's golden streets. The Clyde and the Forth will be blown to smithereens.

"Think of the people manning those lonely snowbound DEW (Distant Early Warning) radar sites at Cambridge Bay and Dye Main in Canada or Thule in Greenland. This is their big hour, the fruit of all those years spent watching for enemy missiles. Our own Baltic Missile Early Warning Station at Fylingdales, Yorkshire, will do its bit too, but the US satellites will be the first to pick up the heat traces as the missiles launch.

"The Attack Warning Red signal will come from the Home Office Warning Officer at High Wycombe. The signal is given to police, HQs and warning points. Also to the BBC, who'll be in their broadcasting bunker at Wood Norton near Evesham, just as in the Second World War.

"The old scenarios (Square Leg, Scrum Half, Hard Rock and other 'war games' exercises) suggest that about 300 megatons will be used on Britain. But the Russians have over 600 megatons for the UK. Three thousand megatons could be used in a 'worse case' situation.

"By the way, Lory," her father continued, "nuclear devices have been used now in Germany, the Gulf, Central America and Afghanistan, despite what the British media might tell you contrary to the fact."

The film finished. The audience got up and wandered off into the darkness (only a few had stayed to the end). I felt depressed, had done so ever since we'd left Kaspar the day before. We raced through the darkness to get the last ferry over the Fal river. We saw the gaunt silhouettes of gigantic ships anchored further up the estuary (a couple of tankers were listing over).

When we reached the King Harry chain ferry we found it had been burnt to a cinder. The moonlight gleamed on the water. We scoured the shore until we found a tiny rowing boat with one broken oar. It took us ages to paddle across the creek, between the abandoned ships.

It was late now – eleven or so – but we managed to cadge a

lift off a chain-smoking widow. We were just about the only people on the road. The woman muttered about losing her husband years ago to cancer. It was an event of such significance, it seemed to dominate her life. She dropped us in the centre of Falmouth.

This deepwater port, once home to the Mail Packets that sailed to the West Indies, Brazil and Canada, was now devoid of all life. Gone were the liners, steamers, pleasure cruisers, fire-floats and troop ships. The quays and streets were gloomy. Hardly a light in any window. Garbage everywhere. Ropes clinked against masts but all the boats looked as if they hadn't been used for years.

We wandered through a smashed doorway into an old theatre, an ancient music hall venue converted into a cinema. We sat amongst the rubble, playing the torch over the recently renovated stucco and gold. The cinema screen had been slashed to bits. The graffiti included the usual items – *I WANT TO FUCK LUCY* – as well as some more acerb phrases: *INGLESE MORIRE*, and *SMASH THE YANKS*.

The night was turning into a silently-screaming horror movie. We walked up to the train station. Two men lay face down in pools of blood. Fæces littered the floor. Swastikas had been sprayed in silver on the walls. Glass everywhere again. How bland and ordinary the town looked by day: the hotels and bars, the holiday flatlets, and how unreal by night.

Up a road we found a glorious tropical park. The whole place had been left to run wild, like every patch of ground we passed. The grass was knee-high. Here we shared wet kisses inspired by the thick, dark leaves. The girl was in ecstasy, loving these broad-leaved gunnera. We discovered a brick alcove where we bedded down.

The next day we hung about the beach. The refreshments kiosks had all been boarded-up, or raided, or burnt-out. Along Gyllyngvase Beach we spotted two swimmers. The oil slicks didn't bother them, it seemed. A jet, plying the rarest altitudes, looked as tiny as a satellite. It looked so small it couldn't harm anyone, I thought. Difficult to imagine that 19,000 pounds of explosives were being carried to some far-off target.

The girl pulled me into the exotic undergrowth on the strand. The grass was thick underfoot, like the floor of a rainforest. She flipped up her yellow T-shirt and pulled me to her breasts (which still had suck-marks from the night before). She grasped her breasts and pointed a nipple onto my tongue.

It was hot and humid in amongst the vegetation but I felt bone-dry. She poured liquid into my mouth. Our bones snapped and cracked as we made love furiously. The ivy-dark plants shivered in the breeze.

Her kisses were like exquisite insect bites, or the soft flutters of butterfly wings. I had three fingers inside her as I knelt behind her. She lay on her side, pushing her bottom back rhythmically. She groped blindly behind for my cock.

A sharp cry from the beach brought us out of our passion-soaked reverie. We peered through the fronds, flicking away the flies.

A van lay on its side. It had slid off the road. The doors were open and a collection of bizarre objects had been scattered over the sand: a bundle of television sets, boxes of rotting fish, some live chickens, which ran away, and some bottles of milk in crates. But the milk was *green*.

A man, badly shaken, argued with three black-suited policemen. They grabbed his arm. He shook them off, and started running up the beach. He didn't get very far. The police caught up with him and started punching him until he was senseless. Then they bundled the body into their car.

The collection of bits and pieces on the sand looked like the dreamscapes of the crazier Surrealist painters. A girl scuttled out from her hideaway behind a hut to examine the leftovers.

I dressed and went to speak to the little girl. I asked her about her parents.

'Got none,' she told me. She was about six with scraggy limbs and long, tangled hair. She looked like a runaway from a Pre-

Raphaelite painting entitled *'Remorse'*. I smiled as she raced barefoot about the beach, trying to catch one of the chickens.

In the trash I found an out-of-date magazine which had a picture-story of the floods in Florence, Varanasi, Cairo and New Orleans. The Nile, the Ganges, the Mississippi and the Volga had flooded a few weeks ago. The sea-levels were apparently rising. I looked at the sea next to me but it didn't seem to be any higher. The photos of the fires in the flooded towns were spectacular. The oil slicks from the cars and basement tanks had been lit by vandals.

I was still absorbed in the magazine when the girl ran up, shouting. But it was too late: the police had returned. They came over to us, looking like aliens from some forgotten Fifties B-movie, and told us we were under arrest. We argued, but knew it was useless to run. They took us to a dilapidated police station and with no further ado threw us into a smelly green cell. Fæces and urine spattered the floor and walls. We crouched on the bunks for two hours until we were interrogated by a sergeant with a thick West Country accent. He asked us about the corpses we'd seen at the train station. He said we looked too healthy.

The girl kept asking to use the telephone. The sergeant eventually conceded, and she rang her father. He fixed it and ten minutes later – after a few more pointless questions – we walked free. Drugs, money, politics, murder – they couldn't pin anything on us. The girl's father was too well-connected, it seemed.

'Let's get the hell out,' I said.

ELEVEN

The Underground Caves

NIGHT IN THE DUCHY: hoots, screeches, sqwarks and songs – the usual symphony of night noises (owls, bats, birds). The strange creaking of the trees; clouds eating up a horned moon; the ocean a sheet of silver. The moon, nearly full, lit up our night walk. Through dark woods and fields we passed, like wraiths. We stepped over lilacs and buttercups then broken glass and twisted metal. The night scents changed from flowers to oil and refuse. I could taste a little of Autumn on the air, that special dampness and edge in the atmosphere.

We walked swiftly, through a burnt-out Jerusalem, a decimated Thebes, a blasted Antioch. Vega, the Summer Square and the Pleiades flashed overhead. Trees, poles, masts, huts – everything was frozen. The Earth had travelled two million miles around the sun since the night before but all seemed so still. I saw a distant bonfire, the headlamps of a car miles off, but nothing else.

The girl stripped off and walked naked. I was not surprised to come across a telescope mounted on a tripod. It had been trained on the moon, which had since moved. No sign of the stargazer. We strode along the cliffs and hills.

'Ishtar, I'm so hot,' the girl murmured.

I watched her slim moonlit figure skipping through the dewy grass., She took my hand and placed it on her womb, then inside her. She made me lick my fingers. She tasted delicious. She laughed, and danced, spinning madly with her arms thrown wide.

I was kissing the ground she danced upon, and waltzing with her and generally having a great time, when we heard a really eerie sound: loud, menacing laughter. We froze. It was scary to hear such a sound in that stillness. We saw the glow of a fire on the brow of the next hill. Slowly, carefully, we crept up to the ring of light, clambering over barbed wire, walls and hedges.

'Don't get too close,' whispered the girl. 'I don't like the look of this.'

I thought it was just a bunch of drunken kids. Then we heard that evil laughter again. No, it was not a teenager's bonfire party. No music, for a start, and no yells and whoops. The sound was too sombre.

Sitting around the fire beyond a hedge were the gnarled forms of strange creatures. Their faces looked stonily at the flames. A dark figure in a cloak read out of a large leatherbound book, looming over the people. He was wearing an ugly, hairy mask and horns. Oh no, I thought, not another amateur coven of druids. As the ceremony progressed we caught the words on the wind, along with clouds of incense:

'Lucifer, Baphomet, Aradia...' The names of the old gods of the witches. This was the real thing, the girl told me:

'Six men, six women, and a man impersonating the Devil. They're conducting a Black Fast. He's reading from a *Book of Shadows*. They're trying to concentrate on some object or person, to cause them harm, or death. They're real witches, too: because most of them are pissed – stoned yet malefic.'

I watched fascinated as the leader bade the coven focus on the world's politicians and war-mongers. They were trying to avert the war, trying to blast the minds of the people in control. It was astonishing to watch these middle-class husbands and wives, these farmers, estate agents and lawyers performing a sabbath next to the age-old barrow on the hill. The goat-man took a cup round.

'That'll be menstrual blood, goat's blood or lager, depending on how serious they are,' whispered the girl.

One of the initiates spat out the liquid – it must have been blood. But then she grabbed the cup and gulped at it. This went on for a while. I was getting bored. Then I noticed the rituals has stopped. The man in the goat's mask was turned our way. He couldn't have heard us, though.

The goat-man pointed. Another man stood up and peered towards us over the smoking fire. There was some arguing, then the second man started to run down the hill. We turned and ran.

'It must have been my influence,' said the girl, panting.

What? I thought, but kept running. Perhaps she had tried to avert the Black Fast, using telepathy perhaps, because it might endanger her father, one of the men in power.

Headlights swept across the hillside. We kept running, down and down, until we reached the cliff's edge, without looking back. We dashed along the edge of the cliff, exhausted. We climbed down a gully. I was pretty sure they wouldn't follow us. To make certain of it, we dived into a cave.

The moon, westering, shone into the cavern, which went back further than we had first thought.

'This is a Dragon's Lair,' whispered the girl as we waded through the cold water. 'Or perhaps we'll find the Minotaur, or smugglers.'

She was in a happy mood, not at all upset by being chased down a hill by a witches' coven. She laughed.

'Did you see their faces, so bored and drugged-up? Are we

going to stay in here? It smells odd.' We looked around the cavern with the flashlight; it was ankle-deep with the water, dotted with boulders round and smooth like dinosaur eggs.

'I was taken to a coven once,' the girl continued, lighting a cigarette and sitting on a rock. I passed her the last of the wine.

'It's great fun, all that chanting, dancing and ritual. You get initiated by someone of the opposite sex. The men are Pan, Lucifer, Dionysius; the women are Diana, Aradia, Hecate.'

She stood up, unsteadily, taking another swig. 'So I am Diana, you are my Lucifer, god of light, eh? We will sleep together and our child will be Aradia, Goddess of the witches!'

She was happy, babbling away. 'You are my etheric double, my spiritual replica, my self-haunting, my shadow body. You are the Sun, I am the Moon, and watch out when I'm Full!'

The moon, in answer, rippled on the water in the cave. The girl raised her bare arms to the moon. She smiled.

'Shall I perform the Drawing Down The Moon rite for you?' she wanted to know.

'God, no,' I replied, looking at the moon warily. I was shaken up by the witches' meeting up there on the hill. I had my own rituals (and they didn't involve guys dressed in hairy black masks drinking blood).

I grabbed her, pulled her onto my lap. She giggled, spreading her legs wide, rubbing herself on me. We kissed. She hitched her skirt around her thighs. The wine bottle fell into the water with a splash, then I could only hear her gasps above the water lapping softly.

I squeezed her firm breasts, her smooth hips, ran my fingers up and down her warm back. She smelt divine. She held the back of my head, drawing me onto her nipples. She buried her face in my neck, making me laugh. She rocked her pelvis faster, nearly coming already. She kept stroking me, stroking me. She drove me wild.

She gyrated faster, working herself up into a frenzy. I gripped her tightly. Her groin was so hot over my erection. She undid my shorts and took my prick inside her. She was soaking and slippery, smooth as silk inside. She ground down on me fiercely, writhing in circles. My feet were cold in the rockpool. Her loud gasps echoed around the cave.

She tented me in her hair, sucked my neck, my chest. She felt delicious, as big and open as the sea. I gripped her bottom hard, pulling her down and down, thrusting upwards crazily. I pumped inside her and she slithered about like a snake.

After her first orgasm, she spent hours moving through many others. I lost all sense of time. She kept rubbing herself over my lap, sliding me out to rub my penis over her clitoris, rising and falling with her labia just around the tip, then sitting on me rapturously, swallowing me whole. Sometimes she liked to slide her lips along the length of my cock, her clit brushing back and forth over the glans, her lips enclosing my shaft so softly. She could do that for a long time, lost in an erotic trance. Once or twice she slipped down to take me into her mouth, tickling the plum with her tongue.

Something splashed in the water behind us, some big fish, but we ignored it, and kept rocking to orgasm.

She asked me stand up. I slipped on the rocks and we both nearly fell into the water. She laughed manically, giggling hysterically. Then she climbed up me, gripping me tightly with her thighs. She loved being in the dragon's cave.

She thought she was being fucked by a dragon. I thought I was being fucked by the moon.

She worked herself up to a scorching orgasm, really extraordinary, ecstatic and tumultuous. I felt seared to her, fused atomically. We swam in the moon-time, overseen by angels. We burned together brighter than Saturn. She threw her hands to the moon, fingers splayed. I held her body as she writhed furiously.

In the silver light of the moon she looked dæmonic, her mouth open in orgasm, her eyes blazing. Then she was gasping loudly, grinding her cunt down onto me. She flung her arms around my shoulders. She was fucking me so fast, really hard. So

115

loud, her voice at orgasm, echoing round that black cave.

I realized that *she* was the dragon, *she* was the Minotaur. She was expanding in every direction. She was becoming mythical. She was in a frenzy, utterly beyond everything, fucking me *so hard*, so fucking hard, so beautifully hard, in so deep. It was tremendous, a tumult of transcendent fucking, sex beyond sex.

Her body in my arms, her thighs around my waist, her head thrown back, her mound going crazy over my cock. I couldn't hold back any longer, and flooded her womb. We orgasmed into one, so hot and sweaty, sweet, sticky and messy.

As she calmed down, panting, I slipped on the stones, and found the water much deeper, already around our knees. The tide was coming in, flooding the cave. The high tides were approaching, as the moon swelled to fullness.

The girl took my hand and put it between her legs. She had the Biblical Flood inside her, the streams of the moon's bloodwater. There was blood on my fingers, dark stains in the moonlight. She grinned. Her teeth shone.

We had to wade waist-deep in the cold sea to get out of the cave. I was shivering. We took our wet clothes off and climbed up the cliff. I was exhausted, and flopped on the ground.

The girl pulled me over. We rolled in the dry grass. I could hardly move; I ached, and was bruised from a fall on the rocks. Her energy astonished me. She pulled me inside her, again and again. She said she felt sore, but wanted more.

More – too much – not enough.

The stars span as we made the beast with two backs. Out at sea a flare from a ship made a red arc in the sky. I thought I'd seen everything but then we saw dolphins breaching about a mile out to sea. The girl clung on to me as we watched the animals curving in the moonlit sea. I had seen everything. I couldn't see anymore.

When we got back to our camp we rolled up in the blankets and slept so deeply we didn't wake until the sun was high in the sky.

TWELVE
———
The Swimming Pool

THERE WAS A fucking killer whale in the swimming pool. You found it first, you passion-soaked girl, you green-scaled mermaid, writhing over me deliriously. Half-asleep, you reached behind and squeezed me inside. I was euphoric. You gasped softly, murmuring in your dreams. I love the way you moan 'Come on come on come on,' with your face agleam in the morning sunlight. I held your soft arms and pulsed inside you, timing my thrusts when you pushed your ass back.

Gasping, afterwards, I said: 'I feel like God.'

And you said: 'You are.'

Blissful loving, two essences touching, outside-inside-all-about-loving love.

You said: 'I want to bypass God and go for the heart of things.'

I said: 'We're on the Orgasm Trail and winning.'

This was loving beyond the event-horizon, in the silence of the sea-light. When you smiled it sounds trite to say it but nothing mattered except that moment.

You rolled off me and pointed to the shimmering blue ocean beyond the scorched trees.

'At the bottom of the sea is a gigantic fish waiting to explode into a loving heart the size of the universe.'

You turned to me with molten eyes and said: 'Our romance is more powerful than a nuclear holocaust.'

We were in each other, so deep inside.

'This love is a kick in the eye for God,' you said. 'A stab in the heart of patriarchal culture. We've got to be soft as raindrops, to prepare for death with a big laugh – the giggle of enlightenment.'

I was with you, that's all that really mattered to me. Selfishly, I clung on to you.

'I expand in all directions like a constantly exploding bomb,' you said, licking your tongue down my belly.

Daedalic love. You all the time murmuring: 'This love is infinity-plus-one. You're the one. No more waiting at bus stops, no more counting out money, no more scrounging for food, no more huddling round the fire, no more listening to people droning on and on and on.

'Love like an ocean, full of rip tides and cross-currents, bottomless, full of bizarre creatures and orgasmic dolphins,' you whispered, giggling.

In the empty streets of Porthleven you picked up a stray cat. It climbed over us and we looked at the twin claws of West Cornwall: the Lizard and Land's End, those two chunks of land sticking out into the sea like the jaws of a dragon. St Michael's Mount looked like a Gothic fairy tale castle. Before us lay the sweep of Praa Sands.

Insects buzzed; magnetic eyes; bare feet; warm water in a plastic bottle; handfuls of cereal; you dressed in your long T-shirt only; me in shorts. Brilliant sunlight.

As we walked through the dust and light I thought of the houseboat we'd come across in one of the overgrown creeks on the Helford River. Attracted by music – Bach's *St Matthew Passion* no less – we climbed onto the boat. No one answered our calls. Inside we found the remains of a meal; a tape-player slurred the choral music – the batteries were going flat; there was rope everywhere.

Then, as we climbed back out of the boat, we noticed there was twine running from the boat into the trees, string tied from tree to tree, twine running everywhere, like a spider's web. A man strode through the trees, with a shotgun. He thought we were going to steal his boat. His wife sidled up, a mass of facial bruises. He said she was feeling 'under the weather', but the weather was blissful. Only later did we realize that the woman's hands were tied behind her back.

The old Castle of St Michael's Mount loomed in front of us as we walked West along the sands. The tide was up around the Castle's skirts.

'I remember wading out there as a kid,' you said. 'Dad carried me the rest of the way. We came back in a boat.'

You flattened a slim hand to shade your eyes from the glare as you stared at the church on the Mount. It looked completely deserted now.

Marazion was a one-street town devoid of all life except a ten year-old kid wearing a bandana sorting through piles of trash. He squinted at us for a moment, then carried on rummaging.

One or two cars had been burnt out; every store front was broken into. An aquarium had been trashed. Attracted by the smell of fish, our cat darted into the depths. A two-foot chunk of a dead eel lay across the doorway, like a section of a serpent. We couldn't find the cat.

We walked through the blistering sunshine, both starving, out of supplies. You talked about the underground caves, the ritual we saw on the hill, the circus in the New Forest, the man in the submarine silos.

I'm sure I saw a waterspout connecting up a boiling cloud

119

with the sea. We were the only people alive, two seers who saw everything. An orange dot in the distance signified a solitary sunbather. The radiation levels were perhaps too high for most people (but they gave a good tan).

We stepped over a sewage outlet (which stank so badly it was impossible to breathe). We decided to rest for a while. You visited the toilets and came back (amazingly) with some water. We popped in a couple of sterilizing tablets after holding it up to the light and deciding to risk it. Gulls squealed overhead. The ocean stretched wide before us.

From here the first moon-ships ought to glide into the sky, I thought, bound for the Pleiades or Cassiopeia. The Cornish beach could be a launchpad for the stars. I watched a tiny microlight aircraft fly out to sea, powered by a little droning motor. I wondered how far the pilot would get. Not even France.

I loved this place, Cornwall, with its pagan cults and stone rings, its tors and barrows, its moors, cliffs and magical spaces: Mên-an-Tol, Boscawen-Ûn, Trethevy Quoit, Rough Tor, Carn Brea, the Hurlers, the Nine Maidens, Dozmary Pool and Fal 'lake'. Sometimes when you squirmed I thought you were a mermaid, a merry maiden, a girl with a fish-tail.

I fell asleep in the dunes, amongst the hissing marram grass. It was sunset when I woke. The sky was fading from pink to bronze. I spotted a satellite sliding over the heavens. No doubt a military device (you told me once three-quarters of all satellites were military).

But you had gone, to the nearby town I guessed. The tide was going out. I walked across the expanses of sand, the sky reflecting purple now in the sheen of water on the wet beach.

I found you, eventually, shaking with fear and excitement beside the swimming pool. You told me what had happened:

'I walked into Penzance at sunset. I found one shop open and managed to buy a little drink, cigarettes and food, at fifty times the pre-war prices. I stashed the carrier bag in the rocks by the harbour, which was strewn with fish and empty boats. The town got darker and darker. I found a copper bracelet in the high street, and put it on. A man started following me. I couldn't lose him. In the end I turned to confront him but he ran off.

'Another man hassled me on the promenade. He had some binoculars with him – a geeky train spotter type. He trained them on a distant city of lights.

'"That's an aircraft carrier," he said, trying to impress me. "Very big. American."

'"It's the U.S.S. *Dwight D. Eisenhower*, nuclear-powered, 91, 400 tons, 2nd Fleet. What's the hell's that doing here?" I replied.

'That shut the man up. I managed to lose him in Chapel Street.

'It was really dark without the street lights. When I lit a cigarette the flame seemed really dazzling. I could see candles behind the lace curtains of Penzance's terraced houses.

'I thought of you, a lot. I wanted you there, so we could run in our heat and darkness faster and faster, to the Edge.

'I want to let go with you, to see what powers will be released. I was – I still am – aching inside. For you, for a child. When the moon rose, I felt better. She is my friend.

'The graffiti on the *Admiral Benbow* pub was funny: FUCK THE YANKS, and BOMB THE BASTARDS. A story in an old edition of the *Daily Bullshit* on top of a pile of junk caught my eye:

Husband snaps his wife in bed with vicar – A jealous husband took pictures of his naked wife in bed with a romeo vicar. Clive Grantham crept into the room early in the morning when they were sleeping in each other's arms. The camera's flash woke up the lovers and the Rev Ian Harris sat up shouting: 'Help! Call the police.'

'I wondered if any more banal escapades were going on behind the chintz curtains of war-torn Britain. Were people still acting as crazily as before the war, like knifing each other in crimes of passion and frustration, still collecting stamps, still gossiping about the neighbours, or getting prizes for matchstick models of World War Two bombers?

'After eluding yet another creep I ventured through the smashed-in doors of St Mary's church in the centre of the town. By torchlight I saw that someone had strapped a dildo onto the statue of the crucified Christ behind the altar. I laughed. It wasn't sinister at all, just silly.

'Down at the harbour I heard a loud splashing in the black night. The tide was going out. I walked towards the noise. It was coming from the tidal bathing pool.

'At first I saw only the water moving as if it was being pushed about by some huge object. Something gigantic was in the tidal pool. As I crept up closer, I was drenched by an enormous wave. It was fascinating: the black water surged about and slapped over the sides of the pool. The water kept soaking me, from my hair to my sandals.

'There was a fucking killer whale in the swimming pool. I froze, watching this fierce creature swim around and around, looking for a way out. It must have been tossed in on a freak wave at high tide.

'It was hypnotic. I walked around the pool. I slipped on the wet tiles. I imagined myself falling into the water and the fish swimming towards me hungrily.

'I couldn't tear myself away. I wanted to help the enormous animal. I couldn't stop looking at its black-and-white body which shone so strangely when the moon came out of the clouds. When you put your arms around me just now I jumped out of my skin.'

The girl turned to me. 'Isn't it the most amazing thing you've ever seen?'

It was. The killer whale splashed us, fighting to get out of the deep pool. Once it nearly flipped itself onto the side. I thought of the poor seals in the Arctic and Patagonia: how terrifying it must be to have a killer whale hurtling over the ice at you, its huge mouth agape.

The girl wanted to save the whale. She tried calling her father from a kiosk on the seafront. She wanted the Army to carry it back to the sea. But her father was not there, only an answering service. She returned to the poolside fuming. The whale breached the water, sending a great wave over us. I thought it might get out at the next high tide, but the girl wasn't so sure.

'I've heard of vandals throwing bricks at whales in captivity, and worse – barbed wire.'

She looked out to sea. 'I wonder where the others are.'

She spoke of the other killer whales in the group or 'pod', swimming out there amongst the oilslicks, slime and radiation. She spoke of the mate and calf searching for the mother whale trapped here. The whale in the pool kept tailfluking – slamming the water with its tail.

'The Navy used to machine-gun whales for sport,' said the girl. 'Ah, look, there they are.'

She pointed out to sea beyond Mousehole. I could just make out the ripples catching the moonlight made by two killer whales. Perhaps they didn't know where their lost mate was, because they couldn't communicate through the concrete sides of the swimming pool. After a few minutes the whales moved away.

We walked past the shoals of fish in the mud of the harbour. I was surprised they hadn't been stolen for food. Beyond the town we saw a distant lighthouse, its giant eye flashing occasionally.

I wanted to go inland, to visit the prehistoric sites of West Penwith: the stone circles of Boscawen-Ûn or the Merry Maidens, to climb through the Mên-an-Tol stone.

The girl kept glancing at the sea, expecting to see a lonely killer whale breach the water again. We spotted the whales again, far out to sea. I wanted to soothe her, to hold her. She walked on ahead, stepping through the rockpools, looking for somewhere to sleep. She was not happy, she was restless, prowling the shore for something, anything.

I wanted to stop, she wanted to go.

Presently, we saw a fire on the sand. We approached, cautiously. Two young women sat around the fire. After a few words, they invited us to sit with them. They were smoking crack furiously, and drinking. I put the bag of wine bottles down. Linda pulled out some red wine and opened it. The other woman, Cim, looked vacantly at the girl. We sat amongst these doped dryads, these two boozy mermaids, and got drunk. I drifted off to sleep, lulled by the heat of the fire, feeling deliciously drowsy.

I woke a while later. It was still dark. The fire had burnt down, and the tide receded 300 yards.

I could vaguely make out the shapes of the girl lying on her back with two caryatids moving gently over her. Linda kissed her on the mouth while Cim crouched between her legs.

The girl was enjoying herself. Linda poured wine over her breasts and licked it off. The three of them looked like the slow-motion figures from some art movie. Everything was soft-focus, blurred.

The girl was gasping, squeezing Linda's hand between her legs. Cim stood up to reveal a shaved slit of livid red between her legs. She knelt over the girl's mouth.

The two strange women moved silently, softly, their gestures hieratic. Cim rolled onto her belly on the blanket. Linda knelt and pressed her mouth into her buttocks.

I drifted off to sleep after a while. They didn't invite me to join them, but I wasn't bothered. I was too drunk, too hungry, too tired.

I was amazed to find next morning that Cim had a baby which had slept in a bundle by the fire through all the love-making.

The girl said she felt sore but gorgeous. She had fantasized about the killer whale in the swimming pool. I was completely in love with her.

We had moments of great pellucidity, utterly absorbed in the present moment. She believed we were actually rejuvenating the

124

planet with our love. We were stopping the world from suiciding, that was her idea.

Sucking her enormous clitoris I could feel every vibration of her soul.

Like two angels we drifted along the Cornish coast, looking for her special beach on the other side of the headland which she had called 'Zanzibar' on a childhood holiday.

She wore some French knickers and a tiny top which she'd stolen from a burnt-out store in Penzance. I wore some swimming shorts and a floppy hat. We looked ridiculous but we met no one. It didn't matter.

There were no social constraints on us now. When we danced we really danced; when we fought, we really bit into each other. We ran through the whole gamut of human emotions in a few days. We pranced round the empty beaches like maniacal kids. We talked faster than a café full of French intellectuals. We drank like fish.

There were no limits anymore, no morals, no stupid table manners. We pissed where we stood, or crouched in the sand. We had found a CD machine and some CDs. For a day or so we played Bessie Smith, Fats Waller, The Beatles and Giuseppe Verdi at immense volume before we got fed up with carrying the thing.

The girl looked no longer like a pale white British subject: her hair was bleached by the sun and was wild; her eyes were full of hunger; her shape was lean and lithe; she was brown all over; she moved like a cat, with complete authority and violence.

She said I looked like a savage, whatever that was. I didn't bother to look in mirrors anymore, and most of them had been smashed anyway, like after a funeral.

We were dropping down into pure beingness, living on the land, so close to it. The rush of water down the throat, the throb of blood in the veins, the pounding heat.

We knew the best places to hide, the best stores to raid. We moved as if tied together. We knew where to go, what to do. We felt really healthy, and pure, so pure.

We moved across the continent of Cornwall towards the lighthouse, hardly touching the ground at times, we were so blissful. I walked behind the girl and watched the rhythm of her body – the swing of her hips and buttocks fascinated me. I liked to kneel down and thrust my tongue inside her, to taste the salty moisture. Turning round, she would look like a witch on heat, her eyes blazing. She would rub her nipples on my chest, her hands would dig down to my balls, squeezing me softly. I lived in fervour, in a fever-pitch of love and lust.

On 'Zanzibar' beach we twirled our clothes around our heads, dancing to music. The girl was a tornado of movement, a brilliant dancer, impossible to catch. She didn't want to kiss 'n' cuddle to Elvis Presley, she wanted to run and jump to Verdi opera, or Nirvana, or Oumou Sangare, or the Sex Pistols. We span around each other, holding on by the tips of our fingers. A convoy of ships slid over the horizon, trailed by helicopters, but we ignored them.

Tipping back a bottle, she poured whiskey down my burning throat. I was in ecstasy, dancing with her so wild, like gypsies, like dervishes, whirling. She opened her thighs wide and pulled me inside her. She writhed, biting my face, my neck, my shoulders. Her hands grasped my buttocks, forcing me in as deep as forever. The music swirled about us and the world span.

Squealing, she ran in the foam, yelping at the coldness of the water boiling about her. She was so drunk, cavorting in the shallows. Below us a shoal of tiny fish darted to and fro. We fell into the sea and felt as if we were being washed up on some unknown shore, an exotic Pacific island. We expected to see giant turtles crawling out of the dunes, or dinosaurs, or pirates. The buried treasure was somewhere deep inside us.

She ran up the beach to fetch a miniature bottle of vodka. She poured it into my mouth and said 'Pretend you're a tiger and fuck me harder.'

She laughed and her legs went wide. She was a jungle

animal, bendy as a big cat.

'Pretend you're a killer whale and ravish me deep.'

She could dance and make love for hours on end. Drunk on vodka, with opera swirling about us and the sea churning at our feet, we made love over and over again.

She liked to fuck standing up, with her back to me and her legs pulled up high, supported by my hands.

She liked to gasp loudly, to whisper, teasingly: 'You're *so big*, so *fucking big*.' She laughed, angling her hips to draw me in deeper. 'Jesus, I love your fucking cock; I want to feel your hard cock inside me, your big hard cock.'

She laughed with the ecstasy, the stupidity of it all. The lost boys we were, the fall-out kids, two nuclear angels.

I was knocked out by the girl. I thought I was dying I felt so alive. It was exquisite.

We stumbled up the beach and lay end to end on a towel, licking each other. We could never last long like this – my hands around her bottom, pulling her wet slit onto my mouth, and her licking my hardness. I slid my fingers between her cheeks and pulled her lips wider apart. I loved to circle my tongue inside her. She groaned around my hardness.

'Suck my cunt,' she gasped. 'I love to feel your tongue inside my cunt, my tallulah, my mini-moos, my fruit-toot.'

She licked my cock at the tip then swallowed it. Soon I felt her fingers in my ass. Playfully, she dragged her teeth around my plum, dabbing her tongue in the eye. It was great to make her come when she was mouthing me, but she wanted to kneel over me.

She turned and rubbed her nipples on my chest. She moaned noisily as she squatted on my mouth. I looked up at her curving belly, her firm breasts and prominent nipples, her wild face and hair, the first stars coming out above her. She whispered obscenities to herself, circling her clitoris on me.

Such violence, such delicious sensuality. I felt so sore, so tired, beaten to a pulp by the elements and the girl.

'Rub my clit,' she whispered in my ear. My hand was trapped between us, fingers lost in her creamy folds. 'My clit, my clit, my clit,' she whispered. 'Don't stop. Rub my clitoris, my brontosaurus. Harder, harder. Make me come.'

She wanted more orgasms. She slid down onto my prick, grinding herself on me. She liked to pull up until I was on the edge of her pussy, then she would ram herself down. She rotated her hips, rocking slowly, gently, back and forth.

'Bugger the Devil,' she said, giggling. 'Fuck the war up its ass.'

I asked her to turn round and she did, quickly, mounting me. What a sight – her swelling hips and magnificent bottom riding my cock. I squeezed the curves of her round buttocks, watching her ass gyrating on top of me. Wonderful. She bent low, brushing her nipples on my knees. The curve of her hips and buttocks from that angle would make a sculptor scream with joy. It was the bliss of Rodin, Michelangelo and Canova all rolled into one.

She arched her back again, throwing her head high. When she reached down to stroke my balls, I came with a shout.

I seemed to be deeper than ever before inside her. I wet my thumb and pressed it into her ass. That set her off.

When she orgasmed she said afterwards it was the best ever. She gasped madly, her womb contracting around me, her body rippling. The juice was pouring from her.

After spending, I uncunted and wiped my pego, as they say in Victorian books.

The music had stopped. The sky was dark, the stars were twinkling above us, the heaven crisscrossed by military and communications satellites.

The girl lay on me for hours, sometimes moving softly, sometimes drifting off into a languid sleep.

THIRTEEN

The Lighthouse

SUMMER BURST ABOUT US. It was a brilliant morning when we decided to row out to the lighthouse. Fever-light, Lizard Light, Longships Light, Wolf Light, Cornwall's lightships. We knew the lighthouse was deserted now, working on automatic.

On the way we'd met an old man staring at the sea with a small boy beside him. 'I bring my grandson down here,' he told us, 'to watch the sea and the rocks. My father died in a shipwreck down there.'

We looked at the emerald sea. Somewhere under it lay the bones of forgotten sailors, rubbed by the rip tides. The waves slammed into the cliff, sending up spumes of boiling foam and mist. We clambered over barbed wire fences, nettles and brambles until we could climb down to the sand. The lighthouse lay some way out. We walked along the beach and saw there was an easier way down, which led to the boats.

This world was so different from the world of our childhoods, from the alleys and the scrap heaps of our glory days. The girl

129

told me she used to explore churchyards with a bunch of German tearaways. I liked to haunt the car dumps and canal paths. Derelict houses, deserted car lots and lonely garages formed the backgrounds of my childhood. The girl said Germany was so clean in comparison with Britain. But in Cornwall we felt we were walking through a new world, a wild land. Summer burst about us.

There was so much light in the air. It danced about. You could take handfuls of it, eat it; it made you glow. The land was tingling with electricity, with radioactivity.

The whole voluptuous world was exploding with light. It flooded down from the heavens, smothering us in a white-hot embrace. The rocks shone, the sand glistened, the sea was a blinding sheet of silver. Gulls wheeled above, Army helicopters buzzed along the cliffs. Prague was burning and London was flooded, or so the radio told us near the boatyard. L.A. had gone way past riots, fires and famines.

We found a boat and set out for the lighthouse. The most difficult part was landing on the rocks. We were battered by a choppy sea but we made it. Overhead the beam of light swung round and round. Inside, the place was derelict. It echoed to the boom and slap of the waves. All the radios and machinery had been ripped out.

We collapsed, exhausted by the effort of rowing, and ate our food. I couldn't believe it when the girl produced a tin of tuna out of nowhere – nothing has tasted more delicious. I noticed a naval destroyer way up the coast, shipwrecked on the rocks. A trawler was floating beside the fractured hull, probably scavenging for things to trade.

Then we explored the rock and the lighthouse. It was a kind of sanctuary, an island in the war. Already the sky was darkening. The storm was on its way. So was the airstrike. It was too late to row back to the shore – the sea was being churned up by a fierce wind. We heard an almighty crash and rushed upstairs.

The sky was bruise grey. Out of the stormlight two jets screamed and soared inland. We saw the orange glow of their missiles. A distant boom. Flashes of light. A curtain of black velvet was being dropped over the Earth. The sea seethed eighty feet underneath us as we stood on the balcony outside the lamp housing. Flying very low, another bomber roared by. The distant glow of some stricken airfield or communications centre grew brighter. Still the lamp swung round and round, casting a silver beam that raced over the crashing waves.

'Look at those black waves,' yelled the girl above the wind. Huge dark waves were slamming against the rocks below. The ocean seemed to be going mad. In the storm the sea turned red then gold then green. Lightning flashes added to the horror. Terrified, we clung to each other, barely able to stand in the hurricane. I imagined the panic in the cities, the sirens, the noise of shattering glass, the screams of children, the falling buildings and the rubble.

The girl pressed her wet cheek against mine, and asked me if I loved her. She had never asked me that before.

We thought we were going to die. The jets might take potshots at the lighthouse, to knock it out. They were approaching very low, below radar-tracking, in from the sea and up over the cliffs. I ran down the stairs. There must be a set of switches somewhere, I thought. It took me ages to find them but I managed to kill the rotating lamp.

The lighthouse boomed and shivered as if it were being attacked by sea monsters. I ducked outside and pulled the boat higher up the rocks. Water and spray was foaming about everywhere. The world was unreal. All the light had died from the sky. The rain came, lashing us. The whole world was full of furious water.

The girl was excited now. 'OK. You wanted Adventure. You got it. Stranded in a lighthouse in a flood during a storm and the first airstrikes.'

Another plane roared over the cliffs. Soon after that we heard a boom and saw flames in the sky. It had been shot down. The whole thing was terrifying – and exhilarating. I understood how people felt in a war, in a battle. It was a visceral excitement you couldn't ignore.

Eventually the storm burnt itself out. The girl surveyed the carnage with glee.

'Our boat's in bits, look. We are really stranded.'

My heart sank as I saw the remains of the boat. We had no way of getting back now. It was too far to swim. The old codger who ran the boatyard had probably forgotten all about us. But the girl soon found another vessel, in one of the basement rooms.

Back on the balcony, I stood behind her, and pressed myself against her. I stroked her breasts. She pushed me away.

'It's started now, the Apocalypse,' she told me. 'So you've got to do better than that. You've got to love me like the black waves down there, ramming against the rocks with pure passion.'

She looked transfigured in the last of the stormlight. The sun was breaking through the clouds, lighting up her face uncannily. She was an angel.

'You've got to love me like the sea,' she continued, staring at me with that mesmerizing look. 'You don't take me like a whore. I'm not pornography. You must love me with the passion of the sea. Your love must be as deep and as rich and as full of life as this beautiful ocean.'

She spread her arms out wide to include the whole of creation behind her. Framed against the livid red clouds, above the bronze water, she looked *magnificent*.

She spoke of the sea, of all nature, while I spoke of the stars. She knew the stars were unreal – cold and hard and distant and maybe lifeless. Humanity might never reach them, she reckoned. But the Earth underfoot was real, the sea was teeming with *life*. She melted with the Earth and ocean, I with the stars. Setting her metaphors against mine, hers always won.

She turned to the waves again. 'Let's get out of here as soon as the sea calms down.'

A Chinese aircraft slewed round under the banks of crimson clouds. The bombardment continued long after the storm was over, a constant rumble over the horizon.

A sky of turquoise and magenta burned at twilight. The smoke of a pyre. We stood out onto the balcony again. The girl, who had sharper eyes than me, saw a figure waving a flag on the stony beach. We wondered what the man meant. Then I twigged, and went downstairs to switch the lamp back on. The figure stopped waving and left the beach.

The sea was dead calm by eight o'clock, as if nothing had happened. Bits of wood, plastic, rope and other refuse had been tossed up onto the rocks. The air smelt fresh. The sky was wiped clear of clouds.

Screeling seagulls dived over the boat as we rowed to the shore. I took the oars while the girl bailed out water. The boat leaked badly. The sea had turned deep azure. Eventually, we landed on the beach. It took a lot longer than the outward trip, because of the tides.

'Thank Ishtar,' said the girl when we pulled the boat onto the stones.

Back at the boathouse the old soak was very concerned about his ruined boat. The replacement from the lighthouse would not do. He had sold it to them years before. In the end we paid him triple what it was worth.

He told us about the ærial attacks. Military camps and airfields (including RAF St Mawgan and Culdrose) had been hit first. He wasn't sure if nuclear devices had been used.

'But the light's worse. It's brighter than I ever knew it,' he added, sniffing and squinting at the sky.

He meant the Cornish light, the famous light of Cornwall. It was even more radiant than usual. As we walked away from the shore, I noticed a heap of crabs the size of tennis rackets behind the boathouse, climbing over each other, hints of the genetic mutation the nuclear war would bring.

We walked in a new land of pure light. The Romans and Phoenicians came and went, the Saxons, Celts, Danes, Vikings and Normans were here for centuries, but they too had disappeared.

The landscape was so rich and colourful, as if it had been newly created. Flowers flared from every crevice – tamarisk, lichen, dog rose, heather, gorse. The granite and serpentine rock base of Cornwall had been washed clean of people. The silence and the bleakness came back.

We could not believe in the attacks we'd witnessed from the lighthouse. I looked back and it was still flashing at us from its isolated spot in the ocean. We came upon a stone circle, another moon temple. The Merry Maidens I think it was – nineteen frozen dancing virgins. The fall-out was in the air, we were told; radiation around 100 rads, but we felt or saw no trace of it.

We climbed over ancient stone walls and through hedges (stepping around carcasses of cattle). The country was like an untamed garden, full of colour and overgrown plants. The scent of pollenating flowers was overpowering.

We frolicked in the aquatinted landscape – dancing around tors, barrows, phallic stones, sea-thrift, cornflowers, fuchsias, hydrangeas. White clouds of hawthorn trees loosed feminine perfumes – the smell of the girl's vulva. She was picking masses of flowers. We found a tiny brook seeping out of an ancient stone well and drank deeply.

The ocean was our emotional centre. It pulsed through us and we hated to be far from it. We were so used to sleeping beside it, on it, in it. We could hear it from the granite cliff-tops or embedded in poppy fields. It was always *there*.

We became the first fish – Devonian age creatures, 400 million years old, walking out onto the dry land with webbed feet. Our speeded-up romance speeded up time, and evolution, and the world. We were out-evolving everything. The girl and I were running through the whole picture-show of humanity, from fish to superbeing, in a matter of weeks. The onslaught of the nuclear war had made everything try just that little bit harder: love, nature, time – everything was accelerating.

'I feel as if I can make love continuously,' said the girl. 'I feel as if I've got the whole planet inside me, as if we are living the whole of evolution in a few seconds, melting it up inside us. We're taking the whole world and absorbing it, blissfully. Isis, I've never felt so *healthy*.'

This wasn't just 'youthful romance' because when we kissed I could feel the landscape vibrating around us. The night shivered as our sparks flew. She was a dolphin, licking me clean. She was so wet and hot. We made love to the light of distant naval flares. Tongues, nipples, buttocks, backs, arms, hands – we bit everything in sight, taking big bites out of everything – big, dolphin-sized, dolphin-smiling bites.

Beyond the lows hills thunder rolled ominously. We had thrown down our blankets on the edge of a cornfield. I imagined the slow process of glaciation on the Cornish peninsula speeding up around us, swamping us in an ecstasy of ice as the next Ice Age smothered Britain. The minerals in the mines below me were tingling. The heather was on fire. The clouds were turning all the colours of the rainbow. We blazed in orgasm, setting the world on fire with our *jouissance*.

In between the ancient earthworks we made love magically. I knelt above her, my penis waving in her face. She kissed up and down the length, and squeezed my balls softly. As she pressed my cock between her breasts, I leant behind, down her back, to slide my fingers inside her, to tickle her clit. She rubbed her nipples on my erection, grinning when I squeezed the shaft between her breasts, pushing forward to slide it up and back. She licked my crown lusciously, teasing the rim with her teeth, and swabbing the tip of her tongue in the eye.

I watched her full, swollen lips, gasping, convulsing violently when she swallowed me whole. I held her head and rocked to and fro gently. Her mouth opened so wide, her huge lips sliding up and down my cock. It was an amazing sensation when she sucked on my balls, encircling the base of my shaft with devilish fingers. Stroking, teasing, circling.

I was close to coming when she cupped her warm hand around my prick, stroking her palms up and down. She gripped me firmly, wanking me into her mouth. When she wormed a finger deep in my ass, suddenly and forcefully, I pumped blissfully inside her. Smiling mysteriously, the girl straddled me, her palm on the back of my neck, kissing me, dribbling the jism into my mouth, her hot tongue delving, licking, toying.

After one orgasm, she lay back in a dream-state, her eyes slitted, a mysterious Leonardo da Vinci smile playing about her full, open mouth. Her whole body glowed pink in the half-light. I sat back on my haunches, between her wide-open legs.

She seemed to be unaware I was there as her right hand dipped to her sex and touched her turgid clitoris. She used two fingers to rub her clit in circles, occasionally sinking them into her gaping peach for lubrication.

I watched, fascinated, as she masturbated herself slowly and purposefully, her eyes closed, her gasps rhythmic, her thighs gently rising and falling. I leant closer, to kiss her smooth belly and tuft, dabbing my tongue over her clit very softly.

Still her fingers went round and around, while I nibbled on the incredibly soft skin of her inner thighs that I loved so. I slid my fingers into the cleft of her bottom, to stroke her perineum. I could tell she was stretching out the approach of her orgasm, stopping from time to time to ride the waves of pleasure, before continuing that hypnotic rhythmic rotation on her swollen bud.

It was as if we were both in a dream world where everything was concentrated in the girl's caresses of her clitoris. A world where every feeling consisted of a gentle but insistent and well-practised circular motion of fingers on a hard nubbin of flesh. Everything was absorbed in her clitoris, in the girl's breathing, in the rhythmical clenching of her bottom and thighs, in the blushes running up her torso, in her quivering nipples, in her open mouth, so that when the orgasm came, it was cosmic in scope, and swamped us both, so closely we were tuned in together.

We could fuck for hours from the side, half-asleep. Often we'd drift off after coming, and press against each other, entangled. An hour or so later, I'd feel her hips very slightly moving, back and forth. She'd clench her thighs very slightly, and push her bottom into my growing hard-on. It was hypnotic, and we could do that for ages before she'd reach round to slide me inside her. Sometimes one of us would doze off for a moment in the darkness, while the other worked back and forth... in and out... round and round.

The orgasms would be incredibly deep and slow, like waves in the deepest part of the ocean – black water rolling over thousands of feet of black water in the total darkness of the night.

While we blazed in ecstasy, American soldiers swarmed over the quaint queendom, convoys were trundling East and West, and missiles were sticking up out of their silos like pagan stones, while in their bunkers the masses trembled...

The moon was just rising as we drifted off. The girl pulled on her clothes and stood up. I woke and looked about. With a shock I saw we were surrounded by people. I dressed hastily. In the darkness I saw many moonlit faces like wraiths. I felt like a fool, like a clown, aroused, bewildered... caught.

The girl went up to talk to them. They were so quiet, just muttering softly. Then, out of nowhere, an aircraft roared overhead. The black shape shot out over the sea and we saw flashes coming from the sea.

'They're after the destroyer we saw earlier,' the girl explained when she returned to me. I hadn't seen anything. The girl always saw more than me.

An explosion ripped through the night air, behind us. The ship was shelling some military installations inland, or maybe a power station. The jet circled and attacked the ship again. More flashes and distant bangs. By the light of the bombs, I saw we were surrounded by hundreds of people, more people than we'd seen for ages. There was something unnerving about seeing so many people in one place, after such a long time of isolation. It was as if we'd forgotten that sometimes humans gathered together in great numbers.

The destroyer was hit. Fires blazed on board. The people around us began to move down to the shore. Perhaps they hoped for a shipwreck, as in the olden days of Cornwall, when a whole livelihood could be washed ashore? The fireworks continued. Hardly anyone spoke. They were silent with awe, or mute with boredom.

The girl dragged me away, over fences and walls.

The ship had moved off. On the beach we could just make hundreds of people standing and staring out to sea. We floated through waist-deep grass and perfumed flowers. More bombers soared above us.

'I'm looking for a comfy bed, or a telephone,' said the girl.

She was thinking of the soft giant red bed she'd slept on in the architect's extravagant house. She wanted to break into another house, to spend the night in luxury. We talked about the lighthouse, the burning ship, the leaking rowing boat. I couldn't forget the incredible light that had been bouncing around all day, like a cascade of archangels. The flames of the sun had burnt into my eyes, my mind.

Away East, there was a glow like the Northern Lights. Plymouth, Bristol and Exeter would surely be bombed. For us, the targets in Cornwall included RAF Culdrose and St Mawgan; communication centres such as Sennen and Goonhilly; Falmouth port and Portreath.

The girl squatted and pissed. 'Get the bed ready,' she said.

FOURTEEN

———

The Zoo

FEW THINGS ARE as strange as a zoo by night. Most of the animals were dead. Cages had been smashed open. Some animals had been slaughtered by vandals – shot to bits by guns for sport. Stupid messages were sprayed on the walls. The stench was incredible. Some of the creatures had been set free. Even so, the sounds were extraordinary: screeches, shufflings, groans, sqwarks. The girls and I walked around the perimeter, peering through the twelve-foot fence

'You know what I miss?' I asked the girl.

'What?'

'The po-faced men walking about the streets, hands in their pockets, staring straight ahead, shuffling to the pub, the laundro-mat, the shops. Men at night, in cars, on trains, in pubs, so many more men than women out and about at night.

'What terrifies me most is a housing estate at night,' I continued. 'All those rows of terraced houses, everyone boxed in, but no one making a sound. It's terrifying. Dead streets. Lights in the windows but nothing happening. Maybe a TV or two, lighting up the rooms all blue. Or a screaming kid – but that's rare.

'The streets of Britain are so *dead* at night. I know, I've walked them many times. Damp, cold, bleak streets. Cars race by, but nothing happens. Gary tries to get his hand up Sharon's blouse by the garage doors, but nothing happens. It's much worse than *Waiting for Godot*, because at least in Samuel Beckett you get profound conversation. In Britain, nothing. It terrifies me. Is it like this in Spain, in Thailand, or Russia, or Africa, so dead at night?'

'No. They're much better or much worse, but never as bland as Britain,' replied the girl, lighting a cigarette as she stared at the zoo.

'That's it,' I replied. 'Britain's so *bland*, so po-faced, so much the same. So *boring*. All those houses are like those cemeteries in Italy with a light on each tomb. Each house is a tomb. Each life is a slow death. Six feet under the ground in a coffin or two feet above the shagpile carpet on a couch watching television, what's the difference? Britain is a place of death. A graveyard.'

'You know,' the girl mused, 'some people will exploit this situation to the max. Organized crime, for instance, and the political leaders. Another small group will always do well, but stay within the bounds of the law: politicians, big business, the multi-national corporations. A third group, the bums and wasters, will moan but do nothing, hoping for hand-outs (which won't come). The vast majority, the middle-classes, will do whatever they're told, unless someone tramples their flowerbeds or cars. Finally, the vulnerable group, who will be in perpetual fear: the very young, the old, and the sick.

'That's how all of society'll react to the war, 'cos that's how they are anyway, all the time.'

She stopped talking. We heard an odd noise. The girl turned off the torch and we crept along the fence. The moon was clothed in clouds, we couldn't see much. There was a chopping sound – a knife hacking away at meat, I reckoned. The girl gasped. We saw

140

the silhouettes of two men cutting into the hulk of some animal nearby, on the concrete floor. They knelt in a huge dark pool of blood. Was it a zebra, or a giraffe? We felt sick. We moved on, unwilling to interfere.

A tiger padded about on wooden platforms. One or two other big cats slept up in the air, on gigantic wooden structures. They were all skinny, with bones showing clearly. The Gorilla House was a mass of ropes and pipes, like a cross between a hi-tech gym and a pirate's galleon. Something rustled in the hay below a platform. We saw gleaming eyes, then the ape loped off, carrying its young.

'I wonder if the killer whale's leapt out of the swimming pool yet?' the girl wondered. None of the animals stood much chance against men. Even the fiercest predator of all, the killer whale, wouldn't last long.

'I feel so sick,' said the girl, turning away from the cages. 'And sometimes I feel as if someone were watching me –'

'– That's just common paranoia –' I said.

'– Someone's got a gun trained on my heart. They might shoot at any moment.'

At that instant I trod on something that slithered away. It was a snake, escaped from the zoo, three foot long. I froze, but the girl leapt a mile, and ran off.

I found her leaning against a standing stone, searching the ground with the torch. I pulled out the water bottle and handed it to her.

'Perhaps we should put the world on suicide watch, like they do with severely depressed prisoners in jails. Let's put the world in a nylon shift, in a bare cell in an asylum, and peep at it every fifteen minutes to make sure it hasn't hung itself.

'This is a bad time for a nuclear attack – Midsummer – before the harvest. There'll be even less food for Afterwards, if there is an 'Afterwards'.'

She continued: 'Did you know the US Government has stockpiled a hundred tons of heroin and morphine and distributed it around the country? The purpose? To put to death the injured after a nuclear war. One mass suicide followed by another. But at least opium death is quick.'

The girl was feeling bitter. She pulled her knees up under her chin and hugged them while I read out her horoscope from the newspaper I'd found in a huge heap outside the gates of the zoo earlier:

Capricorn – You are full of good ideas. The stars are shining on your love-life at present. Anything to do with music, the arts or dancing is highlighted. An ambition could be realized.

'What's yours?' she asked. 'Pisces?'
'Yes.' I said. The girl snatched the paper from me and read:

Pisces – A pleasant journey is on the cards. There's some important business on your mind that needs to be settled. This is a good time for a happy reunion with relatives or in-laws.

It was meaningless. The girl climbed up onto the stone wall. She was in a strange mood. She lit a cigarette and read:

Girl in stabbing found hanged – A teenage girl was found hanged at her home yesterday after her boyfriend was discovered stabbed on the pavement outside.
Come and get it! – A helicopter lowered an 80-foot long glass-fibre trap baited with live salmon into Loch Ness in an attempt by a vodka company to catch the monster.
Class Hostage – Phoenix – A 14-year-old schoolgirl angry over a snub by a friend held her English class hostage at gunpoint for more than half-an-hour.

'I feel sick, boy. I feel sick of everything,' moaned the girl. She threw her cigarette into the gorse bushes and then continued to read from the paper:

Candy Kisses – Traffic wardens – Punks – Brides – Fat Fairies – Schoolgirls –Gorillas – French maid – Drag – Policegrams – Quasi – and more. Ring 2834869.
Don't be a prisoner in your own home – The new 'Lark' is a portable 3-wheeler that will end your search for freedom.

Babysit sex ring is smashed – A child vice ring finding youngsters by advertizing themselves as child-minders and babysitters has been uncovered by police. The children were passed around members of the ring and subjected to "horrific sexual abuse".

'I can't read anymore of this junk. It makes me feel so sick inside, as if I'm not part of this planet, this race,' she whispered. She took a deep drag. 'But look. Here's a silly one for you, boy –'

Tip swallows man alive – Searchers admitted defeat yesterday in their hunt for a man who went missing on a massive rubbish tip. Joseph Smith, 54, vanished while out walking with two of his teenage sons at the weekend.

'That's extraordinary,' I said. 'He just vanished. On a junk heap?'

'Everybody and everything and everywhere is mad,' said the girl, lighting another cigarette.

I looked at her eyes, her hot, dark eyes. She maddened me.

A dreamer in gold, an angel on heat, with her eyes wide and body glowing, she was the passion-girl, so erotic, hot like a constantly-exploding bomb. She stood up on the stone wall, silhouetted against the drifts of bronze-coloured clouds. She was an angel, more splendent than anything in heaven.

Bring down the glaciation upon me, I thought, and the Ice Age and the earthquakes, I don't care: she is *here*. Bring down the passion from the skies. Churn it up inside me. This fever, this ecstasy, with the world burning about us. Blissed-out and kissed-off in passion.

We could hear them but not see them, ranging far out of sight, beyond the horizons of the granite tableland of Cornwall, the aircraft that kept soaring and detonating like technological angels. A cold, fresh wind blew up and the rain came down.

There was big passion in the world but it wasn't concentrated in missile silos, training camps or communication systems – it was concentrated in us, in our bodies, in the rain, the sea, the trees, all nature.

We ran into the woods on the other side of the wall. Rain pattered on the leaves. We kissed, kissed the kiss of life, the kiss of peace, the black kiss, the obscene kiss, kissing hands, kissed-in-the-ring, kissed quick, kissed-out.

It was raining hard. A lighthouse swept the bay below. We moved deeper into the trees. We came upon a giant oak tree which had been decked out with red ribbons. The rain dripped through the leaves and ribbons onto our upturned faces. The girl flicked the hair out of her eyes and embraced the tree. It looked like Christmas, this oak tree with its red ribbons on its green leaves. But no, the girl was right:

'It's for Midsummer, for the Midsummer celebrations.'

We heard some loud bangs from the other side of the copse. I slipped through the trees swiftly and found only an old man in a tweed suit firing a gun into the clouds. He was cloud-bursting, seeding the clouds to make rain he told me (after checking that I was alone and not a member of the military). Now I had seen everything.

When I ran back to the girl, she was still embracing the tree. I wanted to make love with her, against the trunk. She let out a string of vicious obscenities, then said:

'You'll have to do better than that, Mr Cliché. Isn't your love as big as the ocean? Can't you make love like the sea? This wind and rain is fabulous, so hot and tantalizing. I want to run and run. I want a passion that is big and impersonal, not limited to you and your prick. I want something that is wild, and *wild*, and WILD!'

She shrieked and set off at a flying pace. I pursued her through the trees, over fences and hedges, in and out of bushes and ponds.

Ahead of me she changed into a bird, an otter, a rabbit, a horse, a mermaid. I couldn't catch her – she was so slippery. When I transformed into a fox she changed into a bird and flew away. When I turned into a bird she turned into a fish, diving into black water. I couldn't keep up with her, as I was weighed down with our bags and blanket.

Wet through, I finally caught up with her next to a huge brick wall strewn with ivy. She was panting and grinning. She put her hand around my neck and pulled me to her, kissing me deeply, thrusting her hot tongue deep inside me.

'We've got to get out of these soaking clothes,' she murmured. 'I've found us a house, a mansion, a palace. Come and look at it.'

And she led me to the main gates of a dark house. A row of blank windows above a colonnade. An overgrown rose garden. Refuse heaped around the front door. Tyre marks on the cracked paving stones. There were no lights on. The wind and rain blew around in wet gusts in the black night, like a scene out of a 19th century romantic novel, I thought.

'What is this place?' I asked the girl.

'Trewinnard House, Godolphin Hall, Pengersick or Horneck Castles, I don't know. I bet it's warm inside, though. Shall we try it?'

The girl strode up to the House, stepped around the trash and knocked on the giant door. I hung about behind her.

She was Jack the Giant Killer, not me. She could tackle giants, werewolves and dragons, I couldn't. But no one answered. She turned to me.

'Smash your way in, boy.'

Everything she said was a challenge. We clambered in through the kitchen windows. I jumped down into a nest of spiders and yelped, recoiling in horror. I frantically brushed them off. The girl passed through the bags, climbed in and laughed.

She flashed the torch around the rooms. The place was huge. There was a visitors' café and shop, long corridors, many paintings of obscure Cornish gentry, a cash till by the entrance, and many glassed-in exhibits.

'This is where the bourgeoisie come on Sunday afternoons, after a morning spent with the newspapers. They walk about

145

these old country houses and gardens and dream of the older, better, snobbier, upper-class days, the days of the British 'Empire', world wars, Nelson, Churchill, Victoria, Elizabeth I. They sit and sip tea and nibble cream scones at four o'clock, sigh, and go home feeling queasy. It's all such an immense *lie*.'

We tried the lights – nothing. I froze when we heard scuffles from the stairs.

'Only rats,' said the girl.

She was quite calm, as if she burgled houses every night. She wanted to explore the living quarters of the people who owned and ran the house. We crept along a deep-carpeted upper landing and came to a door marked 'Private'. After a little persuasion, I managed to force the door open.

The rooms of the long-departed owners were modest enough. They made their money out of tourists and probably took their Summers in Malibu or the Canary Islands.

The girl reckoned we could barricade ourselves in and spend a restful night in a soft bed. I wasn't so sure: the place seemed too big not to attract attention. What if...?

Then we saw the occult symbols scrawled on the walls. Upside-down stars, red circles, astrological signs, Hebrew letters, hieroglyphs, hieratic characters of all kinds.

The girl played the torchlight over the walls. There were bizarre posters, candlesticks, crystals, demonic African masks, heaps of parchment containing more hermetic symbols. The room stank of incense.

We were in some necromancer's bedroom, an inner sanctum filled with the underbelly of Western religion.

The girl opened a cupboard. It was full of rubber and leather, chains and straps. Sex toys. A wooden chest of shiny surgical instruments.

I wondered what kind of grotesque rituals had been performed in the bedroom. The girl pulled back the black silk bed-clothes: there was blood on the white sheets.

'I'm not staying here. No way,' I told her. 'You're welcome.

146

I'm gone.'

I walked out of the bedroom, back onto the landing, down the stairs and waited for the girl in the high-ceilinged entrance hall. The girl yelled for me – I had the torch. Then, she appeared with a candle at the top of the enormous wooden staircase. She floated down it, the candle flame flickering, her shadow gigantic and outlandish on the walls. She was the perfect ghost.

'I'm not staying here. No way,' I said again.

The girl dumped her bag on the carpet. She wanted a soft bed. She suggested we search the rest of the mansion.

In one of the downstairs rooms we found a giant four poster bed, complete with red plush baldachin – part of the historical displays. The girl leapt on it, giggling.

'Henry the Eighth probably tried to work up a sweat with Anne Boleyn right here, on this very bed.'

'We can't stay here, not with all those rubber masks and chains and bloody sheets up there,' I reminded her.

'Your love must be big as the ocean, and the ocean contains everything,' she said, smiling and spreading her legs. 'So relax and come here. There's all kinds of love –'

'– Not with whips and thumbscrews and knives –'

'– *All I want to do is to lie with you, kiss you, lick you, fuck you.* I love it when you're cooking on heat. Come here.'

She threw off her wet clothes and slid into the monster bed. Her body looked as voluptuous as ever (even though we were both thin and under-nourished). The rain hissed, the wind howled, but I wavered.

'There's wolves outside,' she murmured, in a taunting voice, 'and dragons and witches, all ready to tear you to pieces.'

Smiling at me, her hand moved between her legs under the sheet.

Was I in or out? I plumped, as usual, for in. I undressed and lay beside her. She rubbed her breasts over me, pushed her mound on my thigh. I reached down caressing past the wiry hair into her soaking slit.

Outside the rain roared. Was that a wolf or the wind or a jet I could hear howling? It was Hallowe'en, all the witches and ghouls and devils in the neighbourhood were storming the house. Above us the canopy rippled in the draught. The wood-panelled mediæval room creaked. The candle flickered out. We were in total darkness.

The girl squirmed above me, panting in my ear, her body now vast as the Earth itself. I was making love to a mermaid, swimming in deep black waters.

'Isis, Isis,' she kept crooning. She reached back and jacked the base of my prick. I bucked inside her, orgasming violently and copiously. She laughed and groaned.

The windows rattled, the whole of Godolphin House or wherever it was seemed to be shaking in an earthquake. I stayed hard inside her, feeling her muscles squeezing me from base to tip. She shuffled back and swooped down to my penis, to lick me clean. Her mouth felt soft as feathers. Her tongue tickling the rim was maddening. She dished her back, bringing her crotch down over my shin as she sucked me. She dragged her labia back and forth in short but mesmeric movements over my leg. She often came like that, pressing her clit into my hip or knee or elbow.

With a deep groan, she mounted me again. She was riding towards another orgasm. I was her ghost horse, her hell hound. She gripped my hips tightly and gyrated madly. She took my thumb and licked it.

Her fingernails raked my chest so hard I yelled. She'd do that without warning and it hurt like hell. She knew it'd make me buck fiercely upwards. The bed was so soft and squashy, I put my fists under my buttocks, to ram deeper inside her.

'Squeeze me harder' she gasped when I stroked her nipples. She wanted me to be really rough.

'Bite me. I want a good ride. *Je jouis*. I'm coming.'

When she came her hips were writhing frenetically. She cried out, and collapsed on me with a splash, she was so wet.

I couldn't sleep. The girl was snuggled down beside me, her head on my shoulder, one leg drawn up over my belly, but I couldn't slip away. The windows rattled, the panels creaked, the wind howled. Every noise seemed magnified.

After about an hour of insomnia, I saw car headlamp beams moving across the painted ceiling of Henry VIII's bedroom. I wriggled free of the girl and sat up. The girl murmured in her sleep.

This is it, I thought. Now we're going to be murdered by a group of evil Satanists in a lonely mansion somewhere in West Cornwall. They would notice the smashed windows in the kitchen, I knew it.

I heard voices. They were in the entrance hall. I was frozen, my heart beating wildly. Then footsteps. I grabbed the poker by the fire and waited at the door.

The bedroom door was thrown open. A torch flashed into my blinking eyes.

'Ah, birds sheltering from the storm,' said a sneering male voice. The girl woke up with a start.

'Breaking and entering, what will the Army have to say about this?'

I couldn't see anything but the torch beam shining into my eyes. No one said anything. I felt the girl tense beside me, ready for action.

The man moved forward. There was a woman behind him. I was stunned to recognize the woman – it was Christine, the news reporter we'd met in the New Forest when she was covering a story on the travelling circus. It looked to me as if she had been picked up by this man and brought back to the House for sex. I wanted to warn her, to tell her about the chains and rubber masks upstairs.

Christine was delighted to see me. The awkwardness of being naked in bed and discovered soon faded. The man listened as we exchanged news with a sour expression, his eyes flicking from me to the girl with barely disguised boredom. For a while our conversation was drowned by the noise of a bomber.

Christine persuaded the man to leave us be. He was relieved to find that Christine knew me. Clearly he wanted to get Christine upstairs, to get cracking with his occult sadomasochism. He threw me two oranges before he left us alone – we hadn't tasted fruit for weeks. The girl ate one immediately.

Christine lingered for a couple of minutes. 'Did you know? – half of Germany is wasted, they say, across into Poland and Russia.'

I told her about the sex toys upstairs. She laughed.

'I know all about those things. That's why I'm here.'

I was astounded. Christine, the girl I had gone out with briefly, was into sadism and maybe Satanism. I couldn't buy it. I lay back on the four poster bed after she'd left, thinking furiously.

The girl hadn't spoken once. She lit a cigarette and said:

'So you slept with this Christine? Once?'

'Yes. A long time ago. But – but I didn't know she was – uhh, into this stuff. She used to meet me at the swimming club. She was brilliant at high diving. Immaculate. Not a ripple. Her mother used to make revolting curries followed by prunes and custard. You had to sit there and make 'polite conversation'. She ditched me for a lawyer with a flash car.'

'– And I slept with Kaspar. And others. So what? The ocean is big, big enough for all kinds of love. Come here, little boy blue, come blow my horn.'

She grabbed my head and dragged me to her peeled-apart wetness. She scooted round to uncover my penis. Working on me with those Goddess-quality lips, she had me hard in seconds, swallowing me whole. I trembled. I swiped her slick clitoris with my tongue for a moment then pulled away and jumped up.

No, I couldn't stay in that house, not with them there, not with... all that stuff upstairs. I listened for screams, but none came.

I got dressed. The girl yawned, saying I was over-reacting and that she wouldn't move from King Henry's comfy bed until at least eight. I eventually agreed and pushed a heavy chest in front of the door.

'Turn off the light already,' she moaned.

I lit a candle and I walked about, smoking, checking the windows (which all had window locks on) and wondering what bizarre sex-games were going on upstairs.

I thought of the past – *my* past: the school days; playing under the arches of Victorian railway bridges; the snowy Winters. Our pet dog, Klaus (after Kinski). I remembered my dead father, my bewildered mother. The first (and only) holiday in France, the choppy Channel water.

I looked at the girl sleeping softly in the huge bed. We only had moments left now. Glorious moments, but only moments. The days were being squashed into one, into one intense, sunlit day as we approached Midsummer. The toys of Einstein and Oppenheimer were doing their work.

The rain had stopped. The giants, piskies and fairies of Cornwall had gone back under the hills. Lyonnese was waking up again.

I felt weak and strong, hot and cold, light and dark. The girl's blood was in me. She was sleepy, open, hot in the bed. I loved how hot and soft her body was in the morning. Stars were exploding softly inside her, as if underwater.

I fished out one of her letters from my bag as she slept. The purple paper was wet.

'*YOU BURN ME. Kiss me, lift me out of this life, this day, this world. You make me spin. Such fierceness I feel. I could tear you apart. In my dreams you come into me, with such sweetness and power, so hot and bright. Fill me, dissolve all the boundaries within me.*'

Half-an-hour later we were striding through the ferns and roses, the foxgloves, campions, buttercups, violets, thyme, gorse and seathrift. Gulls swirled in a steely-grey sky. An oil rig burned in the distance, the smoke drifting East above the sea. We traversed the shoreline like hungry wraiths escaped from an 18th century

Gothic novel, climbing over orange and black lichen, over barnacles, crabs, limpets, sponges and starfish.

'We're walking on thin ice,' called the girl over the roar of the waves. 'We've got a day or two, at the most.'

She was collecting seaweed to cook: sugar kelp, serrated wrack, oarweed and eel grass. But it tasted foul after she'd finished with it.

Over the mudflats we ranged, exposed to sun, salt, wind, spray and fall-out.

'I knew a man who lived in a junkyard,' she continued. 'Jim was covered in grease all the time. His mates came round at night and ate sandwiches and drank cider.'

We were making for the Lizard. In Penzance we had escaped from an ugly fist fight by diving into a deserted museum. Most of the exhibits had been torn to shreds. The floor was a layer of broken glass. The place was so desperate – the smashed exhibition cases, the fragments of costumes and model ships scattered everywhere. The information signs had been sprayed over with graffiti: *KILL THE ENGLISH* and *HELLCAMP CORNWALL.*

St Michael's Mount rose gloomily behind us. The sound of the sea was calming after the night before's terrors. We had passed something utterly ordinary and reassuring: a teenage girl reading a magazine, chewing on a chocolate bar. When we got closer we saw she had a rotten carrot and was sucking on it voluptuously. She glared at us. We moved on.

'What's that smell?' I asked the girl as we cross the main road. 'It's overpowering.'

The girl tugged on my arm. 'Wait. Oh shit, I know that smell,' she said. 'Stay here.'

She moved ahead a ways, peering over a low wall. Her hand went to her mouth and she reeled back. I moved closer.

'No,' she insisted, 'you don't want to see this.'

She tried to pull me away, but I wanted to look. So I did.

In the scrubland behind the highway was an open grave

containing some thirty bodies. I gagged on the stench. The girl pulled me back over the road.

We returned swiftly to the beach.

Half a mile upwind of the bodies, I was lost again in a muse of Cornwall – of ley lines and rings, tors and standing stones, chapels and castles, of the china clay quarries around St Austell that looked like moonscapes. It was my escape.

Then I heard the girl shouting at me. I looked up.

A large dog was racing over the sand towards me, barking loudly. It jumped on me and started to bite me. In a frenzy I tried to haul it off. I kicked it and punched it. I couldn't get away from the snapping teeth, the mad eyes, the insane growl. It wouldn't let go.

The girl pressed a knife into my hand behind me. It wasn't sharp at all but I dug it into the dog's neck and belly. I was covered in blood. The dog was going mad on top of me. I kept stabbing at the animal until it fell to the sand. Then I kicked the hell out of it. I picked up a stone and crushed its head, again and again. I didn't stop smashing the dog for ages until it was rags of flesh, blood and bones. The girl was shouting at me to stop.

Eventually I dropped the stone, walked away and fell to the sand. I wanted to weep. I wanted to excuse myself to the cosmos, to say I didn't want to kill any creature. But I couldn't say a word.

FIFTEEN

The Dolphinarium Show

IMAGES FLOODED ME – images of the girl kneeling above me under the swollen stars; of the giant eel in the Aquarium; of the whale submarine in the dockyard back East; of the gardens, the zoo, the arcades, the clifftops and the stone rings...

Five or six cars were abandoned on the beach, crashed together by some maniac. The girl smeared bright red lipstick on her mouth as she squinted in a wing mirror. I remembered the joy rides we'd had in the cars, making love amongst the fake leather and hot plastic.

A fine rain was falling. We wandered inland, around a deserted theme park, dedicated to Merlin and King Arthur, patron saints of Cornwall. A hundred gulls were squabbling over a pile of rotting fish. We waded through mounds of mud and soggy cardboard. The dolphinarium gates were open. We jumped over the turnstiles.

Inside it was dark as hell. We walked through echoing concrete corridors. The place was mute, soft, warm. The walls were clammy. The stench was overpowering. Two bare lightbulbs hung over a circular expanse of water which was strewn with trash.

The large auditorium was silent. The windows and glass roof were filthy. We sat on a wooden bench. I looked around and imagined the screaming kids during the peak holiday season. We stared at the littered water for a long time. Deep water has always fascinated me. Underneath the grimy surface I sensed thousands of gallons of dark liquid.

The silence was disturbed by a ripple in the pool. We watched as the water started to undulate.

The dolphins were coming.

They crashed through the fetid surface. The pool frothed into life. The dolphins squealed. We jumped out of our seats. I could just make out the shadows of the huge fish through the slime, in the half-light. I was sweating in the hot, dim auditorium. It was macabre, these cavorting dolphins.

Then the showgirl appeared. She was dressed in an old tinselled costume. She was a mass of fake red feathers and silver glitter. She was about fifty-five. She carried a tin bucket of fish. The dolphins screeched at her, flipping over and over. The woman raised her arm and cracked a whip over her head. The pool was a mass of seething water and blue-white dolphins. Water sloshed over the edges of the pool.

The showgirl was performing for us alone. Once or twice she smiled at us wanly as she paced around the platform fixed over the pool. It looked as if the woman enacted this ritual every day, for her own pleasure, as if real life – like feeding the fish – had to continue, no matter what.

Squeaking like mad children, the dolphins jumped high into the air, performing somersaults, leaps and tricks while their mistress cracked her whip and grinned insanely. I could imagine this strange showgirl playing with the giant fish at night, throwing in kittens or rabbits instead of fish, her arm around the waist of some disgruntled, chain-smoking, beer-swilling husband.

I noticed the girl beside me was mesmerized. She was rocking backwards and forwards on the bench, staring at the spectacle. To her this was simply another extraordinary event in the love-circus of life.

The dolphins were hungry, on the verge of death. When we looked closer we saw their decay. They grinned like idiots, displaying hundreds of teeth. They were starving. The showgirl threw in the whole bucket and the pool exploded as each dolphin tried to catch the remainder of the fish. They seemed savage. The woman cracked the whip again and again over their heads as they paddled in a line, waiting for more food. She threw up her arm, in a gesture that encouraged applause. The girl clapped vigorously.

The showgirl soaked up the adulation, bowing. Perhaps she was imagining a whole crowd of holiday-makers in her head, a sea of faces surrounding her, like in the old days. She reached down and went to stroke one of the dolphins. The mouth closed and bit her. The woman withdrew her hand sharply. Another dolphin leapt half out of the water, onto the steel walkway, and pulled the woman's legs from under her. She fell, grabbing hold of a steel post. One of the dolphins bit into her leg viciously. The other dolphins were going mad. The girl ran around the pool. The woman was fighting off the dolphin, kicking its snout.

We managed to pulled the woman free. She was sobbing more in rage than pain, though her wound looked pretty deep. The dolphins were snapping at us, leaping up and down, grinning crazily. The dark pool was seething with blood and trash. One dolphin leapt onto the platform and thrashed around. The aqua-show had turned into a bloodbath. The dolphins were attacking each other.

We pulled the showgirl away from them, onto a bench. The girl had wrapped some cloth around the leg. The woman kept asking for us to find some more fish, quickly. I ran into the back rooms and found a broken fridge, its door half-off. I brought back the fish and threw them to the dolphins. The violence with which they lunged for the food was terrifying.

'Get my husband Jack. Get him quick,' yelled the woman. The dolphins were still surging around the giant tank. The girl called for Jack in the back. The woman was seething with anger, but could not stand up. The girl held the cloth around her leg.

Jack turned up, a grizzled, unshaven and overweight guy in his late fifties. He opened the gates and let the dolphins out into the bigger pool, behind the auditorium. Then he rushed to help his wife. He pulled me away.

'Get out, get out. You're *contaminated*,' he shouted venomously. He thought we were radiated, or fall-out sick. He hated having us there.

'Get out, go on, get out,' he snarled. No thanks from either of them. The woman ignored us.

I was about to say something, but the girl shook her head, and pulled me away.

'Leave them to it,' she murmured. So we left them to it.

Outside under a grey rainy sky the dolphins were dancing in the pool behind the building, their babyish mouths agape in wicked smiles. They clapped their flippers together. Too heavy for Jack and his wife to carry to the sea, they would no doubt soon be shot – a bullet in the head each. We didn't want to be there when that happened.

We trudged away from the dolphinarium through the muddy theme park. A giant plastic statue of Merlin the Magician loomed above us, all Moses beard and flowing yellow robes. With his ten-foot blue magic wand and ferocious expression, he seemed to be urging us on to commit some cosmic crime.

Other giant figures were there: King Arthur, Lancelot, Guinevere, a troll and a dragon, huge plastic statues that lit up at night and rotated slowly – Disney gone wild.

Fog was rolling in from the South-West. As we clung together under a tree, we heard a distant sound we couldn't place.

'It sounds like the whales, like the whales in that museum

where I first saw you,' murmured the girl.

No, it was the fog horns from some lighthouse, warning ships that were not there, would never be there. The girl pulled out the orange the Satanist in the manor house had given us, as a special treat.

'Look at that,' said the girl. She held the orange up. 'Such a beautiful colour, such a beautiful texture.'

She ate it, rind and all – I didn't want to touch it. Anything to do with that guy was tainted.

We walked down an evergreen lane to the sea. I was smoking, the girl was talking.

'This is the brief space of ecstasy in between entropy and extermination. The world is upside-down, inside-out, back-to-front. Total disorder.

'Think of those long, blank, echoing corridors and walkways in the big cities. You'd hurry along them in the wind and rain while some alienated drunk would yell behind you at the top of his voice *F-F-F-F-U-U-U-U-U-U-U-U-C-C-C-C-C-C-C-K-K-K-K-K-K-K O-O-O-O-O-F-F-F-F-F-F-F-F-F*. Nice. An everyday occurrence in the cities of the West.

'Think of the shattered nuclear bunkers, sand-filled. The desolation of the flattened cities. Fires everywhere. The blasted-in windows. The infinite melancholy of the post-war dream...'

The girl halted suddenly. 'Oh oh, what's this – ?'

A figure loomed up in the mist. At a road junction a man was shifting around bits of scrap metal, wood, cable and tyres. We watched him working away, lost in himself. Some cars on the far side of the junction had crashed into a petrol tanker.

The man, dressed in blue overalls like an engineer, looked up and froze.

'Well?' he said, in an affected Cockney accent. 'What are yer staring at?'

We said nothing. The man glowered at us.

'What are you doing?' I asked.

The man scoffed. Clearly he regarded this question as stupid, because the answer was obvious.

'I'm Borelli, the artist. Ain't you heard of me? I'm collecting scrap for my latest piece – my last piece – *Nuclear Britain*.'

We watched him working for a while. It wasn't a particularly unusual sight after everything we'd seen.

Then something inside me snapped. I rushed forward, picked up a steel pipe and started to smash the man's 'sculpture', a huge pile of miscellaneous junk.

I went mad, thrashing around at anything in sight. Borelli snarled but didn't approach me. I yelled every curse I could think of, and some the girl had taught me.

I ran over to the cars, pounding at the windscreens, the headlights, the doors. Glass cracked beautifully. It was delicious to bash in the windows, doors and bonnets, to hear the thuds and scrapes. I wanted to get rid of all the tensions inside me, to let everything go in an orgy of violence.

After five minutes I gave up. Borelli watched me with wary eyes. His hands twitched. He looked like he wanted to throttle me. The irony of a little more destruction in the middle of global war seemed to have escaped him.

'What did you do that for, ya bastard,' he sneered.

I moved towards him. He backed away, waving his arms pathetically. I knew he was a weedy little shit. The girl watched me. She thought we were both mad.

I threw down the piece of now-bent pipe and walked away into the mist. I was sweating all over.

The girl followed. I turned.

'Don't come near me,' she said, coldly. 'Don't come near me. Don't touch me. I don't want you near me, your touches, your ideas.'

I looked at her. Her eyes were blazing. We stood facing one another in the fog for some minutes before I spoke.

'My mother's dead.'

The girl frowned. 'How do you know?'

'I telephoned my uncle. She lived near an airfield on the

Wiltshire Plain. A bomb fell –'

I slumped to my knees and started sobbing. The girl walked up to me slowly and clasped me to her tightly. I was beside myself with distress, but I remember the torch clattering onto the tarmac. The girl was kissing my hair.

We must have stayed like that, clasped together in the middle of the foggy lane, for a long time. I remember feeling chilly all of a sudden. Then the girl whispered.

'I want you to burn my womb. I want you to make a fire inside me. I want to womb-burn, to make a child.'

I looked up at her. She cupped my face in her hands.

Her face was streamed with tears.

SIXTEEN

Zero Summer

WE STOOD KNEE-DEEP in the white-pink and lilac heather on the Goonhilly downlands. Pygmy rush, orchids, clover and wild roses were strewn about us, their hot-hued faces open to the sky. Before us loomed the huge dishes of Goonhilly Earth Station. I was amazed it hadn't been blown to bits. Once upon a time these giant dishes beamed the transatlantic telephone calls of businesses and the bourgeoisie. Now they were focussed on enemy satellites.

We approached the cluster of huts nestling under the machines cautiously. The fence had been pulled down. Red lights flashed on the edges of the dishes. A bank of puce and cerulean clouds was drifting slowly down from the North.

A voice called out to us. A woman stood at the door of a hut. We said we just wanted to look around. She was wary – I thought she had a gun – but when she saw we meant no harm, she let us inside. (It was a knife, not a gun). A brief whispered word from the girl was the only security clearance we needed. I knew the girl was related to some VIPs somewhere, but didn't think about it much any more.

Once the place had been full of tourists. The woman took us through the Visitor's Centre, past models of satellites and radar dishes, past the audio-visual displays of telecommunications, and through the restaurant, into a low-ceilinged room full of cigarette smoke. Two men sat at a row of machines and computer consoles.

The woman, dressed in jeans and a red sweater, introduced us to her colleagues.

'This is John Tregeagle. He does the weather reports, because the British must have their weather information. His favourite programme used to be BBC Radio Four's Shipping Forecast, at half past midnight, just before the National Anthem and close-down. Now they broadcast fall-out and radiation levels, if they're on air at all.'

John Tregeagle turned a bleary-eyed face to us but said nothing. He turned back to his computer screen with a sigh. The freckly younger man sitting next to him the woman introduced as Troutbeck, another meteorologist. He too said nothing.

The woman lit up another cigarette, puffing on it furiously. She called herself 'Beany'. She offered us coffee in the restaurant. We sat on orange plastic chairs with a good view of the Lizard peninsula. Black smoke was still rising from the remains of RNAS Culdrose.

'You two are the first visitors we've had for weeks, apart from the Army. We're working here for the government.'

'How come you're still here?' asked the girl.

'I'm amazed we haven't been hit yet. Perhaps the pilots can't see our gigantic radar dishes? Especially since the raid on Culdrose. We're just told to carry on.'

'It's delicious coffee. Thanks,' I said.

Beany smiled wanly. 'It's foul. You just haven't tasted any for a while.'

Beany was happy to have us to talk to – the two surly men in the communications room were driving her mad, she said. They were not meteorologists at all, but government scientists. Beany had pretended, for our sake. She was used to lying to the Army, during their occasional visits.

'The Army people are the worst. Ugly and stupid. They check up on us every couple of days. Cornwall's been ruined utterly. Everyone's gone mad, you might have noticed. No one goes out because of the fall-out. A nuclear device was definitely dropped on Bristol. I'm not sure about Exeter and Plymouth. Pretty much every airfield, communications centre and military camp has been hit at least once.

'We don't see anybody. We are completely isolated here. We hear things, though. Bodies are found in the pools and quarries; the suicides have increased twentyfold; water is really scarce; whales have beached themselves for no reason; you see bonfires at night and wonder what they mean – it's not quite time for Midsummer Eve bonfires yet.

'I saw a man with one leg and no crutches crawling through the heather last week. He said the police had dumped him there. I got the Army to pick him up. We've got some fish if you want some. My son got me in a load before the attacks last week. I've got mackerel, sole, herring, skate and whiting. Freezer still works, too. We get emergency power here.'

Beany lit another cigarette. She was warming up now, really enjoying this chance to speak freely. We enjoyed meeting someone sane, who could give us a more accurate picture of the state of things.

'You hear all sorts of stories, about cemeteries being dug up by bulldozers and the dead being piled in,' Beany continued. 'People are not bothering to look after their babies – many have been abandoned. Gangs roam the streets, killing whoever they wish. The world is in chaos. The governments are trying to review the extent of the damage, but it's impossible to know for sure. The full-scale exchange might happen at any minute. Everybody wants to retaliate, wants revenge. Everyone's threatening it. Things have gone this far, they think, so why not go all the way? There have been mass suicides in Hong Kong and

Vietnam. The IRA are threatening to use their atomic devices in central London, though there's no need, it's already fucked. Hundreds of prisoners in Brazil and Chile have been burnt to death. Washington, Rome, Paris, Baghdad, Jo'burg, Rio, Sydney and many other cities have been hit with nuclear bombs. The outskirts of London has had two hits, officially, thought I reckon it's more like five or six. It's madness.'

We were exhausted enough to listen to Beany for hours. She was lucid and coherent after so many of the damaged souls we'd met.

She gave us a tiny radio so we could pan the airwaves later on. Then she told us an odd story about an astronomer she had known in America, when she was attached to one of the big public observatories.

'Kavan was a bizarre character. He used to appear at parties dressed in a black turtle-neck sweater, looking like a beatnik reject from Andy Warhol's Factory. He was immensely brainy. He knew the stars backwards. When I first met him he said: "I'm the sunrise terminator," and I laughed and laughed. He soon had me drunk, but he only touched bottled water he brought himself.

'He got taken on by NASA. He was heavily into prehistoric astronomy – the mysteries of ancient civilizations: Egypt, the Incas, Babylon and Greece. He worked in Florida. He produced some startling new research papers on black holes and cosmology. He was an ardent pupil of Stark, the leading scientist who talked about 'babyverses', Big Bang theory, superstrings and deep space wonders.

'Kavan married another astrophysicist – Selene. They visited the old launchpads in Florida, marvelling at the crudity and frontier spirit of the early Space Age, now as out-of-date as the Stone Age.

'Selene was passionate about the moon. Eventually, she was accepted for a moon-mission, to one of the new stations. The training was very stressful and difficult, but she got through it. I was there at the lift-off on a bright Spring morning: six million pounds of thrust, burning up five tons of fuel per second. It was very exciting.

'Everything went well until the craft flew around the dark side of the moon. They lost contact. It crashed, killing everyone on board. Selene was three weeks pregnant, but the authorities didn't know that.

'So Kavan threw himself into his work. He went to Arizona, where I met him again. He had nightmares of his wife, crashing on the moon, his unborn child inside her. Sometimes we drove into Phoenix together, to raid the libraries for stuff on the Aztecs or the Persians. We visited temples at dawn, at the Summer Solstice.

'Kavan travelled widely: Mount Aragats, the Caucasas, Brazil, New Mexico. He got friendly with Leon Zarkhi and they exchanged long intercontinental phone calls on quantum theory and radiography. Kavan wrote a book on galaxies, filling it with quasi-Oriental metaphysics. It was beautifully illustrated by huge photographs of the galaxy clusters from JPL.

'Kavan could not ever look on the moon, for there his wife had died. He hated it when the moon swung into the field of his telescope. He would rant and curse. He found a Black Hole in Galaxy M81, and had it named after him. He worked long after we had gone home each night.

'He was obsessed by deep space, every aspect of it. He dreamt of a deep space colony founded on solar winds and ion technology. While the war raged in the Levant, we investigated M87, the largest source of radiowaves in the sky after the sun and moon.

'But Kavan was frustrated. He wanted to go, to fly. But even a nuclear-powered spacecraft would take hundreds of years to reach even the nearest planetary system. So Kavan started talking about 'pure thought' and how it could instantly leap across infinite space. He was going blind as well, from too much squinting into gigantic telescopes and computer screens. He kept in contact with Leon, studying Centaurus A and Gamma Cassiopeæ.

165

'Leon said: "Do you realize that if the Earth were to be made the same again, nothing like humans would be created. Descended from Devonian fish, we're the biggest aberration on the planet." Leon loved to annoy Kavan like this. I slept with him once – with Leon, when he over visiting.

'Like Leonardo and Einstein, his heroes, Kavan thought he was onto something really important. For hours he pored over his star charts and main-age sequences of suns, making indecipherable notes in childish shorthand. He babbled about the End of the Sidereal year and the End of the Age of Pisces, and all that New Age nonsense.

'Then came the news from Washington that the telescope was to be used to monitor enemy activities in space, just like we're doing here at Goonhilly. We had to send daily reports to the Pentagon. Nobody drove along the interstate now. Arizona was as bleak as the surface of Venus.

'Kavan said the full-scale nuclear attack would be like the first few seconds of the universe during the Big Bang. At Mission Control they were panicking to get some shuttles ready for the exodus of the politicians and billionaires. In Las Vegas people were spending millions of dollars before time ran out. You couldn't move on the Strip.

'When I last saw Kavan he had taped some thick spectacles onto his regular pair. He listened to the time-music of the stars in a daze. Most of his days were spent intercepting the transmissions of Russian spies. The new light in the sky fascinated him. He would sit outside and watch the dust storms boiling through the empty desert. I flew to England a couple of months ago. Kavan sent me messages occasionally, full of silly things like "Would Venus like to climb aboard my space rocket?"

'He spoke of the dawns in Arizona which were now blood-red every time. He talked of the Event Horizon, his favourite topic – truly the boundary of the unknown, he said. His messages became more and more garbled. He was deteriorating rapidly. Sometimes he said "Our galaxy is drifting towards the Virgo cluster of galaxies. But we won't crash. We'll melt."

'He died strapped to a chair at the base of the telescope. Sand was pouring in through the open hatch. He had been too weak to move. I imagined his soul shooting up through the telescope, up and out into deep space, flying towards M87 or some supercluster, past the moon and the crashed shuttle containing the remains of his wife…'

Beany stopped talking. We were on our fifth coffee.

'That's a sad story,' said the girl.

'Yes,' replied Beany with a sigh. 'I suppose I was a little in love with Kavan, though he was so neurotic and unapproachable. Since my divorce… Well, let's not talk about that now. It doesn't much anyway. Not now.'

'Guess not,' I muttered.

Beany brightened. 'Are you hungry?'

We said we were starving. We accepted some food from Beany – she said we might as well have it. We had two or three days left at the most.

'Listen to the radio,' she said. 'Then you'll know. You'll hear an ear-piercing scream just before the Big Bang.'

Summer burst about us. Light soaked the landscape. We lit a fire on the beach, in one of the coves – Church Cove, Poldhu Cove, Godrevy Cove, Kynance Cove.

'Look,' you said, showing me a newspaper, 'here's the best epitaph for you: *Last seen wearing blue jeans and a black leather jacket.* Isn't that *the* epitaph for all of youth from World War 2 onwards? *Last seen wearing blue jeans and a black leather jacket.* It's marvellous. Much better to have that appearing in the local rag instead of "The family of Mr X would like to thank all relatives and family and friends for the flowers and messages of sympathy sent to them in their recent loss."'

'But there won't be any epitaphs,' I replied after a moment.

The girl brushed sand from her hair. 'Good.'

An hour later, the girl had drifted off, and murmured in her sleep beside me, then woke. I was staring at the clouds.

She looked about sleepily, then wriggled. 'Shit, I'm burning,' she grumbled.

I had long ago given up on thinking of considering being bothered about sunburn. I figured that the atomic blasts, when they came, would be beyond factor infinity sun tan lotion.

The girl rummaged in her bag and pulled out a bottle of sun cream.

'Put some on,' she pleaded. She lit a cigarette and rolled onto her tummy.

I lifted up her long T-shirt. As usual, she was naked underneath it, and so brown I couldn't tell if she was burnt or not.

I spread the lotion over her back, bottom and legs. She murmured, loving it. I kneaded her skin gently, tracing my fingers down her spine. She trembled a little.

I bent down to kiss her buttocks, massaging the sun cream in deeper. I could knead and press her delicious bottom for hours, completely mesmerized by her marvellous globes and the wet furrow between them.

She moaned softly, arching her back. I caressed the length of her pussy lips, which were already wet and pouting. She groaned again when I slid two then three fingers inside her.

She was dragging deeply on the cigarette as I parted her cheeks and rubbed her clitoris in circles. She loved that, really grinding her bottom around, smearing her moist labia over my palm.

I glanced about, but there was not a soul to be seen anywhere. Nothing but the grass shivering in the wind in the dunes, and sand trickling down into our hollow.

The girl was lost in an erotic bliss. I leant down, my nose pressed in her pucker, drawing her hard clit into my mouth. She ground her ass about wildly, round and round. I wormed my tongue as deep as possible inside her. She moaned louder. From time to time I licked along her vulva, tonguing her asshole. She quivered.

She wanted me inside her desperately, reaching around behind blindly to grasp me. She shifted up onto all fours, knees apart, back dished, ass high. Her cunt was wide open.

But instead of ramming in deep (which was very tempting), I bent down to gamahuche her again, my face buried in her dark heat and tangy liquid. She flexed her bottom against me, pushing up and back, up and back. Her breath came ragged and fast.

When I curled my tongue around her clit again, she orgasmed explosively. I gripped her thighs, pulling her cunt onto my tongue as she convulsed, pressing her ass back to me.

We were swimming in pure light, and there would be 'No Future'. Good.

It was one of the three or so days of Midsummer. Good. The moon was nearly full, the nights were luminous. Was that Bach's *St Matthew Passion* we could hear, faint on the breeze? Distant choir music, making the world even more sublime.

You swam through our memories, these hot and blistered weeks, replaying them: the smashed Aquarium, the submarine man, the arcades, fairgrounds, circuses and theme parks, the rain-telephone box, the boatpark, the caves, the rituals on the hills, the first airstrikes we saw from the lighthouse, our bizarre wedding, the whole extravaganza of Britain in burning-out decline.

From our corner of reality, we surveyed the crying world. Last night I panned the airwaves, picking up a babble of French, Arabic and Chinese voices. A robotic recording of emergency procedures. A pirate station playing backmasked heavy metal music.

The world was hiding in basements, bunkers and make-shift shelters. But the Summer seemed as if it would never end.

Sometimes the sky was gashed open and the acid rain poured in. We luxuriated in the intense heat. Our skin crackled and peeled. Our eyes were screwed up into wrinkled holes. Despite the horror, we lived in a timeless state of rapture. The Cornish radiance melted through us. We swam before breakfast. The sun was a ball of flame in the sky, shining through a dangerously thinned atmosphere.

Anyone seeing us would be startled to find two aborigines, lost in a sun-crazed dreamtime. We shed our clothes and layers of skin, like lizards. We basked in the blaze, feeling rapturously alive. There was no going back now, to the old life, the old ways.

'I want something big and passionate and wild, *wild*, WILD!' you cried, cartwheeling over the expanse of sand.

In the brilliant morning we dived into the sea. Like sliding through stained glass it was, liquescent, deliquescent, incandescent. Colours vibrated around us. Shoals of fish shivered through us. We didn't eat – we got our energy from love-making.

You peeled back my foreskin and licked me. It was like taking raw opium to feel your mouth on me, your hair cascading around my thighs. You tongued me softly, soft as an angel's wing. I fainted away. My legs were jacked out so wide. You rammed your fingers in my ass, grinning at how much I liked it. Your lips drove me wild.

It was like being fucked to death on opium.

Passion like this only occurs once every billion years, once every universe.

You kept exploding love-bombs inside me. We were bursting in a chain-reaction of love. Orgasms were like nuclear ground shocks, our hot breath was like heat waves. Our love-making was a ricocheting blast wave.

Love like ours was shocking in its brilliance, its intensity. We perspired in the tropics of Cornwall.

Your fist encircled me, masturbating me rapidly over your erect clitoris. In the sunlight's fire we rolled over and over on the hot sand. The silver bullet of a bomber roared overhead. We watched the smoke-trails of missiles.

When the air fizzed you became more aroused, pushing your full bottom out and round. Your thumb in your mouth, you gyrated madly on all fours.

I crouched high on my heels, to press deeper inside you, barely able to hold onto your writhing body. I slid out of you, gripping my cock, and exploded come over your back and globes. You mizzled for a second, but I was already rammed back inside you, reaching round to your clit, rubbing it with two fingers.

You knelt up, twisting your neck to kiss me. I pulled out and rubbed my cock along your ass. We often did that, my penis caught in the hot cleft of your buttocks.

You undulated against me, sliding your bottom up and back, up and back, bent right over, then you whispered: 'In my ass, in my ass.'

You guided me inside your butt, groaning. You felt so snug, so hot. I kept circling your clit as I rammed you deep, until you came, giggling, pitching us forward onto the sand.

We dozed, then you knelt up and fished something out of your bag. You giggled as you strapped on the dildo. Who knew where you got strap-ons from. You spat on my ass and quickly pressed inside me. It hurt but I didn't care anymore. I was instantly aroused, a solid, painful erection, hard as a marble statue of Dionysus. You laughed quietly as you fucked me. I think you came before me.

The sun was turning us into ocean-mad wraiths. We were devils and angels. We were turning into post-atomic creatures, beings of light, of bliss. We powered the planet and it fed back into us.

Legs wide, mouth wide with desire, you absorbed the hissing trees, the boiling foam, the fizzing sky. All nature's energy was being sucked inside you.

We lived at the end of the energy-chain. We were transforming the energy of the bombs into passion. Atomic power grew out of the metals and minerals below us, in the mines, and we could sense the copper and tin expanding, cracking open the mine-shafts and rock-faces. And below that, the rich seams of uranium and plutonium.

We expected the Earth to open up and swallow us. I loved the idea that there were 500,000 earthquakes each year – that's what the Russian scientist we met on the train outside Dover said. Furheil said there's a river that runs under the sea with an annual flow six times larger than the Nile. There's a cave in Greece 4,500 feet deep.

And suddenly, ten thousand years ago, the world warmed up by sixteen degrees. Then we had the 'Little Ice Age', between 1400 and the mid-19th century. I thought of the frost fairs on the frozen rivers of Europe. Then came the dustbowl disaster, the ozone layer and greenhouse effect. And now this intense heat. The global climate was controlled partly by volcanoes. There was nothing new in such extreme weather changes, we'd had big temperature changes before…

We looked out at the sea South of the Lizard and expected to see an island being born – a new Atlantis, all steaming water and red smoke, with lava pouring from a fresh crater.

I had the musky, salty taste of her honey all over me. I hated to wash now, because I loved her smell. I loved to taste her on my lips and chin after I'd been licking her for hours, through countless dreamy orgasms.

The girl still liked to bathe now and then – though that usually meant using a rockpool as a jacuzzi. But with the sun so strong, the tidal pools were nicely heated.

The tide was rushing in. We watched it slide in and out, every wave running up to the rocks with such violence, each wave weighing hundreds of tons. Every wave was fresh, new-born, a one-and-only creation.

Your love-making was like a Flood, washing us with waves of desire. As we lay on the stacks of warm rocks ten feet above the water, spattered by the larger waves, we stared abstractedly at the ocean, mesmerized by its magic motion.

You saw something dark and huge move down there, jolting me when your grabbed my arm. I jumped up and squinted into the water. Something black and shiny was swimming down there. I thought it was a crashed angel.

My mouth was so dust-dry, I couldn't tell you what it was. You smiled. I could see you were linked somehow with that fabulous whale. You shared secrets I could never touch.

Swiftly, you slipped into the sea before I could stop you. I fell over the barnacled rocks. You swam down. It was all blue and purple below the rocks. The whale came back and swam around you. When it surfaced and blew out a plume of water I shouted with joy – and fear. I couldn't tell which was you and which was the whale.

When you broke the water your face was transfigured as if by a vision of the Divine. Your eyes shone, your face glowed. You dived again, and again.

When you climbed out of the sea you gave me the kiss of life. I clung onto your drenched mermaid's body and rejoiced. You took a sip of wine and felt instantly drunk.

'What's it like to swim with a whale?' I asked.

You smiled broadly, leaned towards me, and gave me a long, hot, wet, deep kiss.

'I want a daughter, a precious child named Isis, full of promise for the future, the No Future. She will be beautiful. There are lots of things I want to tell her. She will be free of fathers, and men, and all the hurt and hatred they create.'

You turned to me and said: 'I'm staining my lips the colour of life, of blackberries, of pomegranates. I'm darkening my eyes for magick and mystery. I have such energy. You only touch it now and then.

'I dream of passion, and strength, of losing myself, of going over the Edge, of wildness.

'I want to be wrapped in dark velvet and taken down into a special place of heat, tenderness, wonder and exquisite pleasure.

Can you take me there?'

It was a big question, a cosmic question, an ultimate question. I looked at you, stunned. I was falling in love with an amazing girl.

Later a star fell softly out of the black sky . We watched it curve out of the heavens and hit the water with a loud bang and a great wave. It wasn't some splashdown of a forgotten, fifty-year old moon mission, or a meteorite, it was a satellite, shot down by God knows who.

Last night I had heard the jargon of the defence package on the radio: C3, SAC, DCS, BMEWS, COCNAADC, Green Pine and Giant Talk radio networks. The Russians had gigantic radar ships – big liners and cruisers fitted with enormous spheres and dishes as wide as the ships themselves. I recalled the huge globes of the anti-missile radar centres we saw near Plymouth. Since 1945 there have been over 2,500 nuclear detonations. In the atmosphere we had over 100 rads, so Beany had told us at Goonhilly. Luckily, in Cornwall we escaped the major dose of heat and blast waves.

DEW, AWACS, NORAD, ASM, CEP, TEL, TNF – the whole war machine was lumbering along, battering everything in sight.

Passing through our bodies, through our kisses and our orgasms, were the transmissions, on UHF, FM and the very low frequencies, of submarines, ground stations, satellites and High Command Centres. No one had a clear overall picture of events. Nobody knew for sure what Iran, India, Israel, Brazil, Pakistan, America or Russia were doing. There were no doubt millions of secret deals, spies, and messages hurtling back and forth too.

Yesterday in a sun-dazzled grove we had seen a convoy of mobile missile launchers, tanks, howitzers, armoured personnel carriers, cranes and mobile bridges trundling by. The savage rockets thrust up into the sky, while a bespectacled nerd waved at us from the turret of a huge tank. We hid behind some bushes.

Following the convoy trudged a squad of soldiers, carrying

machine guns, gas masks, and NBC protective gear. Soldiers in love with their M-16 5.56mm rifles and the FAL 7.62mm infantry rifles, from Vietnam to World War Three. Army recruitment adverts were full of this stuff:

If variety is the spice of life, here's a vindaloo – Will you be able to cope with some of the world's most sophisticated military equipment? Equipment like the Fox armoured car, the 105mm artillery gun, the JAVELIN ground to air missile or an 81mm mortar? You will become intimately acquainted with the Self Loading Rifle and General Purpose Machine Gun.

Further along the lane, near Chygarkye, we came across an abandoned truck, piled high with TV sets, hi-fis, washing machines, dishwashers, microwaves, all the useless junk of consumerism that was even more useless now there was no electricity to power it.

Flies buzzed around the corpses of two dead sheep and a goat further up the lane. At the end, at another crossroads, a man held us at gunpoint until we realized he was dead. We approached slowly, and found he'd been propped up against a wall with rope, perhaps as a sick joke.

We passed a reservoir sunk to grey mud and climbed over a barricade that blocked the way into a derelict hamlet. A hotel front had been blasted out in some personal vendetta, so we were told by an eleven year-old boy in rags.

As night fell yesterday we had seen another bizarre sight that would have really surprised us before the war: a couple were making love standing up at the bottom of a drained swimming pool. We heard the man panting as if he'd just swum the Channel.

On a cliff near Polbream Point we saw three human heads stuck on some steel poles driven into the grass. Not some trick or treat this, but a political killing. The girl reminded me that it wasn't so long ago that Oliver Cromwell's head had been displayed at the Tower of London. Britain was merely returning to a savagery that had been there all the time. Civil wars and revolutions boiled under the surface.

Looking inland, we had seen a black box being parachuted into a field, but we didn't dare approach it. As we walked down to the beach, the girl read out the index of a classified ads magazine:

Index – Animals & pets... Gardening... Household Security... Freezers...
Beer & Winemaking... Leathercraft... Television... DVDs (Adult)...
Camping... Antiques... Banknotes... Cameras... Coins & Medals...
Metal Detectors... Militia... Smokiana... Holidays Afloat...
Sports...

This captured perfectly the hobbies of the British people: gardening, DIY, collecting, football, beer, television. Sex and celebrity were the national obsessions, but what people did more than anything, apart from watching TV, was shopping.

'You see more people shopping than doing anything else,' said the girl. 'In any town, anywhere, always shopping. Or you used to. What is there to buy now?'

Boy shoots Dad dead – California – A boy of 13 shot dead his father in a row over his school report.
Salmon run – Oslo – Hurricane gales have smashed open fish farms in West Norway and allowed thousands of salmon to escape. "This is the largest escape by the fish ever," said a spokesman.

We rested in a field on the edge of the heathland. After a meagre meal from one of our last cans, we lay down together. The girl was on her back, her thighs open, my fingers stroking inside her. She was so creamy; her lips were softly distended; her legs so wide apart; her hips flexing gently. I caressed her thighs, the exquisitely soft skin of her inner thighs.

She arched her back gently, eyes closed, in a dream state. She was musing again:

'We're all responsible for this Apocalypse, this global suicide. You, me, everybody. Instead of working, trying to live, through all the pain and the ecstasy, we're giving up. We are not fighting. We haven't got any guts. We don't want the Future, and yet the Future is right inside us. Our child…'

The girl took my hand and placed it on her womb.

'We've got to grow up, even if no one else is going to. We're not doing anything to save the planet, are we? We're on this beach, swimming with whales, but we're not *doing* anything.'

'We can't do anything now. It's too late,' I said.

'Always the male's reply.'

She turned to me, gave me the full force of her dark, ochre eyes.

'Boy, we are the only people who can save the planet. We are the only souls who can stop the fire. Because we *are* the planet. I am, you are. We *are* nature. We've got to stop the fire, the holocaust. We've got to love so hard we'll stop the burning. We can do it.'

'Show me.'

'We are the apotheosis of humanity, the Couple, the Lovers. We are the highpoint of evolution, the top of the global tree. This deathwish is killing us all. We've got to stop the fire.'

I looked deep into her blazing eyes.

'Show me.'

SEVENTEEN

Holocaust Autumn

SHE WALKED ACROSS the hot sand of the cove towards me as if she were treading a tightrope. Her arms waved to an imaginary crowd. She had wine, cigarettes and a tin of cherries she'd saved. I lay on my back. She straddled me and poured some wine into my mouth. She began to rock her hips back and forth, gently. I clutched her firm buttocks. She threw her head from side to side. She sat back on me, saying 'I want it deep inside me.'

She smelt of heaven. She looked so proud, and high, her belly pressed forward, flicking her body backwards and forwards magically, her clitoris rubbing on my cock. The juice poured from her.

She was incredible. She pressed some cherries into my mouth, laughing. We were drunk on sunshine, wine and desire. She was murmuring to herself all the time.

'Everything seemed to be much the same. Yet while we ate and slept people were organizing our deaths in secret. While we lived, they planned our deaths.

'I reject having my death organized for me by utter strangers, by people who don't know me, and don't care for me. My death is sacred, my sacred act, mine own. I do it – no one does it for me. I can accept a passionate murder, in lust or despair, but not this cold, cunning planning-for-death by middle-aged grey-faced idiot suits who can't empathize with anybody.'

She was working up a manifesto as she worked up to an orgasm.

'I loathe the impotent narcissists, our 'leaders'. I despise their bodies, their limousines, their grey suits, their blandness, their conferences. I hate their complacency.'

The wind blew cool over our naked bodies. She thumped my chest, and scratched me. I pushed up into her deeper, higher, harder. She leant down to kiss me. She was all erotic motion, a witch on heat.

'I hate this war,' she gasped. 'It's spineless – all done from a great distance, manipulated from bunker control rooms by men fiddling with the knobs on a computer console. It's a big video game for them. They 'score' hits like they 'score' women or drugs.

'No nuclear power has instant communication. It takes hours for real decisions to be made. It makes a mockery of the whole computer/ satellite/ laser/ digital system. By that time all 'strategic' advantages will have been lost, the defence complex will have turned out to be useless. The world is going up in smoke.'

We sat up together, still inside each other, our limbs entwined. I sucked her prominent nipples. She pulled me tightly to her. I caressed her spine gently. She shivered.

'How do you know all about this?' I asked her.

'My father showed me everything. He took me around some of the communications and military centres when I was younger. You wouldn't believe the amount of money governments spend on arms.

'My father showed me around the central government war

HQ at Hawthorn, near Bath. It's so right that the government should hide in the Wiltshire Plain, the centre of magical and prehistoric Britain, with its twin Stone Age sacred sites of love and death: Avebury and Stonehenge.

'The US President, meanwhile, will be ensconced in flying war rooms made from converted Boeing 707s or 747s. The Hawthorn war headquarters is a labyrinth of escalators, corridors, steel doors, computers and air shafts – over 4 million square feet underground. Five hundred staff have been beavering away there all through peacetime. It's like being in a science-fiction movie, going down into the bunker, which can house up to sixty thousand government staff.'

To me she was an angel of profound beauty. Her eyes glowed, her body felt utterly voluptuous, her skin smelt of the sea. She caressed my face, cupping my cheek.

'You don't understand, do you, you poor boy? You don't understand the billions and billions of tax-wrenched dollars it's taken to put this nuclear war together, do you? It's our fault, too. We've lust-soaked ourselves into suicide. We're more alive than anyone else on the planet, and yet we're powerless.'

She threw back her head and laughed like a fiend. I stared wide-eyed at this luminous being, this astonishing creature.

She had the power it seemed to me to set the world alight. She said two lovers make a whole world together, their love becomes a world in itself. I dissolved the boundaries between our self-made world of love and the outside world at war. Everything was bound up together – by her, by love.

She caught me up in her enormous angelic wings and took me on extraordinary flights. Ever since I had met her at the seaside resort on the other side of England, I had fallen deeper and deeper in love with an angel.

'Do you really understand why men build these weapons?' she continued, as her hips rose and fell in waves, with my hardness deep inside her. 'Think of all those underground atomic tests: they were all to kill people, and as many people as possible, in as short a time as possible. Commonsense, rationality and morality do not figure here. It's utter madness. You come out of those underground military operations rooms clutching your skull and screaming silently inside.

'The whole multi-billion dollar war operation is so over-protected by the holy lies of patriarchy.'

She opened her eyes and looked at me.

'No, don't laugh, boy, it's true. It's shit. Truly *shit*, in every sense of the word. *Shit. Merde.*'

I wasn't laughing, I was dazzled by her voice, her words, her splendour. She fed a nipple into my mouth, and held the back of my head. I thought I could taste a hint of milk form her nipple. She carried on murmuring:

'Only one bomb, low yield, 200 kilotons, is everybody's problem. All the nuclear power station 'accidents' are chicken-feed compared to this. The system works because they kept it out of sight. Missile convoys didn't trundle through towns by daylight until now (well, not too many British towns). People didn't realize they were *surrounded* by billions of dollars of death machines, in their own lands, *right next door.*

'Do you realize that in Britain you're never more than a few miles from a communications centre, an airbase, a military camp, a radar station, a power station, a nuclear bunker, a training centre, a Special Forces base, an arms dump, a weapons factory, an army barracks, or a command HQ?

'Now we've got radiated oceans, invaded countries and soldiers everywhere,' she said. 'Between 150 and 300 rads you suffer from nausea, fever, vomiting, skin hæmorrhages, mouth ulcers, loss of hair and affected bone marrow. A total dose of 450 rads means half of healthy adults die.

'Nature is reacting with animals going crazy, crops dying, lurid sunsets, a fucked-up eco-system. All water tastes foul. We can't halt the Collapse. The Zero Summer is upon us. It's Autumn already, Winter in June, the solstices confused. Rain, hail, hurricanes, floods, earthquakes, everything mixed up together in the death cauldron of superpower oblivion politics.'

'Britain used to be a magical continent full of warring tribes,' I said, '– the Celts, Romans, Normans, Saxons, with great heroes like Boudiccea, King Alfred, Henry V and King Arthur.'

The girl looked at me like I was mad.

I carried on: 'And then there was the reign of Elizabeth the First, Gloriana, ruling over Albion at its greatest – Shakespeare and the Elizabethan Age. Then the British Empire... Now it's just an 'unsinkable aircraft carrier', a forward nuclear strike base for the Americans.'

'You idiot,' she snarled. 'Britain's always been invaded by one kind of force or another: nomads, Indo-Europeans, Phoenicians, Romans, Celts, Jutes, Angles, Saxons, Normans, French, Dutch, Spanish, Germans and now Americans. There never *was* a 'British' people, or a 'United' Kingdom. *'United'?* Ha! It's *never* been 'United'. *Never.*

'Britain's always been a forward strike base. Now it's the 51st State of the U.S.A. *Hey, gimme a cheeseburger with tomato relish, over easy, sunny side up, large French fries and a medium Coke – to go.'*

Such intensity of love-making, such tenderness and together-ness. She began to push back at me harder, her whole body rippling fluidly, her breath now coming in the short, loud gasps before orgasm.

'All the housing estates of the world will look like those stone houses on the cliffs up there, with no roofs or windows,' I said.

She flung her head back and squinted at the flocks of seagulls wheeling overhead. The cosmos was spinning around us, myriads of stars. As we made love our leaders were making all the right decisions down millions of miles of red-hot telephone cables, connecting hidden underground bunkers with hidden missile silos, all the military equipment for so long kept safely out of sight, blended in with the landscape.

Making love under a burning crimson sunset, we could imagine the hysteria of billions of people surging through us at orgasm. Faces wet and hearts beating fast, we orgasmed tumultuously, irradiating the agony of millions of stranded souls.

We woke to a sky of xanthic light. Everything was drenched in gold. High Summer had been rushed into full-blown Autumn. The trees shone with red and bronze leaves. The yellowed grass became wet and verdant. Flowers raged in every crevice. The dunes glowed in the golden light. The landscape was turning into a dreamscape concocted by some psychotic geek on a super-computer. We walked in a loudly-lit movie set which had no edges. The air throbbed so hot we perspired like athletes. Deep within us, we burned by day and melted in passion by night.

The girl ran down the dunes yelling and carrying a card-board box of clothes she'd found. She slipped on a dark blue evening dress printed with silver stars. She had taffeta, silk, lace, velvet, wool and satin in the clothes box, and a multitude of colours: emerald, copper, damson, chalk-white, mahogany, saffron, ebony, amethyst.

'How stupid we were to be taken in by fashion, to buy all this crap,' she laughed, prancing about as if on a catwalk. She flung the clothes and high street carrier bags into the sea, which soon scattered them.

'A world built on vanity and ego-boosting. Cosmetic surgery, breast and penile enlargements, celebrity, gossip, Hollywood, *junk*.'

The girl ran about in the surf kicking up the sodden garments. She was enshrouded in bronze light. Her skin glowed as if she'd rubbed it down with the sun itself. Catching hold of her was like trying to net a falling star.

In the thermogenic landscape we made love frantically. I licked her buttocks, her enormous clitoris. With her knees in the sand, she arched her back, pushed her hips high and bucked violently.

We ignored the warship in the bay, the aircraft flying over it like vultures swooping onto a carcass, firing sheets of white flames. Booms echoed around the cliffs. The ship retaliated with anti-aircraft guns but was soon smashed up. Later there'd be acres of trash washed ashore, including corpses, adding to the fish, eels and octopuses we'd already seen.

We ignored all that and made love like two whales, facing each other, undulating. Making love with the passion-girl was like heaving about on a wind-tossed sea, every touch a hot wave, kisses like spray, her body rippling and wet. She was dripping with lust, I was hard as whalebone.

Two roughnecks were up on the cliffs, watching the ship sink and jeering at us. They'd probably wandered out of some nearby institution. We ignored them. We were igniting, we were beyond them, beyond the thugs on the cliffs, beyond the professional thugs in the jet fighters hitting 500 knots on their bombing runs. Someone somewhere thought it was still necessary to have these out-dated ships about. They'd have no ports to return to, no support, no orders.

When we heard the crash of the bottles the louts were throwing down the cliffs at us, we decided to move. We made no reply to them, we simply moved away.

'We can't have these freaks frying our brains,' muttered the girl. The skinheads shuffled off, after a few minutes. Further along the cliff was a group of people 'spotting' nuclear missiles, fanatics like the anorak-wearing, thermos-slurping train-spotting geeks.

It was good to move, to pound the wet sand, to be in motion. The light seemed even brighter than before. Sheets of lambent flame fell around us, discarded by the Sun-God up there. Dark brown and green seaweed lay underfoot; on the cliff faces bloomed scarlet and pink flowers. In the Midsummer madness the season was extending backwards and forwards. We tasted Spring in the air and also the bite of Winter.

The moment was full of potential. If only we could harness it.

'In European folklore on Midsummer Night the sky opens up and you can see forever,' I said.

The girl turned to me: 'You're dreaming again, Friedrich.'

Ah, yclept passion-girl, you are fantastic.

The bombs had blown up the calm streams of Time. In the catastrophic fragmentation colours blossomed madly. Never seen such saturation. We lived in the heart of a rainbow. Impossible to photograph it, or to paint it. The girl tried once, in St Austell, I think it was, to put the light onto paper. Impossible. Best to live in it, to live it.

A-bombs, H-bombs and neutron bombs were going off all around the planet like fireworks. Children clapped and cheered. In the air, F-16s, Jaguars, Tornadoes, Mirages, F-4s, MiG 21s, Su-24s, Blinders and Badgers flew, burning up enough fuel to take any city into the 22nd century. Missiles screamed their death-wails: AGM-86B, SS-20, SSBS-S3, Polaris A-3, Minuteman III, SS-NX-17.

Over the landscape ranged the missile launchers and tanks: Pershing 1A, Lance Honest John, M-110 howitzer, Frog 7, SS-C-16. In the seas slid the lovely submarines, bristling with warheads: *Delta*-Class, *Yankee*-Class, *Lafayette*-Class, each sub delivering more explosive than all that dropped in the Second World War. On the seas roamed the aircraft carriers and frigates. In space, satellites of all kinds orbited, tracking, mapping, communicating.

We could feel the atmosphere buzzing with commands, counter-commands, decisions, arguments, prayers, from every radar base, jet, ship, satellite, submarine and Command Centre. Washington, Moscow, Sao Paulo, Tokyo and Baghdad were dead, but the commands kept flying from thousands of bunkers.

'I detest being raped,' said the girl, out of nowhere. 'This holocaust is global rape.'

Rape, murder, suicide, genocide, megacide – none of the words were strong enough.

She was wearing 'un jean avec un T-shirt' as the French would say. Big deaths and little deaths – *l'amour et la Morte* – we experienced them all.

She pressed my hand down the front of her jeans. Behind us an abandoned radar establishment loomed out of the dark, grey on grey concrete. Hot stars span above, somewhere, beyond the illumination of the sun.

The girl sucked me into her body aura, magicking me into an erotic stupor.

We were turning into nuclear angels, creatures of pure phosphorescence. When we made love we ignited sparks of lust all about us, the sand rising in circular waves from our conjoined bodies, dusty ripples on the beach. Our kisses became more feverish, our touches more frenetic. She felt divine, her face gleaming in the sun.

'Quick,' she gasped, 'we haven't got much time left.'

She closed her thighs around my fingers in a tight scissor grip.

'Fuck me before it's too late,' she said, hanging onto my neck, kissing me.

I hated that phrase 'it's too late'. It was a hopeless thing to say, at any time, in any situation. My whole being reacted against it, violently. Too late? No, never!

But it was. The girl unbuttoned her jeans, her eyes burning into my soul. My hand was buried inside her furnace-hot gash. She was twisting her body around gently.

'Will you never listen? We'll never be together after tomorrow. We didn't do enough, we didn't care enough.'

I silenced her with a deep, soul-searching kiss, then said:

'You're not Christ or Krishna or Buddha. You can't take on the whole world's pain, the world's sins. That's the egoism that's led to this mess.'

She had a finger and thumb around the base of my penis, jacking me slowly. I still felt queasy. Earlier I had retched into the sand. Now I felt cocooned in her love.

But she saw me as somehow responsible for the bombings. I was male, and she saw the catastrophe as largely man-made. Men see masses, but women see individuals, she explained. Men generalize, women particularize. The girl generated tolerance and humility, where I saw only billions of blackened, dying souls.

'You shouldn't say "nuclear war",' she said. 'It shouldn't be a *word*, it should be a *scream*. You should scream, not speak.'

She let out a couple of yells that reverberated around the cliffs. My ears popped. I felt sick again. I began to throw up. The girl screamed again, testing out her reactions to the global rape.

I had blood, sand, sugar, saliva, sperm, water, salt from the sea and her wetness on my hands. I loved it.

All the liquids in the body were pouring out of us. We lapped at them like cats. As I vomited the girl kept rubbing my hard cock, as if she were soothing a baby. I couldn't resist her, and convulsed in her deft grasp.

She kept rocking slightly to and fro. She murmured, leaning into my ear.

'We've got one day or so left, boy, in which to run through all of evolution: from mammal to religion, from cetacean to factory, from fish to Apocalypse.'

We had a day in which to fulfil everything, all our wildest dreams. I loved the passion-girl when she spoke like this. I grabbed her, wiping my mouth on my shoulder.

'One day in which to stop the fire, to halt the decline, to slam the rot back into the faces of the 'leaders'.'

She lit a cigar we'd found in a deserted house on top of the cliff. We had slid down the dark serpentine rocks of the Lizard peninsula into another secret cove. It was washed smooth by the out-going tide, and about the size of a tennis court.

'You realize when the tide comes in we're buried?' I said as I dumped our bags on a rock shelf.

'Good,' she replied, sucking on the cigar. 'Look.'

Out beyond the surfline a group of killer whales were swimming in a row. The girl told me they were quiet because they were resting. They swam gently through the water. Then they started to take shallow dives.

'They're so beautiful,' she murmured.

But I wanted to set the girl free. I wanted to escape from her matriarchal power. I didn't want to cling onto her anymore. I wanted to untie the umbilical cords of passion that connected us belly-to-belly, mouth-to-mouth, eye-to-eye, genitals-to-genitals. She kept stroking me, up and down, smiling softly, more enigmatic than anything Leonardo da Vinci painted.

I told her we had to part.

She was surprised for a moment, then softened.

'You'll be back,' she said. 'You're romantic. You need kisses.'

She was right, and in the end it was she who left me. She told me she didn't need me, at all.

'You're just there to fend off attackers. And I don't even need that now I've got this gun.'

She squeezed my penis hard in my shorts.

She grinned. She knew she had me, hook, line and sinker. I was a foolish fish and she could dangle me wherever she wished.

'Women don't need men at all,' she went on. 'Except as impregnators, and even then we can have a giant sperm bank – and no men. Just a deep freeze of seeds, and a world without men. Bliss.'

All the arguments were in her favour. She had the world under her thumb, but a few men had escaped, and had set up on their own. These Presidents, kings, ministers, governments, soldiers and army chiefs were now about to burst the bubble, to overthrow Mother Earth.

Vermilion dust was falling from the sky. The girl stepped from the waves looking like Venus being born. She smoothed her hands over her nude form, washing herself with sunlight. She smiled, throwing back her long wet hair.

'Come here, neophyte. Let me initiate you. Put your morning erection into my *vajra-vesapravartna*. Let's fly up into the Celestial Spheres. Let's rock and roll into one – conjoin in the *unio mystica*, the spiritual conjunction.'

She grinned, warming to her mystical theme.

'O *biddhu, mudra*, my Third Eye is weeping *soma*-juice. Come, thrust your long *lingam* into my seething *yoni*. Let's Shiva-and-Shakti, eh? Come burst my Cloud, you *tantra-mantra-yantra*-boy, you *kundalini*-genius, you spine-climbing freak.'

Her mouth grew big as the sea. Vermilion dust fell from the sky. My skin tingled. She licked my ear and murmured:

'Push deep into the spiritual zones, dear. Go for *wu*. Crush your swollen ithyphallus into my waterlogged temple, yes? See how it feels to be one of the Gods!'

She clawed me into her heat and wetness, all the while muttering religious gobbledegook.

'This is *Klim, bija, Ram,* ah, Ying fucks Yang, bliss.'

She reached into her bag and produced some cherry-red lipstick. She yanked off my T-shirt and drew moons and stars over me, and made up her face like a shamaness. She loved to play, she loved to play.

'Come on, boy. I anoint you with the blood of Christ, the tears of Mary and the sperm of the Devil. Set me on the *via illuminativa*. Self-illuminate me, my *logos*, my soft *Nous*, my nourishing Neo-platonic One.'

She pressed her fingers inside her minge, then into my mouth.

'– I bless you and hold you and keep you. Come, suck *satori* out of me. Squeeze the *soma* into bliss. Climb the *chakras* quickly. Blister your way into the Tenth Sephiroth and burst all the stars about us! This is where the fireworks start.'

She was groaning madly and writhing over me. She squeezed my body fiercely, riding me hard.

'Come on, boy. Soak up our *karma*. Suck the blood of religion right up to the top of the *axis mundi*.'

The girl moaned, orgasming wildly. I pulsed inside her, expanding voluptuously. An orgasm of dark spasms and white flames. Her lips were as large as the pyramids, soft as the Nile in flood. I shivered and pumped everything inside the witch-queen.

A rogue wave washed over us, startling us out of our rapture. We screeched as the sudden cold, and climbed up onto a ledge. The girl pulled on a shirt, kissed me and popped a pill into my mouth.

'It's not LSD or some such,' she said when I protested. 'It's a relaxant.'

She dressed while I watched her in my hebetude. She placed me on my back on the ledge, and folded my arms across my chest, like a pharaoh in a sarcophagus. She sat smoking the rest of her cigar until I dozed off. Then she left me, half-covered by the blanket, on the rocks at the base of the Cornish cliff. It was getting dark.

I woke up in the brilliant morning. No sign of the girl except a letter. My head felt heavy, my body ached. I lay in the shade of the cliff, under the cool rock. I stashed away some of our stuff, then climbed into the rising sun. The half-chopped-up carcass of a horse lay on the grass, flies buzzing around it, eyes eaten out. Trees had been lopped down as if some psychopath had just discovered the slash-and-burn tactics of industrial Amazonian deforestation. Graffiti in huge letters on the stone walls read: CHARLIE'S BACK AGAIN, and CHILD-SEX AVAILABLE, ENQUIRE WITHIN. Also a row of swastikas over-painted with the circular nuclear disarmament sign.

I had blood stains on my T-shirt. I took it off. Was it menstrual blood, I wondered? Or that of a horse perhaps?

I looked about: nothing and no one in any direction. Just the eternal Cornish wind blowing... and grass... gulls... distant smoke... sunlight...

I sat down to read the girl's letter, crouched on the grass:

'I am going to meet God,' she wrote, 'who wants to see me one last time. I smell of you. You are in my deep dark places. I want you to fill me with gold and silver stars. Find me calling you on 5072 in the rain-telephone.'

I guessed she meant me to find a telephone box with the number 5072 on it. She would call me.

That morning I had had another strange dream:

The girl was a lion escaped from a Russian zoo. We were lost in a glade surrounded by gigantic electricity pylons. A herd of lumberjacks were cutting them down with steel saws. The pylons hissed like trees, waving madly. Overhead flew black helicopters. They lowered rescue cables but we couldn't grab hold of them. You dropped from a tree like a white cat and fell onto my shoulders. Finally, we managed to escape from the mass of crisscrossed electrical cables on the ground.

Then we were in a Latin American city. Everyone was blind, wore eye-patches. It was Pentecost. Fires were lit on the mountains. A group of fat ladies played bingo in the street. A man was having his head caved in with a hammer down at the docks. You went about shrieking "Pastel Shades for sale! Pastel Shades for sale!" Strawberries slipped from your mouth. Bees crawled into my mouth and made honey.

In a white nightdress you stood on the captain's deck of a pirate's galleon. Dwarfs cavorted insanely. A mob were on the rigging. Hail fell. You seared your skin to mine. You choked me with your tongue, your body climbing up me. As we made love another man pushed into you from behind. Your nightdress became a birthdress, a white wedding dress. We all drowned in the taffeta. Someone let off a smoke-bomb. Seagulls cried above.

When I woke the birds were still there, circling over the scraps we'd left on the beach below.

I wandered into a backyard strewn with plastic kids' toys, and through a door into an old house. I found some ancient chocolates and ate them rapaciously. A boy of about six lurked around a corner, startling me. He watched me silently, then said:

'Those are daddy's.'

I asked him where his daddy was.

'Dead,' he replied, staring at me with shark's eyes. Then I heard a frail woman's voice calling from upstairs.

'Tom, Tom, Tom.'

I left the house quickly. A smoke-screen of brightly-coloured leaves fell from the sky. I found refuge in a cemetery. An old man hobbled up to speak with me, clad in non-descript trousers and sweater, like a relic from mediæval Britain he seemed. He told me trade in the funeral business was slack.

'People drop dead in their homes. The telephones don't work, so I never find out about the corpses 'til it's too late. Burial's out of fashion. They burn 'em or tip 'em into the quarries. Atomic apathy rules.'

A girl with a skin rash on the side of her face skipped up to us. The man offered round a bag of sticky sweets, which tasted months old.

'I see you don't bother about fall-out either,' he said, looking at me with a wry smile. 'It's all a bunch of lies anyway.'

Time moves slowly in graveyards. Yellowed leaves fluttered down onto the tombstones. It felt like melancholy Autumn – as it always is in a cemetery. The old grave-digger told me not to go to Mullion, Helston, Gunwalloe or Truro, because, his very words:

'A plague's broken out.'

He pointed to Belle, the little girl with her rash.

I had a vision of archaic, mediæval Britain ravaged by plague. I expected to see King Arthur riding across the moors on a white stallion, or hordes of dour Dark Age warriors swarming over the furze. Instead of this we got Army trucks sputtering along the narrow lanes, with gasmasked soldiers waving inanely.

The cairns and maens and ancient earthworks of Cornwall were all empty. Fire, water, flesh, jewels or quartz were no longer buried in them anymore. The tribes of old England were long gone, long dead. Yet the sunlit days were as halcyon, as epicurean as ever.

In a deserted, ransacked café on the B-3293 I pinned up a note for the girl on the cracked notice board, in amongst the many other missing persons messages and photos.

She could be anywhere.

This war merely exaggerated what was already inside everybody, all the paranoias, the neuroses, the hatreds.

I sat under a bright yellow sky raining fall-out and read a heap of newspapers, some of them dated February and April, before the war had started. Wars have no monopoly on horror. It exists everywhere, everyday:

Dog kills owner – A man bled to death on Sunday night after his pet Alsatian bit him on his wrists and legs.
Thailand death toll rises – At least 171 people were killed and 500 injured in an explosion of more than a million electric detonators in an overturned truck.
Typhoon – At least 800 people were feared dead yesterday after Typhoon Jackie hit central Japan causing floods.
Lovers 'strangled tell-tale sister, 13' – A schoolboy murdered his sweetheart's little sister to stop her revealing their secret affair, a court heard yesterday.

Even before the war, people were murdering each other in bizarre and violent ways. Chopped to pieces and burnt in an incinerator... hacked to death for stepping on someone's toe... hung; battered with hammers... drowned... strangled. An amazing variety of deaths, of violence, of torture, of pain.

Bruges – A 33-year-old Belgian woman has confessed to killing eight of her ten children.
Tiff horror – Thomas Brown, 36, burned himself to death in the street after a row with his lover in Crumpsall, Greater Manchester.

In the news a mother watches TV while her child is sexually abused in the same room... a man rapes a 70 year-old grandmother... another rapes an eight-month pregnant woman... a Florentine killer specializes in murdering young couples – 18 of them... politicians claim humanity will be wiped out if homosexuality is taught in classrooms, and so on. Sometimes I wondered if I was living on the right planet. Speed the carnage up of everyday life and you had a war.

Day was hieing. Falling stars dropped through a sunset made of equal parts of purpurin and bice. The smokefall felt like the accumulation of every Autumn evening I'd ever experienced. I stepped over stinking seaweed and slimy pebbles in some vast debris-strewn cove on the West side of the Lizard peninsula. Crimson washed over the sky now and I was madly missing the girl.

I missed her presence, her voice, her touches.

Her eroticism took in the whole world. She wanted a love that engulfed everything and she taught me how to look at everything in a fresh, sympathetic way. She wanted someone who could 'go over the Edge' with her, as she put it, who could really soar.

She was looking forward to the nuclear holocaust. 'It'll be the *lux fiat*,' she said. '"Let there be light", the First Creative Act of God.'

Under the empurpling afterglow I wandered through an obliterated caravan site. Only metal frames were left of these mobile holiday homes. I thought of the petty squabbles and fragmented joys of the holiday-makers who had come down here from Doncaster, Norwich, Liverpool, Coventry and Yeovil.

I glimpsed the sad remaining shreds of humanity: the burnt corner of a mattress, empty beer bottles, an empty flower pot, shrivelled soup packets, a Pokémon cuddly toy. Life was so fragile, so easily tipped into death.

On the radio I had heard the last, desperate broadcasts. Someone was raving into a microphone on a pirate radio station. Terrorists and activists were doing all they could to hit their targets, but the world governments had sealed off their bunkers. Global war rendered global terrorism somewhat redundant. The cities that had not been bombed were living in an emergency state of curfews, riots and rations. Hypermarkets and superstores had all been raided by hordes climbing barricades. Many crowds had been dispersed using live ammunition. Insurgents in Indonesia and Bolivia had got hold of supplies of napalm. The world was turning into a moonscape out of Hieronymous Bosch.

Again and again I wondered where the girl was. She said she

194

had gone to meet 'God'. Perhaps she was busy rewriting the *Book of Genesis*, careful to edit out all traces of 'man', 'mankind' and Adam. I suspected that 'God' was really her father. It made sense that she might meet him one last time, before The End.

I was amazed to find a broken boat riding up the surf in the cove: inside it was a box of *Bibles*. I picked one up. All the pages had been ripped out except for the *Book of Revelations*. I jumped a mile when I heard a scream from the cliffs forty feet above me. A woman in a dark tan twin-set suit scuttled down the cliff path, followed by three harassed, peevish males. The woman ran over the sand towards me; quite a sight.

'Have you wicked man found our boat? Our *Bibles*?' the bedraggled woman asked me. She fumbled with her tortoise-shell spectacles and peered at me.

'Thank the Lord we found them,' she sighed and snatched the sea-wet *Bible* from my hand. I wasn't sure exactly who these religious freaks were – Jehovah's Witness, Mormons, Methodists, Christian Scientists, Anglicans…? They seemed to be a mixture of everything Christian and evangelical and self-righteous.

I shrugged. 'The boat ran aground here,' I told them.

The woman snapped at me. 'Wicked man. Pagan. Sinner. Come on, Harold. Get these holy books away from this blaspheming heathen.'

Her three helpers muttered 'Praise the Lord,' many times, as they picked up the books.

At the end of the beach was a pile of broken wood and canvas, vaguely recognizable as a one-time Punch and Judy Show. There was a bicycle near by. I picked up the bike, but both tyres were flat and the front wheel was buckled.

Halfway up the hill was a stone well, decked out with coloured ribbons. I threw in a nail for luck (there was no point wishing now – and everyone was wishing for the same thing). I had no coins, but had picked up some nails, for no particular reason.

The radio and TV stations had all disappeared now – they had spent weeks closing down. There always seemed to be some band of nuts who'd try to get a broadcasting service going again.

I passed a throne made of a natural rock formation and imagined the girl sitting in it, like some Goddess or High Priestess. Thus enthroned she might be able to sort out the Islamic fundamentalist brotherhood that was terrorizing women in the cities of the Middle East (gang rape was the least of the atrocities).

In the distance I saw a group of wild horses. I was surprised that no one had shot them for meat yet. Even from half a mile, I could hear the sound of their hooves on the grass.

I wondered how the dolphins and whales were coping with the warmed seas. Sometimes the tide brought in whole shoals of dead fish.

The wind over the fields was strong and dry, like the Mistral or Sirocco. My skin was baked to a cinder. The heat was intense, like a wall. It was difficult to move in it. The desertification of Britain was fully in progress.

I walked around a black lake, which stank of burnt plastic and sulphur. It wasn't empty but it was definitely undrinkable. I imagined a huge monster at the far end of the lake, hurtling towards me under the surface. My heart stopped when I saw a stationary wave near the outlet of the pool, but then I realized it was set up by the flood gates.

The hissing grass, hot wind and expanse of empty landscape made me feel erotic. I wanted the world to rain, so that the exterior drenching water would reflect the sweet wetness that would be inside the girl when I met her. Inner and outer. Inner – *in her*. So it would be all drenching wetness and wrenching sweetness when we met. But there was not a cloud in the sky.

Flamethrowers were being used in some Central American and Far Eastern countries, finishing off what the bombs had started. Words like 'liberty' and 'peace' were no longer used by anybody, even in jest or irony. Survival was everyone's priority.

Survival and violence. The babies (world governments) had been given too many toys to play with. The naughty little boys (politicians and military generals) were usurping their guardians (mothers and taxpayers).

I thought of some people who would love this atomic apocalypse: Arthur Rimbaud, the Roman Emperor Nero, Alexander the Great, Napoleon Bonaparte, Genghis Khan, the Marquis de Sade, Adolf Hitler.

We were paying the price for our alienation, I thought. For years it hadn't been necessary to meet anyone in the flesh: the telephone, computer and television did it all for us. I thought of the empty office blocks which had been set up by the espionage agencies to record and monitor international phone calls. All those civil servants must be huddled in bunkers now, if they were lucky.

Someone had once asked "Where was God when the bomb was dropped on Hiroshima?" But where was God now, when every submarine or jet could deliver ten or a thousand Hiroshimas each?

Humans had been around for – what? – 100,000 years, or maybe two million, or however you classed 'humans' – but now was the first time in history that people had created machines to wipe out all of humanity, the girl told me once.

'But why would they do that?' I asked her.

'I know,' she said. 'It's completely crazy. You can't imagine any other species doing that, wasting so much time and money and human life on manufacturing mass global death.'

I sat in the dunes of Cornwall, amongst the rustling marram grass, and looked at a disused tin mine, gaunt against the sky. Blue Vega shone overhead.

I watched the satellites speeding silently from horizon to horizon. I listened to the voice of the universe and it said: *tick-tick-tick*. The Final Countdown, the Meltdown, the Falldown. Far underneath me Uranium-238 decayed softly into an atomic sleep.

197

I imagined the conversation taking place at that moment between the girl and her father:

Father:	*Hello child. Would you like to fly my B52H bomber?*
Daughter:	*O yes, Daddy. You're so strong, so hard, so good at destroying other people. Can I hold this Trident II D-5 rocket in my hand?*
Father:	*Certainly. But don't squeeze too hard. It might –*
Daughter:	*Oooh, Daddy. It's so big and hard and cold. Ooooh!*
Father:	*That's right, dear little pet. It's for killing those Commie bastards, Arabs and Chink gooks.*
Daughter:	*Oooh, Daddy, I love your authority* (thinks: you vapid idiot). *Can I sit in the holy computer seat?*
Father:	*Yes. How does it feel to be in control of COCNAADC?*
Daughter:	*Oooh, great, Daddy. All these buttons and lights.* (thinks: Yikes, these guys are CRAZY).
Father:	*This is where we control the Theatre of War.*
Daughter:	*What happens if I press this button, marked in red 'DETONATE EUROPE'?*
Father:	*Whoops. You've done it now. Europe's dead. Great, huh?*
Daughter:	*Oh Daddy, did you really have to do it, to kill Europe?*
Father:	*Er, yeah, honey. That's the way it goes in male war –*
Daughter:	*Oooh, Daddy. You're so strong, so authoritarian.*
Father:	*Thanks. Do you like sitting in this ATB-jet cockpit?*
Daughter:	*Gosh, I love it. It gives you a sense of Power.*
Father:	*Yeah, that's what we like about these jets:* Power.
Daughter:	*And this AGM-69A Short Range Attack Missile is fired at people and kills thousands of them?*
Father:	*Er, uh, yeah, uh, I suppose so.*
Daughter:	*Does it* have *to be like that, Daddy?*
Father:	*You know it does, child.*

At night I go to sleep to the sound of A-bombs exploding. In a thousand computer centres around the world I can hear the hiss of incoming satellite calls, the susurrus of middle-aged men making 'decisions' in board rooms.

Here on the dunes of Cornwall, it was so peaceful I could believe in anything but a nuclear war. Wait a minute – those flying dolphins swimming through the atmosphere have got sub-noses, like Pershing II missiles: W84, SSM, airburst, 40-kiloton yield.

I can see the flights of Tu-95 *Bears* coming in for another dropload. The scream of towns burning after a W78 Minuteman III ICBM 330-kiloton yield ATTACK.

My darling, what is your launch mode? Mode is hot, HOT. Do you hear the sound of flying dolphins, blasting up out of the ocean, transmutating into roaring missiles? This and other floccinaucinihilipilifications.

My launch mode is hot.

I sat on the dunes of Cornwall and gasped for water and dreamt of LGM-30G Minuteman III missiles: with their Triple MIRV warheads with penaids; Mark 12A with 335-kiloton thermonuclear warheads; length: 18.2 metres; speed at burn-out: 15,000 mph; range: 7,000 kilometres.

I dreamt of the Vought Corporation's Miniature Homing Vehicle – a cylinder 12 inches in diameter, 13 inches long which is ejected from an F-15 fighter at a speed of 17,5000 mph. Sensors home in on the target and the onboard computer guides the cylinder to its target using mini-rockets. It destroys the victim not with explosives but by simply smashing into it at 17,500 mph.

Is that a submarine I can see raising its spikey black metal head over there? Soviet *Oscar* Class, a cruise-missile submarine fitted with SS-NX-19 anti-ship missiles...

MX missiles: 95-ton, 3-stage, solid-propellant missile with inertial guidance using gyroscopes and accelerometers.

I thought of the military satellites in geostationary orbit above me, like technological guardian angels, whispering in my ear about secret manœuvres, with their atomic clocks that lose only one second in 30,000 years. Atomic time beating away, like my heart, counting every utterly insignificant and minuscule fraction of a millionth of a micro-second. And all those strange globes, cubes and dishes of the radar systems, the oddest additions to the landscape.

For years the 70,000 nuclear warheads of the globe had been on constant alert. Now every missile was vibrating eagerly in its silo, like a spoilt child waiting to be taken on a Christmas shopping spree to buy that special thing it has been lusting after for months. Missiles were like eager football players, itching to get out onto the field, to smash the enemy, to score a direct hit on some quaking township.

Britain lay under dense clouds of fall-out drifting over from decimated Berlin, Warsaw and Moscow. Poor old Paris... that ancient whore of a city had finally bitten the dust.

I thought of the girl and her desire to STOP THE FIRE, as she put it. I remembered a friend telling me that he didn't think women really understood how truly violent men can be.

The world is on Panic Alert, Attack Warning Red. Forty thousand megatons are ready to go. The world is on a tripwire, a highwire balanced between Suicide and Death. Twenty major nations were getting ready for the 'big firework' (another of the girl's phrases).

I've probably sat next to nuclear scientists or atomic chiefs on the subway, going to work, or in cinemas, or bars and cafés. They're all around us, I thought. Everything was upside-down. Noah's Ark was now a hole sixty feet square cut into the bedrock, lined with lead and concrete and furnished with water, food supplies, plastic chairs and outdated magazines. Two by two we file into the Ark, carrying a gasmask and a roll of toilet tissue.

Take some Uranium-238, encase it, add a little 'heavy water', fire some atoms at it, and watch. The perfect recipe for a disaster. Around the world scientists had been working away like Faustian alchemists, searching for the Philosopher's Stone, nuclear power. The atom bomb was the Philosopher' Stone *par excellence*, and it would grant immortality. The Faustian pact with the Devil – the demon in all of us.

I still hadn't found the rain-telephone box.

There was amazing light on the planet, though. Fervid orange glows in the sky. I wandered through piles of detritus, barbed wire, glass, metal, paper, sodden cardboard boxes, black plastic and old clothes.

I wanted to touch the firm round breasts of the girl, to feel her nude body embracing me. I shaved, cut my hair, and washed in a rockpool violet-hued with iodine. I wanted to kiss the Goddess, to suck her swollen clitoris, to hear her orgasmic gasps.

I was blue. I walked like a castdown archangel across wind-swept Cornish beaches. I wanted the girl straddling my shoulders, my tongue deep inside her honeyed heat.

I wanted to see all the people I'd known. I wanted them to climb out of their cubby-holes in the sand, to leap from behind the prehistoric burial mounds and moonstones, to come down out of the clouds.

I was moving into the heart of the light.

It was so bright I couldn't tell where the sea began and the sky ended. I lived in glory because I was starving and parched and exhausted. It was nearly The End. (I wished the girl was there – she had a knack for finding water, and could locate those Cornish wells which were so overgrown and hidden).

My eyes were wildly open and I lived in a kind of bliss. It was bliss to be sane, or to be insane (but what difference was there now?), to be utterly alone, to be able to do absolutely anything.

I stumbled over dunes, menhirs, cliffs, moors, fields, paths, lanes. I wanted to find her, very quickly, before the incineration.

I felt sick. I was falling apart. I felt radiant, and irradiated. When the girl finally meets me, I thought, she won't recognise me: I'll be a nuclear angel.

Eventually I found the phone box, painted red with a black plastic receiver with the magical number 5072 on it.

Good, I thought, and waited and waited for her call. I got up, smoked, paced about. I walked down to the beach, still within earshot of the telephone. I itched, stretched, sang, muttered, cursed. I ached for her to call me. I yelled at the sky and sea.

It was like waiting for a telephone call from God, or from a nearby star. Minutes seemed like light years.

I looked up. There goes another missile, I thought, watching the vapour trail. MSBS M-4, 150-kiloton yield, ready for impact, primary target: Bristol, Plymouth, Leicester, Hull, Aberdeen, Cardiff. I waited, and waited, and waited, scratching, mumbling, walking, lounging... waiting.

Here I can bring my story up to date at last. I have written it here, in pencil, on scraps of filthy paper, beside this telephone box, on the dunes of Cornwall. I am still waiting for the girl's call, so we can compare our stories.

The telephone rang. The noise startled me out of a deep stupor. I fell over as I scrambled towards the kiosk. I snatched up the earpiece.

She: *Hello? Boy? Crash-crash, this is Radio Trash. Is that 5072, 5072? Over? Over? Do you have time for lerrrv?*

She sounded delicious, but very far away. The line hissed and crackled. Was she on the other side of the planet? The girl could be anywhere, even in one of the stations on the far side of the moon.

She: *Echo five, come in.* Ça va? Va bene? Nasisiniz? Prusht taza?

She was speaking in many different languages; I had no idea what was going on.

She: Wa'aleiykum as salaam wa rahmat Allah wa barakaut! *Get your feet out of the dung. Stand up straight. Move into the sunlight.*

She cackled with laughter.

Me: *How come the public telephones are still working?*

She: *They aren't. I got my father to fix this connection up for us on preference category 3, through an emergency switchboard.*

Me: *Where have you been?*

She: *I told you. To meet God. I've been to an Apocalypse Party. Everyone was there. Old schoolfriends.* Zda-nekd nelkdy-te-jeste-uvidim? *The Burndown is today. Tonight. Look up and you'll see a balloon with "Deutschland" printed on it in Gothic lettering. Hello, Moscow. Get out and clean the streets.*

Her voice was drowned in static. I want you, I want you, I thought, but said nothing. I waited for the static to die down. It did, after a minute or so. I lit a cigarette, and stood outside the telephone box, smoking in the brilliant sunlight.

She: *Shoot and destroy. Slash and burn. Protest and survive.*

Me: *Do you see Venus, burning brightly?*

She: *Yes, I see it. This is the Year of the Serpent.*

Me: *How do you propose to avert this global catastrophe?*

She: (Laughing) *First we've got a few airbursts, to set the children screaming. Next up we'll have the submarine missiles fired on the world's major cities. There will be ground attacks, causing blast waves, hurricanes, ionizing radiation and firestorms. Plutonium-239 is set at super-criticality. Just ten kilograms is enough, and the effects should be, to use that well-worn media phrase properly for once, DEVASTATING.*

The atomic clock is set at one minute to midnight. In nuke-speak that means PANIC ALERT. Every warhead is on primary ignition. Nothing can alter the Countdown. It's the Maximum Fake-Out. Missiles primed for Cairo, New Orleans, Kiev, Lima, Melbourne, Seoul, Chicago, Santiago, Calcutta, Johannesburg, Tehran, Singapore.

Congratulations, World, you've won tonight's Star Prize: a weekend in decimated Berlin for two! A crashdive into the trash of advanced capitalism.

Me: *Stick the knives in deep. You're good at making people squirm.*

She: *Don't bland me out, faker. Here, listen to the children screaming in a billion atrocities. Hear the wail of a billion middle-class married couples as they survey their flattened homes and possessions from their bunkers.*

I wanted to ask her: where was she? Who was she with? What was she doing? I wanted her so much, but listened to her polemic entranced. I couldn't keep up with her soaring mind.

She: *Stuff philosophy back down the throats of the layabouts who propounded it. This is Instant Alert, way beyond the reach of post-structuralist hermeneutics or Cartesian metaphysics. Oh look, is that the world crying? No, it's just another shower of rain. I'll wait for the rainbow.*

Is it raining where you are, boy?

Me: *Tell me where you are. Where are you?*

She: *Not yet, not yet. Don't rush me. What are you wearing?*

Me: *My shorts. Nothing else. You?*

She: *I have a white and green cotton Summer dress on. No knickers and nothing else except leather sandals. Ah, there's the rainbow. I knew I'd see one.*

It was raining on my telephone box. I couldn't see the rainbow, but I had a hunch that the girl must be near.

She: *What good did Plato do for us after all? He was the first European fascist, that's all. He stitched us up good. Look at the sky, there's the real deal –*

Yes. A missile was burning itself out in the ionosphere. The telephone line crackled again. It sounded like frying eggs. The girl was talking again, softly, sweetly, savagely.

She: *Bless the Republic for making us flinch every time we hear a police siren. Bless us in our daily toil as we crouch below the shockline in our bunkers. Bless the Holy Father for creating this megaton death –*

Me: *How is your father –?*

I blurted this question. There was a pause – I'd said the

wrong thing. Then:

She: *Not yet, not yet. Wait, boy, wait.*

Can you really understand, boy, just how much people worked their backs off trying to put together a reasonable life? Do you know just how much people worked *for their lives? Can you believe that a tiny minority of immature idiots are going to blow up all that work, all that pain and toil? The lunatics have been let out of their asylum. There they are, streaming over the neatly trimmed lawns, into their limousines, clutching briefcases, pills and speeches.*

Me: *You sound just a touch bitter –*

She: *– Bitter? Moi? Ha! What about* my *children? Are the leaders going to rob me of everything? I am pregnant, boy. By you, boy. I am terrified, and the child's inside me, growing.*

I didn't know what to say to this. She was pregnant?

She: *I have our child inside me, symbol and flesh of our joined-together love. A changeling. A witch's daughter. Love acting from the Outside in. Deep love.*

You have been living your days around my menstrual cycle. Now the big blood-magic has done its work. I am quick. I'm on fire.

She said she was on fire. She's on fire.

I wanted her. I wanted to see her, to feel her belly, to dip my fingers in her holy womb-blood. Instead I had a plastic telephone receiver, an old phone kiosk and the windswept dunes of Cornwall.

Me: *I want to see you.*

She: *No, damn you, no. Not yet. Curb your male violence. Wait. Be soft. Listen to me. The Everglades in Florida are twenty feet under hot water. The gantries of the old NASA moon rockets stand up amid crocodile-infested swamps.*

Wait a minute –

There was silence, then static. I hung on, waiting. It sounded like she was talking to herself. I could just about hear her, above the hiss and whirr of Secret Service data recorders.

A few minutes later she was back on the line.

She: *Sorry. I just couldn't speak anymore. They're raping every-*

body. Are you scared?

Me: *Tell me where you are: I'll be there faster than a ground-to-air missile –*

She: *– Yes, but not yet. Wait.*

     I glanced at the sea and saw a group of dancing dolphins. They zoomed over the blue waves into the air, becoming atomic missiles. A flock of seagulls swooped around the telephone box. The air was filled with the roar of rockets and inertial guidance systems.

Me: *We're not walking on thin ice anymore, we're being dropped into boiling hot lava.*

She: *Once I was a mermaid, swimming in the primæval oceans with shoals of bright fish and dolphins.*

Me: *As you say, this is the Maximum Fake-Out. They are exploding their egos above our heads.* **Ruat** coelum!

She: *It's been a fantastic Summer. Remember the submarine silos? The aquarium, the sex shop, the fairgrounds? Remember the dog that attacked you? The killer whale in the swimming pool? Remember all those things, boy, boy?*

Me: *Of course. It was only yesterday. And the sunken reservoir? The bonfires? The witches' ritual on the hilltop? That night we spent in the train? That occult mansion? The lighthouse and the storm and the missile attack? That night in the cornfield and the bombing of the ship? The zoo, the museum, the garden maze, the army camp in the middle of that stone ring? Do you remember all of that?*

She: *Tell me your dreams.*

Me: *A lunatic was with me. We were trying to sleep, but I didn't want this clinging creature around me. I had to lock him out. He kept pushing at the door.*

     In another dream I had a new 'brother'. Mother told me about him. He had a great sense of humour. My grandfather died in another dream, and in a post-holocaust landscape we ran away from horrible men. I used my flying powers and we flew to a cabin. We escaped.

She: *You are autistic, autoerotic, stuck in the mirror phase,*

phantasizing about incest and rape. Psychotherapy would not help you.
It's too late for men.

> *I have a girl baby growing inside. I know it's a girl. I*
checked.

I could not make sense of much of her words, except
the part about a baby. I wanted to know about her father. Had
she seen him? Had she met 'God'?

She: *Yes, I have met him. He was evacuated out of the capital a*
few weeks ago to some dark retreat in South Wales. But he wanted to see
me, one last time, his only child, his rebellious little daughter. He met
me at a disused airfield at Portreath, in a helicopter, with his guards. He
was wearing an NBC-suit to protect himself from the fall-out and
radiation. He spoke to me through a little microphone and speaker. I
could see his weary eyes behind his metallic blue visor. We couldn't
kiss.

> *He said I was radiated, and would die within weeks, or*
maybe days, if I didn't come with him, to be nursed somewhere in the
Brecon Beacons. I refused. He was mad at me, but he left, with three
other helicopters. I had him drop me off here –

Me: *Where? Where are you?*

She: *In good time, boy. Be patient, boy. Do you know this*
conversation is being recorded? It's all automatic, and in 24 hours those
recordings will be so much ionized dust.

I waited in silence.

She: *My father told me of a recent attempt by German terrorists to*
knock out the US Defence System in the Pentagon. Two lesbians and
two homosexuals, from Berlin, stormed the Command Centre. Their
inside contact was Sue Papen, secretary to Harry Rohe, the defence
chief.

> *Kat Meer, Diane Jones, Zel Zelsky and Dez Bethall – heard*
of them? Typical left-wing terrorists, you might say. Their main weapon
was the 'orgasm gun'. This is true: it's a chemical weapon which can be
fired at men to give them an instant ejaculation. It leaves them crippled.
Dad had told me about it before. You use it before rape or some violent
act, and it renders men momentarily helpless.

207

These terrorists were aiming for the US War Machine, the big Phallus of Lies, Violence and Big Bucks. Sue Papen gave them top secret information, and the terrorists planned their night attack for months. Black Friday was their attack date.

The day before, a colleague of theirs, Toni Debray, had shot the Pope in the Vatican. He was a very happy assassin, later mowed down by the Pope's guards in one of the baroque, velvet corridors of Rome.

Well, the terrorists got quite far into the Pentagon. They entered the compound at three a.m., the dead time, moving swiftly towards the computer centres. They shot and knifed many guards and scientists. They managed to knock out a number of computer banks before they were surrounded. There was no way out. All of them were killed. The headlines should have read: LESBIAN TERRORISTS STORM PENTAGON WITH ORGASM-GUN. But of course not a scrap was leaked. They failed to stop the war. My father knew I had sympathies with them.

Me: *Who is your father?*
She: *Haven't you guessed yet? Let's talk about sex.*
Me: *What? Sex?*
She: *Yes. Why is it that men are so obsessed with sex? Why sex and not love, why surface pleasure and not DEPTH?*

The sun was lowering in the sky. I sat on the sand outside the telephone box. My arm ached from holding the receiver. And still the soft voice of the girl talked on and on, and still I was utterly mesmerized.

She: *Go on, ask me if I'm pushing a Hershey bar into my mouth, licking it all over, or if I'm pulling the gusset of my French knickers into my wet crotch. That's what you want to hear, isn't it?*

And I thought: yes, you passion-girl, rolling in the blue surf, your small round breasts naked, your face covered in red moondust, your hips swinging beautifully along the shore, your hot caresses, your angelic dark eyes, all of you so hot and gorgeous.

She: *You poor boy. Making a myth out of me is dangerous. You'll be disappointed and I'll be dissatisfied. You sack-clothed idiot. I'm not here for sex: I'm pregnant.*

Me: *You fake me. Where you are? I want you. You're delicious.*

She: *I'm not 'delicious'. I'm not an 'angel'. The reality is: I'm pregnant, which is more than gorgeous, more than angelic, more than everything. I suppose you are rubbing yourself, imagining me there, leaping up from behind a stone to lush you up good and proper, eh?*

She was right. I was touching myself. I wanted her. I wanted to know where she was, so I could swoop into her like an angel.

She: (Sadly) *I am totally alone. There is nothing left. This world will die in one day.*

Me: *Stop this shit. Stop it and come here and let's make love, in a cove, moving like two doves, you and me –*

She: *– You want love? At this time? At the End of the World?*

Me: *What else is there? I mean, WHAT ELSE IS THERE?*

She: *I'm tired and I'm alone and What Else Is There? You're not here. I saw a whole forest of trees today, flying over the moors; not a leaf on any one of them, all barren. Winter is here, and it's only Midsummer Day.*

The girl's voice oozed melancholy. Above me in the hemisphere of sapphire stars glinted magically. I wanted to kiss her, to kiss her, to kiss her.

She: *And a shoal of fish ran aground. I stared into their tiny, shining eyes.*

It was deep dark night now. A million memories suddenly swam into my mind. Masks; garden parties; television; clouds; houses; factories; fingers; clothes; colours; food; mountains; rivers; boats; trains; cars; mothers; fathers; tables; doors; chairs; churches; pools.

Faces began to swoop down out of the sky towards me. All the people I had known or seen. Friends, tramps, movie stars, TV personalities, children, a queue of pensioners outside a post office waiting at nine a.m. for their money. All those faces, all those people, zooming in and out of focus.

She: (Softly) *I feel insular tonight.*

Me: *Do you? Come here, my love. Let's go. Come to me. Vite, vite, plus vite. Now, now.*

She: Ahlan wa-sahlan. Ja peklo volam k pololi.

Me: *What? What?*

She: *I said: "I summon Hell to aid me".*

Then she laughed. It was gorgeous to hear that sound, that so-rare sound, of laughter.

She: *Excuse me a moment, I've got to piss.*

I heard the phone being put down.

Me: *All the houses and towns and villages, all of them to be burnt? All the music, sculptures and paintings made, all the books written and emotions sustained, all of them to go? For ever?*

All of the pain and the ecstasy? All of the gods and the goddesses? All of the homes and the trees and the people and the animals? All of the memories? All of the futures?

There was a pause, then she came back to the telephone.

She: *Yes. All of them will be burnt alive.*

Her words cut into me like hot wire. So this was the mass-suicide so eagerly desired by men in their insanity?

Me: *All of it?*

She: *Yes. All of it to die. All of it to burn. The maelstrom, the conflagration, the scorification.*

The telephone went silent for some time. A cool wind was blowing from the calm sea. The moonlight turned the surface silver. I lay back against the old red box, exhausted. I couldn't speak anymore. There was only one thing I wanted to hear. The girl finally said it.

She: *Meet me at Zanzibar Beach. Remember where it is? But don't come to me with all your old expectations – of love and romance. Don't ruin your chances, boy. Don't come to me expecting everything to be like it was before, all rosy and sweet. I'm changed. I'm growing. I've got a child inside me, expanding, growing.*

So don't bring your archaic notions of love with you. Forget all that.

We're going to begin again. We don't want to repeat the mistakes of the past ten thousand generations.

EIGHTEEN

Nuclear Winter

FUCKING YOU WAS like fainting, you passion-girl, in the heat of the beautiful day, in the light of the brilliant morning.

Jesus, you fucker, you fucking gorgeous being, blinding me with your passion-soaked love, coming down out of the clouds with your clothes billowing, laughing as the sun dazzled you, your soft mouth falling on me as we embraced in the radiance of the beautiful morning.

You were wet, hungry, livid with lust, frantic with fever, wind-blown across the mouth blown, passion-soaking me. Hot, hot, hot. Splintered, dazzled, with fevered eyes she slid my soul inside hers. We danced the death of the five thousand, the five billion billion.

We co-formed, we love-kissed, we passion-blissed. Kisses made by angels in the furnaces of heaven. There was nothing else now, just this, just you, just our love, the all-together-now love.

The world was lit up as if the moon had crashed into the ocean. A light so intense I squinted through shocked eyes. Out of the coruscating, rippling sheets of silver, you were a mermaid, a dolphin, a killer whale, a siren of the sea. Your eyes gleamed madly, your body glowed with the light of a billion galaxies.

With trembling hands I touched you, put my hands upon you. In your eyes swam the shivering remains of molten suns, collapsing white dwarf stars.

Your kisses were those of an angel, a mermaid, all bronze and gold. Closer than ever before our hearts beat together. Our tongues danced the music of the spheres.

Fucking you was like fainting into eternity. You beautiful beautiful passion-girl. You were sun-drenched, storm-wrenched and rain-wet. Excited beyond belief and in-deep, swollen and swooning.

Amazed, bedazzled, we danced through a landscape of crashed cars, burnt-out houses, raided supermarkets and storm-trooped villages. We danced through the smashed Western world. We ran through towns razed to the ground, through fields of burning corn, along clifftops soaked in blood, oil, tar, detergent and snow.

Down the ocean boulevard, past the swimming pool, in and out of the lighthouse and the dolphinarium, through the boatpark and circus and zoo we ran, with bodies hot and eyes shining. The grass sang, the trees hissed, the electricity pylons buzzed and the storm above throbbed and cracked.

You were so wet in the hot Zero Summer. Your teeth sparkled white in the stygian darkness of the thunder storm. The sun flared through enormous rain-clouds in the East. Your mouth opened so wide you took in the sun, the sky and the sea. Sex glowed through us. The heat was sultry, torrid, tropical.

Incandescent angels we were, shooting through the darkness and the light. We spent the whole day, the whole year, the whole era, making love.

'I can't wait to see the fireworks tonight,' you said, smiling.

Yes: the most expensive, the most dazzling firework display of all time – those billion-dollar nuclear missiles.

When the orgasms came they were tumultuous. I felt melted, drowned, blissed-out. We must have looked like two idiots, standing there on the beach. I wasn't aware of anything but you, you voluptuous maniac, you sun-scorched dream-girl with your hoarse voice and long wild hair and your staring green eyes.

I licked your neck, elbows, wrists, belly, knees, ankles. The sun burnt us up, deep, good and tight. You were as watery as an Amazonian jungle, drowning me on your rain forest floor, my face sunk in the lichen and fronds, the rushes and sedge.

You gasped madly. Your clitoris was a fish, wriggling and eager to hook an orgasm out of the sea's ooze. I loved this wet-wet passion. I pushed four fingers inside you, then my fist, my arm, my head, until you had all of me.

We squirmed on the sand like two mad eels, like two halves of a chopped worm trying to find each other, like two snakes writhing around each other, making concentric spirals in the sand.

'Our love is bigger than nuclear war,' you murmured, adding, 'Fuck me, fuck me, fuck it to me good.'

You gouged me gorgeously, your body arching up to the silently exploding sun. The sea boiled about our ears. There was water everywhere. I was blinded by the sun and drowned by the ocean. You bucked back onto me, rubbing your clit fiercely.

'Baise-moi. Vas-y. Ah, plus loin, plus profond. Ma chatte est pleine. Bourre-moi bien. Dans mon cul. Je vais jouir...'

You cried out as the orgasms of all the gods and goddesses coursed through you. I orgasmed like the chain-reactions inside the Bomb.

Big, wet and succulent orgasms. Earthquakes, volcanoes and tidal waves were as nothing compared to our catastrophe of love-making.

'¡Si!... ¡Me coro!... ¡Si!... ¡Mas fuerte!'

We fucked more powerfully than stars implode, more ecstatically than universes are flashed into being.

You were bendy as a jungle cat, purring and splaying your

thighs wide, fingers gripping your toes high in the air, staring at me through slitted and marvellous eyes, rubbing your clitoris voraciously in circles. I watched your labia opening and closing like a flower's petals around my prick.

You bent your knees back under your chin, so I could be even deeper inside you. You were dripping wet, the ocean flowed from your conch. You dragged my face into your wetness, all the while groaning, bucking your mound towards me manically.

'Fuck my cunt hard. Hard. Harder,' you whispered.

Your body was pink in the flush of orgasms. You spoke to me in a low, excited whisper:

'I want to fuck you all day. I want to fuck and fuck. I want you to fuck my brains out. I want us to fuck until we can't scream anymore. I love this passion, of mothers and sons, fathers and daughters, sisters and brothers, this incestuous passion-fucking.'

We lay side by side, legs entwined, kissing, writhing gently. Your thumb was in my mouth, my fingers in your mouth, sucking and licking.

Making love with you was like being on the ocean, rocking up and down slowly; like making love to a whale, so liquid and deep; you took me down to the dream-depths.

'We're Adam and Eva, the last people,' you said, smiling.

You pressed your hand under me and into my ass. I spread your round buttocks and did the same, my fingers and penis deep inside you. You moaned and turned your huge mouth to me once more, kissing me so voluptuously. My world became nothing but your vast lips and tongue.

As we fucked on the sun-baked beach in Cornwall, the rivers of the world were flooding in Florence, Cairo, London, New Orleans and Moscow. Tidal waves devastated Indonesia, Japan, Florida. Televisions and radios were dead. In Rome, Sao Paulo, Beijing and Los Angeles hordes rioted for the last time. There was no electricity anyplace.

People were murdered and had their gasmasks and anti-

215

radiation suits ripped off them. Millions had crammed all the drugs they had into their mouths. Streets were littered with overdoses. Skyscrapers blazed, unattended. The hills were full of wide-eyed families, crouched under tarpaulin or in make-shift pits, waiting in frozen fear for the final moment.

In Bethlehem, Jerusalem, Varanasi, Lhasa and Mecca crowds surged through the pulverized streets, begging for deliverance to Allah, Jehovah, Kali, Zoroaster, Jesus, Krishna, Buddha... to any deity would might listen, who might be able to help. Muezzins wailed from the minarets of the Maghreb, as they have always done, and the faithful bowed five times to Mecca. In Prague suicides lay in mounds, clutching copies of Kafka and Goethe. Mormons held hands in rings reciting prayers in bunkers in the Utah desert.

Black clouds of death drifted over Europe. Packs of ravening dogs followed hot on the heels of the plagues of rats to strip clean the corpses. Chemical and bacteriological weapons didn't seem to stop them.

The dense fogs reported flying above some built-up areas were not from fires, but were millions of insects.

Bugs. Bloody, sodding bugs. They were the only things that would definitely survive the war. (One of the reasons we stayed around the coasts was there seemed to be fewer insects there).

Battered bombers raced from Iran, Libya, Bangladesh, Vietnam, China, South Africa and Argentina towards America, Egypt, Russia, Australia, Korea, Israel, India and Japan, and back and forth, crisscrossing trajectories in red, green and white on the giant video screens of the world's war rooms.

'The 'world' isn't dying. *Some* people are killing *all* the people, a minority slaughtering everyone,' said the girl, rolling off me for a moment, 'but the world itself is still there, and it'll be around a long time after this Holocaust.'

The girl rose with a grin and leapt up onto a rock. She thrust her hips forward and pulled apart her glistening labia.

216

'Look!' she yelled. 'This is where real power resides among people. Right here.'

She cackled with laughter and sailed down upon me through the æstival air. She sprouted wings and claws and landed on me with a squeal, tearing at my baked flesh.

In the sudorific heat we basked, making agamous love. She wrote secret messages in occult languages on my back as I thrust into her, deep as forever, moulding my mouth around hers, delighting in the feel of her flaming lips. Her mouth was a flower in full bloom – iris, rose, lily, gladioli. The sky changed colour every time we touched.

'This is our last noon, our last twilight, our last day,' said the girl, 'so we shouldn't sit about gassing blandly about sugar and tea and gossiping about 'nice things'. We should scream. I will scream. Listen –'

And she screamed at the top of her voice. As if in answer we heard a very distant boom.

We had a last swim in the sea, a last dance on the sand.

I told her we were travelling towards the Virgo cluster of galaxies at a million miles per hour, or two hundred and seventy-eight miles per second.

She yawned. She hated numbers ('men's stuff').

'This is the last of everything,' she said. 'Our last kiss, our last shared glances.'

Beyond the rocks a group of dolphins leapt out of the sea. We ran onto the cliffs, following them. Down below us five right whales were stranded on the shore. The girl climbed down to the gigantic creatures. She stroked them and sang to them and tried to cover them with water. You could see the fear in their eyes as they felt the full weight of gravity acting upon them for the first time. They were massive, and there was no way we could move them.

'At least after tonight there'll be no humans to come along and hack them to pieces,' the girl said ruefully.

We kept running to the sea and fetching tins of water; but it was hardly enough, and eventually we gave up. We couldn't save the whales.

We moved away from them, up the cliffs, unable to bear seeing them die.

The minutes were ticking by. Never had we been so aware of every second, of every single moment trickling through our fingers like sand. Savouring each bubble of time, but unable to stop the atomic decay down to Zero Time.

Dea—. I was afraid to say the word. D**th.

Satellites, computers and communications centres around the globe were buzzing on emergency power. You could see the air being crisscrossed with fizzing blue lines of electronic energy. The atmosphere was charged-up with technology, with infra-red sighting systems, radio waves, lasers and ultra-violet signals. I wondered if the whales down on the beach could intercept the voices filling the air around us, and what they would make of it.

Lima, Seoul, Baghdad, Osaka, Wellington and many other cities had been hit the day before. Our turn was next. They would wait for night. Above us we saw the streaks of jet-trails: second-stage missiles heading for the continent. Hope, faith and laughter had long since died.

We ran into the fields to collect together the stuff we'd need for the final night. A group of horses galloped past us, throwing back their magnificent heads. Britain hardly looked the same anymore: fields were burnt or littered; trees were scorched, or leafless, or split in two. Plumes of smoke rose from distant towns, the wreckage of the Goonhilly Earth Station sending up the biggest poisonous trail. Poor old Beany.

We passed some oak trees decked out with red ribbons, relics of an earlier age. Drains and heaps of trash stank. Bones lay about – of pigs, cows, goats and chickens. And humans.

We came across a few corpses, including someone the girl thought she knew: Kaspar, the anarchist we'd met in the Brighton riot, and later in the architect's house, the girl's one-time lover. I muttered I didn't think it was him, and walked away from the girl, kicking at a rat. She stood, frowning, looking down at the smashed-in skull.

'The blood's gone,' said the girl, catching up with me. 'The blood's in my womb now, nourishing my baby. The moon is full, and it is Midsummer Day.

'The tides are high. Everything is expanding. I am pregnant and growing. Nothing can stop me growing. Not death, not the war, not anything. We've loved so hard, and hard enough, I feel.'

The strangest thing was the silence. No birds, no tractors, no cars, no people, nothing. Just the wind breathing through the grass (and one or two insects buzzing).

We had found ecstasy in entropy. In amongst the national collapse we had found a deep and long-lasting love. Maybe it was delusion. Maybe the hypothalamus in our brains was merely pumping us with ecstasy. But in our self-delusion we were magnificent.

Never had the girl looked so beautiful, walking through the blasted landscape naked, with just a ragged T-shirt over her shoulders. She was as brown as chocolate. She was completely transformed. She pushed her belly forward as she walked, proud in her pregnancy. I walked utterly naked. I couldn't have cared if anyone saw me.

We were stunned to hear music drifting on the air. We climbed on top of a fallen standing stone to see a group of people frolicking in a nearby field. About twenty people were dancing to the merry sound of accordions, recorders, fiddles and skin drums. Two or three children beat on the drums happily with wooden beaters. Some of the mummers had blackened faces – others had blue or red or green faces and hands. They threw sticks and teazers into the air, shouting. An 'Obby 'Oss – the Hobby Horse of mediæval fairs – span and dipped in the centre. A horse's head and a cloak.

Someone saw us and called us over. We must have looked bizarre, standing there on the stone, nude, silhouetted against the golden afternoon sky.

Hardly a word was spoken as we joined in the dance. I saw a sea of haggard faces as I jigged with the girl. She beamed. Some of the women had flowers in their hair – myrtle, jonquil, and white roses.

This was the happiest we had seen people for a long time and still we danced with the band of merry makers. No one seemed to notice that we were naked, and a couple joined us, shedding their clothes.

But the day was wearing on. We left the folky, pagan group. The girl dived into an empty house and came out with a bundle of things. She held her nose. The stench was incredible – a whole herd of mastodons must have been decaying in there.

When we had gathered together a heap of useful items – candles, rope, tins – we sat down in the shade of a tiny Norman church.

The girl pulled out a torn piece of paper. It was her father's last message. She read it out loud:

'The nuclear assault on Britain and Europe will occur at two or three a.m., the dead time. Every kind of warhead will be used: SS-18, T4, CC-NX-4, SS-NX-20, MSBS-20. Total world nuclear delivery in the full-scale exchange will be between 30,000 and 50,000 megatons. In other words, maximum blackout, a comprehensive wipe-out that will destroy every city, town and village, and all the livestock, plantcrop and animal kingdoms of the world.

'The chances of survival in the open are minimal, on any of the Western continents. Winds and atmospheric changes will send radiation around the globe within ten days, with levels in excess of 500 rads. Blast waves and heat flashes will create firestorms over major cities and communications and missile emplacements. Ground shocks will cause major earthquakes and tectonic shifts.

'There are over 20,000 targets, some soft, some hard. In the panic of the exchange, major computer communications centres will be demolished. Without higher command, the military groups will make many mistakes. Nations aiming to hit Europe include Iran, Iraq, Libya, Russia, India, South Africa, Korea, Indonesia and Argentina. The colonial countries will hit back at their one-time colonizers.

'In the panic to disarm and depth-charge submarines there will be dog-fights between bombers and jets, satellites and the headquarters of nuclear nations. In the collisions that ensue, some subs will be destroyed, leaking out radiation into the oceans, in all directions.

'The blast waves and heat flashes on the West Coast of America will constitute a holocaust in themselves, making a molten mass of atomic energy. New York and Washington will receive at least ten missiles each, some from pirate submarines in the Arctic ocean. Moscow will be sunk under at least fifteen megatons. As many command centres surround Moscow itself, many of these will be knocked out.

'More mistakes will be made. Some missiles will explode on the home-sender's ground. As delivery systems, in the form of bombers, satellites, subs and underground silos, are overloaded with cross-referenced targets, confusions will ensure ignition and targetting mistakes. There will be faulty launches and some missiles will explode in their silos.

'Launch mode is *hot.*

'The number of people killed instantly will be about a thousand million or more. The number of people killed in the next hour after detonation will be approximately 600 million. In the next five hours, over two-thirds of human life will be dead or dying. After two weeks the number of people surviving is estimated at about two hundred million. Of these only twenty million will be alive after six weeks.

'The politicians evacuated to the stations on the moon will be looking at a planet which will have been subjected to about thirty thousand nuclear explosions. There is a star in the galaxy for every person ever lived on Earth. And there is a fragment of a nuclear explosion for every person living on Earth now. Every human being will receive their own dose of the Holocaust.

'With the huge amount of nuclear megatons being exploded in such a short time (two or three hours), the effects on the atmosphere and ecosphere are hard to predict.

'All animals apart from insects will be destroyed, or fatally wounded. The soil will become barren. The power-failures will mean even more mistakes in the launch centres. The communications network, which has powered the planet with news, entertainment and decisions for decades, will be destroyed overnight. Without any clear picture of the situation, no nation will be able to decide on the next course of action. There will be no burial of the dead, for instance.

'Bombers which have delivered warheads may be able to ride the blast waves, but they will return to airfields decimated by the enemy. Many will crash. Warships will be the first to be hit by marauding enemy fighters. No frigates, destroyers or aircraft carriers will survive the first hour of the exchange. Subs will survive, but no dockyards will be left after the first hour. All airports, harbours, shipyards, silos, bunkers, command centres and sub-arctic bases will be the first targets of any force.

'Some regions, in which nuclear bombs will be detonating simultaneously, will become pure firestorms: Northern Europe, the Far East, the Gulf, the Levant, European Russia, and the West and East Coasts of America. Even the deepest fall-out shelters and bunkers will be smothered by flying debris from five hundred or more major cities as they are vaporized. Billions of kilograms of fission and fusion. A million out-of-bounds zones. One gigantic waste land.'

It was Midsummer, in the Year of the Snake, the Year of Thirteen Moons, the end of the Age of Pisces, with Pluto in Scorpio and Neptune in Taurus, and the number 666 printed on all the missiles.

And God looked at the thermonuclear detonation, and saw that it was *good*, I thought.

And we looked up into the heavens and we saw an angel standing in the sun. And we saw four angels at the four corners of the Earth, staring at us with eyes of ice. And we saw the New Jerusalem coming down out of the clouds, and we saw that it was *good*. The Word was made Flesh, the Alpha and the Omega reigned, and we celebrated the Death Of The Five Thousand, no, make that the Ten Billion Billion.

The City of God was a boiling mass of atomic light. We heard bells peeling and human bones cracking. And we saw that all this was *good*. Was that a voice we could hear?… a voice crying *'My God, my God, why hast Thou forsaken me?'*

The girl said we were witnessing the death of religion, of culture, of faith, of all people.

'As it was in the Beginning,' she intoned, 'so it will be in the End. All the connections between sex, violence, power, money, child abuse, rape, big business and poverty have been made.'

The girl stood behind me. To our left the whales were dying on the darkened strand. The sky was full of smoke. We saw the glow in the East brightening – the false dawn, the new clear dawn, the nuclear war.

The walls of heaven had cracked open and we saw hundreds of angels tumbling down to Earth, each one leaving a smoke trail. There were angels all about us, zooming manically, their wings folding back to reveal the grey, black and orange shapes of nuclear missiles.

The sun burst through the clouds. We began to prepare ourselves. The girl drew a circle on the sand, nine feet in diameter. It was a magic circle, she explained. She placed four candles at each of the cardinal points. She drew other shapes in the sand with a knife: moons, stars, astrological signs, letters. She lay leaves she'd picked from some botanic garden on the sand outside the circle. She held my shoulders and stood me in the centre on the sand.

'Now, you are going to be our Robin Goodfellow, our Puck, our Green Man, our Jack-in-the-Green, our Fool. It is Midsummer and you are the King, about to be sacrificed.'

Christ, I thought: she's going to kill me.

But the girl had other ideas. She stood behind me and ran her fingers lightly up and down my penis, erecting me gently, like playing a flute. I would be her Pan, her Goat-God with cloven-hoofs and fiendish horns. Already I could feel my legs sprouting fur and hooves.

I turned and kissed her. She was as radiant as hell, her mouth as hot as an atomic fireball. She ate me whole. She ground herself on me, licking my ears and my tongue, in tiny movements that drove me wild.

She could turn despair into ecstasy, boredom into beingness. She crushed me in her arms and we made love feverishly. Another nuclear firework glittered through the evening sky. Dark blue waves washed up the shore. Dolphins danced beyond the rocks.

She tipped some perfumed oil over me, rubbing it into my skin. She was murmuring to herself, about what I couldn't say.

She was seething – with lust and passion-soak. Her tongue was like a lizard's, licking me with maddening dabs. We perspired in the hot rush of sex, diving like fishes into the blood of passion, drowning like witches as we screamed in orgasm. Her mouth was bigger than the sky, a deep crimson rose of bliss, kissing me, kissing me.

The girl put furs on me, and antlers and bells. We danced like American Indians, like shamans, lifting our knees and arms rhythmically, head down, caught up in a trance. We pounded the sand in the magic circle and chanted. The girl wound ribbons around us – taken from an oak tree. She strewed us with flowers.

'Speak the unspoken things,' she murmured. 'Take me down to the places of heat and energy. Take me over the Edge. I am ready for the darkness.'

When she said things like that I thought I would burst with

joy. But I didn't know what to do. Where was the 'Edge'? What was it? And how could I take her over it?

She was pregnant.

She was pregnant and she was hot with life. Life was surging through her. There was more fire inside her than in any atomic bomb. She didn't kill a million people when she exploded – she created them. Already we could feel the Earth shaking as thousands of megatons scattered pain and madness over the body of the planet.

Clouds hot and orange loomed large and low. Our candent love-making was lightening the sky. The Full Moon was rising. Below us the tectonic plates manœuvred obscurely. New mountain ranges were formed as we fucked.

Christ but God I was hot. The heat from the molten white core of the planet gushed into our orgasms. Your eyes were so hot, so radiant. The sky rippled with a million flickering silver flames.

Then the cold came: there was ice everywhere. Icebergs rotated slowly in the bay. But we were burning. The icebergs toppled and slid into my head. Another missile hit some airfield or town, thirty miles away from us. The firestorm was building over Southern Britain. Warm water dripped over us. We choked on crimson dust.

Ecstasy and death kissed us. We were being transformed. I felt new arms, new limbs appearing on me. You became a chimera, a lion, fish, bird, gazelle, moving through a portfolio of mythical beasts.

You were a witch-girl, flaming me up into ecstasy. Ecstasy flickered out in points of light at the ends of your hair. There was a delicious sense of being alive, breathlessly alive, so hot and feverish. Passion burnt us in a heap of flames and water flooded us in blood-coloured coolness.

In the tropical madness of thermonuclear explosions we became everything we'd hated, everything we thought we'd left behind: gods, cages, houses, trucks, nightmares, skyscrapers.

Making love with you was like writhing with an angel

covered in silver paint.

Making love with you was like coiling around a serpent under thousands of tons of azure water.

You wore dresses of purple silk and swam six feet above the sand in a sky of sepia. When I grabbed you, you said I was an ogre, with a black head and eyes of blood-red. The icebergs cracked again and more whales fell upon the land, offering themselves up as a sacrifice.

'Stop the fire,' you said.

You turned to face the moon.

'Give me a Full Moon Fuck,' you groaned.

Kneeling behind you, I rubbed my face in your wetness, spreading your buttocks apart and burying my tongue in your ass. I hugged you close. You rocked your hips back at me, round and round, up and back, back and forth. I held my cock and pushed it slowly inside you. We made love gently. I squeezed your breasts as you rolled your bottom around. You bent forward, clasping your ankles, wrenching your hips about madly. I pumped into you deeply, moving faster, harder. You pushed back onto me fiercely. You opened your mouth and swallowed the moon. I yelled as the orgasms overlook us. You were so juicy, ramming back to me, going wild with desire.

'Fuck me harder. Fuck me good,' you groaned. 'Ram in deeper – in in in in. I love to feel your hard cock inside me.'

I pushed in as deep as forever. We were hot, hot, hot. We orgasmed in brilliant flashes of white and hot deep dark explosions of loving. The full moon fell out of the clouds. The girl threw her arms high, to welcome the moon like a witch. I pulsed inside her, gripping her asscheeks. She turned her head and kissed me.

'We are brilliant creatures,' she whispered above the roars. 'We've sucked the energy out of the world. We can STOP THE FIRE. Orgasm me.'

Surrounded by fifty million children on the beach, all of them staring at us silently, we made love furiously. She hit me, licked me, kicked me, scratched me, thumped my sides as I pounded into her voluptuously. Her eyes opened wide and she laughed wildly as I banged into her very fast. She hooked her knees behind my arms, splayed her legs wide and held her ankles. Fierce loving.

She bunched her legs up beneath me, so she was doubled up, her knees under her chin, her body opened up for very deep thrusts. I rammed inside her deeper than ever before. Six strokes shallow then one deep. Pulling out to the lips and teasing her.

'Forget the sex yoga, that *Kama Sutra*, Taoist stuff,' she grunted, 'and fuck me hard.'

We fell over the Edge. Going deep, and then deeper still.

'We live in a New Clear Reality,' she murmured, stroking my blood-wet face. 'A Universe of Light. I'm so happy to be young and in suck. To be blissed-out by the idiocy of my lover. It's Christmas Day, Independence Day, Day of All Saints and All Martyrs. This is Idiot Day and Get-Married Day, Armistice Day, D-Day, Departure Day, the Winter and Summer Solstices in one, the End of the post-war, post-apocalyptic, post-everything era. Hail Mary. Kiss me.'

She giggled, poured perfumed oil over me and pressed a chocolate into my mouth.

'Eat me,' she ordered.

We started to gnaw at each other's shins and wrists, like animals. She put another chocolate egg into my mouth, licking me like a jungle cat. I spread my legs and she squeezed hers together, lying on top of me, trapping my hard-on. We rolled, and she undulated underneath me like a mermaid. Her hair swamped me. She bit my nipples.

A siren from some distant lighthouse howled like a woe-begone wolf. She swivelled, lowering her humid, peeled-apart slit over me, taking my prick into her mouth, stroking me, sucking my balls with swollen lips. I held her clitoris between my lips. It was as big as a galleon. It filled my mouth, an ever-expanding fruit.

Our bodies were stretched so wide, so open, as far as we could go.

She pressed a finger into my ass. I was straining upwards into her mouth, so high. We were so sore we could barely touch each other, and barely resist touching each other.

A bolt of lightning flickered out of the livid copper-hued clouds, a flame from the dragon's nostrils. I thought of the negatively-charged cloud bases igniting with the positive Earth and the positively-charged upper clouds. Cumulonimbus, nimbo-stratus, cirrus. Convection cells. Ball, fork and sheet lightning.

After the initial leader stroke the lightning connects up with the Earth, ionizing the air to temperatures in excess of 30,000° C. Energy in excess of half a million volts. That's power, I thought, that's real, natural power. There are 1,800 thunder storms on the planet at any one time.

'What's your launch mode?' asked the girl mysteriously. 'What's the nitrogen level in your soil? How are you charged-up, negative or positive? Is your launch mode hot? Cold? Anticipated? Negated? Delivered?'

Boom, bang, crash, crack, rumble, rumble – the blue forks and snakes of lightning fizzed about us, travelling at one-tenth of the speed of light. The ocean roared, the Earth shook, the sky boiled.

We saw rainbows, hail, mist, rain, snow, hurricanes, tidal waves, volcanoes. We saw a mirage printed on the clouds upside-down, of all the cities of the world burning, burning. We saw the *brockenspectre* – the image of ourselves like a shadow on the ochrous clouds: the image of a girl writhing atop a boy on a beach pulsing with light.

The Milky Way scintillated above. Flash-floods poured from the rivers and the lakes. Avalanches of snow and ice fell from grey crags. Then came the *klugelblitz* – the famous ball lightning, zipping past our ears, spinning out into the blackness over the ocean.

The sand was whipped up in miniature whirlpools. Amazing

rainfalls, raining cats, dogs, pitchforks, fish, crosses, human skulls and dust from the decimated deserts. Every meteorological extravaganza was thrown at us.

We saw extraordinary visions. Steeples and towers crashed about us; we saw cascades of bodies intertwined with the flying debris of ice rinks, fairgrounds, circuses, leisure parks, arcades, mazes, cinemas, caves, pools, zoos. We saw toys falling from the clouds – rag dolls, yoyos, puppets, skipping ropes, soldiers, animals.

All of human culture seemed to be up in the atmosphere, spinning, zooming, falling.

Cathedrals fell through the air, and trains, squares, statues, houses, trees, parks, lamps. Cornwall was booming and blazing with a chain of storms whipped up by hurricane winds racing off the blast waves inland. Europe, Asia, Africa, China, the Americas, Antartica – the whole planet was boiling into nothing. It was an Apocalypse lasting not a hundred days but two hours.

We were making love inside a cloud. Rain ripped into us. We slid down rainbows and caught snowflakes in our eyes. Lightning sparkled about our writhing bodies, caressing us with millions of volts of electricity.

'Remember when people asked "What would you do in your last four minutes of your life?"' the girl mused. 'You could tell all the men were thinking about squirting their dead juice into their latest flesh-phantasy. But where are the warning sirens? The panicking crowds?'

But we were doing exactly what people dreamt of – making love manically as the bombs dropped. In the last four minutes people didn't rush out and screw frenziedly. They didn't cheer, or shoot heroin, or sing songs. No. They stumbled, slipped, cowered, fell, urinated and defecated helplessly. Screams were drowned by the crash of rubble and the roar of the blast waves.

The girl drenched me with oil and sweat. We kissed. I pressed blood-soaked fingers onto her belly and breasts, nuzzling the child within her. She cackled like a witch, climbing up my body, locking her legs around my torso, bucking up and down crazily.

The air was full of dirt and debris now. The cyclones clashed above the smouldering ocean. Sheets of lightning collided with each other, like mile-wide panes of glass intersecting and smashing.

Each nuclear explosion creates 300 or so products: the sky was full of smoke, mist, gas, ash, dust, a billion combusting elements – sulphur, mercury, potassium, lead, gold.

A loud crack we heard could have been the pulverized lighthouse collapsing down the cliff. The false sunrise illuminated our faces with a weird fuscous glow. The world was puking, slobbering, choking, bubbling, steaming and wheezing like a senile old man on his last legs.

This was the zero hour, the dead time everyone had dreamt about. If only the people of ancient Babylon, Egypt, China and Rome could have been here; if only the priests and saints of mediæval Hell-fearing Europe could have been here: they would have loved it. This was the Big Bang to end our little universe.

Fucking her was like fainting into bliss. She thrashed around me while the world about us churned into dust. She was magical and I knew she could stop the Apocalypse if she tried hard enough, if we loved deep enough.

The girl held my head and said, 'Religion clings to a once-glorious Past, science looks to a better Future, but both of them were wrong. They both looked the wrong way, not to the present.

'So what about the present time? What now? A nuclear crucifixion. We're all on burning crosses.'

The girl opened her mouth and screamed but I couldn't hear a thing above the roar of the whirling wreckage. The thermonuclear Jehovah had stitched us up good and proper. We heard nothing but a billion shrieks all piled up on top of each other.

We raided the chicken farms and drank the holy water of irradiation. We entered the Death Shop and bought two kilos of holocaust. We grabbed fish from the air as they flew about like pollen on the breeze. We suffocated under millions of pounds-per-square-inch of air pressure and blast waves. We wandered around the atrocity exhibition and marvelled at the exhibits: human skulls, rotting flesh, tears set in glass boxes, mutilated bodies, engulfed houses, razed cities, fragments of fall-out blown up under microscopes.

We stood in the wrecked magic circle holding on to each other so tightly. The candles and leaves and flowers had all been ripped to shreds. Bonfires blazed behind us on the cliffs, flapping in the wind.

The girl gave me the five-fold kiss of occultism.

I was babbling. 'Listen to the voices of the angels,' I said.

Sure enough, high in the air, beyond the crash of waves and the hiss of rain, beyond the howl of bombs and the bellow of thunder, we could hear the voices of all the angels of the world, singing, mewling, bleating, screeching. We looked up and saw the stars and planets all shimmering. I was aquiver, slithering into the fabulous embraces of the girl.

And then, suddenly, it all came down on top of us. The whole world collapsed about our ears, on top of our bodies. This was the final airstrike, the Maximum Fake-Out, as the girl once called it.

It was our time to die.

We looked up and saw four candent angels zooming in towards us out of the black-red sky. They turned into dolphins, into whales, into missiles. With a horrendous crash they exploded somewhere behind us.

'DON'T LOOK AT THE FIRE!' yelled the girl.

The beach shook in the missile onslaught. We gasped as we watched the night implode upon itself. The sky shrank, as if receding before a tidal wave. A flash lit up the clouds. Then the intense heat, after a few seconds. We fell to the sand, writhing like speared animals.

A boom followed, which we took in our bellies, like thousands of windows breaking simultaneously. Time and space inploded upon themselves. We felt the rush of the hurricane, and the heat flashes of the bombs.

'WE'VE GOT TO MAKE LOVE WHEN IT HITS US. WE'VE GOT TO MAKE LOVE WHEN IT HITS US,' yelled the girl, again and again.

We were making love; we were talking, kissing, dancing – we were having a wild time. What more could we do? I wondered.

Another roar, another missile shot by overhead. The ocean responded with a tremendous mashing of waves. We were drenched. We crawled slowly up the beach.

Flames crackled above us. The roars of the sea, the storms, the bombs and the blast waves were deafening. The girl screamed to me:

'DON'T LOOK AT THE FIRE. DON'T LOOK UP. LOOK AT ME. LOOK AT ME! KISS ME. KISS ME.'

We were nude and burning. The girl wrenched her thighs wide and pulled me inside her. She was gasping in my ear but I couldn't hear her.

Out in the cities, in the streets, on the plains, in the battle-zones and the skyscraper towns, nothing was heard but the screeching wind which was hurtling around the globe, trying to equalize the pressure on every continent. The sky was scorched red, like a wound that would never heal. More flashes overhead. The girl threw me onto my back and straddled me gently.

I pushed into you, you so beautiful girl, you lithe witch-girl, with your hot eyes, your glowing face, your delicious body fucking me.

Rage and lust and agony burned your face. We were hotter than the bombs, the storms, the sea. Our bodies dislocated themselves, tracing beautiful arcs in the air as we made love. Stars crashed into the atmosphere. A million telephone boxes around the world exploded. Even the cathedrals exploded. Skyscrapers were torn down like paper huts. Trees became fireworks, igniting and burning up in seconds.

232

You were gorgeous, eyes shining, mouth open in a screaming smile. Soaked by the sea, we were forever bound up together by our love-making.

Swamps and marshes were fired into deserts in moments. Oceans froze and uncoupled with the Earth beneath them. The freed-up glaciers tumbled down from the North. Mountains collapsed. New hills were formed, new islands. Volcanoes sputtered like Roman candles.

We clung to each other. Passion-girl, you're beautiful with your body on fire, the baby in your womb lit up by our passion-soak lust-fever. Rainstorms bled over us. We were opened as never before. I pushed into your hot womb. You orgasmed in a flash of flames and pure energy.

'OH ISHTAR,' you bawled. '– LOOK AT THAT FIRE! SUCK IN THAT FIRE, EXPLODE IT ALL OVER US!'

Heaven, Earth and Hell shook and rang. We rejoiced in the air bursts and ground shocks, the firestorms and blast waves. The girl was magnificent, sucking in all the fire, all the pain and sadness of the world, all the centuries of hatred and agony, heartache and toil. She sucked it all in and made it beautiful again.

What a paradise we made of it, of blinding light. It was a brilliant day, a beautiful day.

I thought of all the people who have ever lived, all those billions of lives. But now there was no more Asia, or Africa, or Russia, or China, or Antartica, or America. No more England, no more of anything for us.

She was so gorgeous, sliding and splintering over me. We were squeezed together, fused together by heat and love.

We died, orgasmically, melting deliciously into each other. You in me and me in you, fading into the Zero Summer.

The fires would rage for months afterwards. The sky would be black, choked with fumes and wreckage and fall-out. One or two humans might crawl out into the open, in the more remote parts of the Southern hemisphere. The moon would rise over an exhausted ocean.

Deep in the black water whales might still be swimming. A herd of whales might have swum deep, to avoid the explosions and earthquakes. They might surface from under the shifting pack-ice in the Arctic, or in the empty subtropical seas. The moon might be shining dully from behind clouds of smoke. The whales might sing to each other in their eerie, high-pitched voices, wondering how much longer they had to live.

J.R.R. Tolkien
The Books, The Films, The Whole Cultural Phenomenon

by Jeremy Mark Robinson

A new critical study of J.R.R. Tolkien, creator of Middle-earth and author of *The Lord of the Rings, The Hobbit* and *The Silmarillion*, among other books.
This new critical study explores Tolkien's major writings (*The Lord of the Rings, The Hobbit, Beowulf: The Monster and the Critics, The Letters, The Silmarillion* and *The History of Middle-earth* volumes); Tolkien and fairy tales; the mythological, political and religious aspects of Tolkien's Middle-earth; the critics' response to Tolkien's fiction over the decades; the Tolkien industry (merchandizing, toys, role-playing games, posters, Tolkien societies, conferences and the like); Tolkien in visual and fantasy art; the cultural aspects of The Lord of the Rings (from the 1950s to the present); Tolkien's fiction's relationship with other fantasy fiction, such as C.S. Lewis and *Harry Potter*; and the TV, radio and film versions of Tolkien's books, including the 2001-03 Hollywood interpretations of *The Lord of the Rings*.
This new book draws on contemporary cultural theory and analysis and offers a sympathetic and illuminating (and sceptical) account of the Tolkien phenomenon. This book is designed to appeal to the general reader (and viewer) of Tolkien: it is written in a clear, jargon-free and easily-accessible style.

754pp   ISBN 1-86171-057-7   £25.00 / $37.50

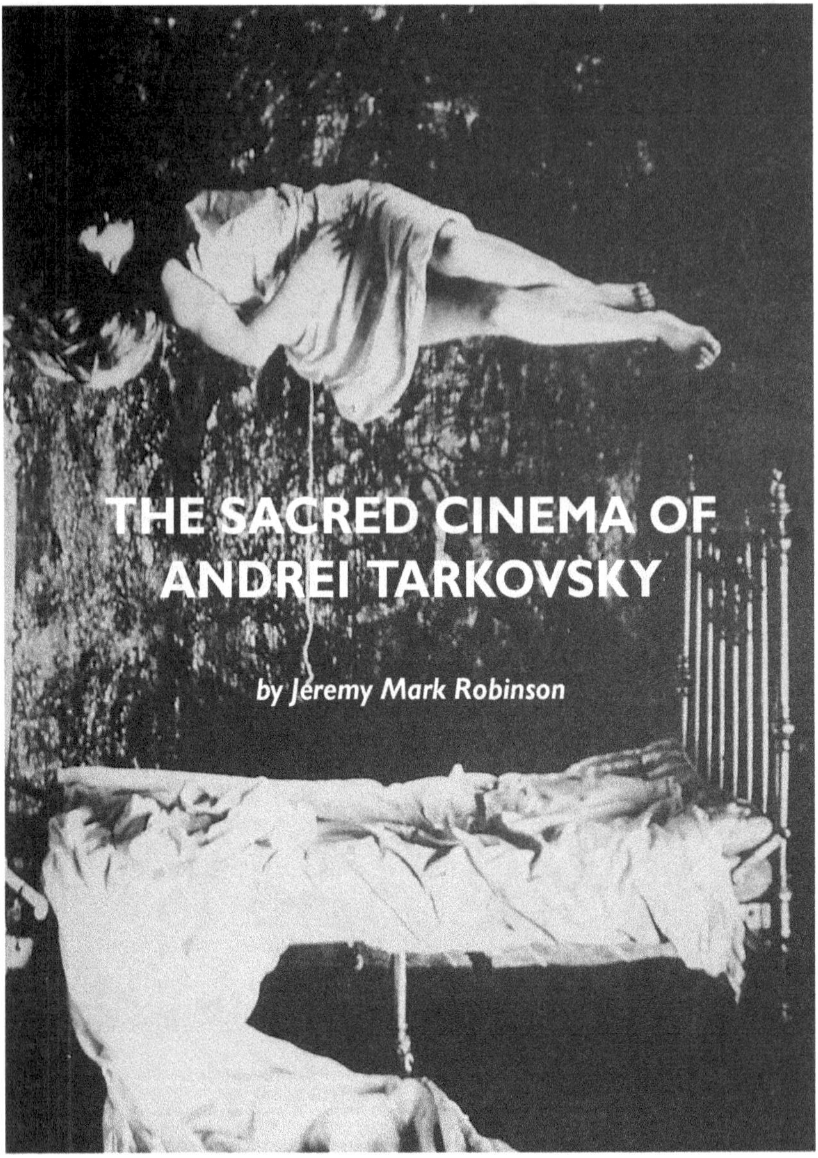

THE SACRED CINEMA OF
ANDREI TARKOVSKY

by Jeremy Mark Robinson

A new study of the Russian filmmaker Andrei Tarkovsky (1932-1986), director of seven feature films, including *Andrei Roublyov, Mirror, Solaris, Stalker* and *The Sacrifice*.

This is one of the most comprehensive and detailed studies of Tarkovsky's cinema available. Every film is explored in depth, with scene-by-scene analyses. All aspects of Tarkovsky's output are critiqued, including editing, camera, staging, script, budget, collaborations, production, sound, music, performance and spirituality. Tarkovsky is placed with a European New Wave tradition of filmmaking, alongside directors like Ingmar Bergman, Carl Theodor Dreyer, Pier Paolo Pasolini and Robert Bresson.

An essential addition to film studies.

Illustrations: 150 b/w, 4 colour. 682 pages. First edition. Hardback.

Publisher: Crescent Moon Publishing. Distributor: Gardners Books.

ISBN 1-86171-096-8 (9781861710963) £60.00 / $105.00

The Best of Peter Redgrove's Poetry
The Book of Wonders

by Peter Redgrove, edited and introduced by Jeremy Robinson

Poems of wet shirts and 'wonder-awakening dresses'; honey, wasps and bees; orchards and apples; rivers, seas and tides; storms, rain, weather and clouds; waterworks; labyrinths; amazing perfumes; the Cornish landscape (Penzance, Perranporth, Falmouth, Boscastle, the Lizard and Scilly Isles); the sixth sense and 'extra-sensuous perception'; witchcraft; alchemical vessels and laboratories; yoga; menstruation; mines, minerals and stones; sand dunes; mud-baths; mythology; dreaming; vulvas; and lots of sex magic. This book gathers together poetry (and prose) from every stage of Redgrove's career, and every book. It includes pieces that have only appeared in small presses and magazines, and in uncollected form.

'Peter Redgrove is really an extraordinary poet' (George Szirtes, *Quarto* magazine)
'Peter Redgrove is one of the few significant poets now writing... His 'means' are indeed brilliant and delightful. Technically he is a poet essentially of brilliant and unexpected images...he never disappoints' (Kathleen Raine, *Temenos* magazine).

240pp   ISBN 1-86171-063-1   2nd edition   £19.99 / $29.50

Sex–Magic–Poetry–Cornwall
A Flood of Poems

by Peter Redgrove. Edited with an essay by Jeremy Robinson

A marvellous collection of poems by one of Britain's best but underrated poets, Peter Redgrove. This book brings together some of Redgrove's wildest and most passionate works, creating a 'flood' of poetry. Philip Hobsbaum called Redgrove 'the great poet of our time', while Angela Carter said: 'Redgrove's language can light up a page.' Redgrove ranks alongside Ted Hughes and Sylvia Plath. He is in every way a 'major poet'. Robinson's essay analyzes all of Redgrove's poetic work, including his use of sex magic, natural science, menstruation, psychology, myth, alchemy and feminism.
A new edition, including a new introduction, new preface and new bibliography.

'Robinson's enthusiasm is winning, and his perceptive readings are supported by a very useful bibliography' (*Acumen* magazine)
'*Sex-Magic-Poetry-Cornwall* is a very rich essay... It is like a brightly-lighted box. (Peter Redgrove)
'This is an excellent selection of poetry and an extensive essay on the themes and theories of this unusual poet by Jeremy Robinson' (*Chapman* magazine)

220pp   New, 3rd edition   ISBN 1-86171-070-4   £14.99 / $23.50

THE ART OF
ANDY GOLDSWORTHY

COMPLETE WORKS: SPECIAL EDITION
(PAPERBACK and HARDBACK)

by William Malpas

A new, special edition of the study of the contemporary British sculptor, Andy Goldsworthy, including a new introduction, new bibliography and many new illustrations.

This is the most comprehensive, up-to-date, well-researched and in-depth account of Goldsworthy's art available anywhere.

Andy Goldsworthy makes land art. His sculpture is a sensitive, intuitive response to nature, light, time, growth, the seasons and the earth. Goldsworthy's environmental art is becoming ever more popular: 1993's art book *Stone* was a bestseller; the press raved about Goldsworthy taking over a number of London West End art galleries in 1994; during 1995 Goldsworthy designed a set of Royal Mail stamps and had a show at the British Museum. Malpas surveys all of Goldsworthy's art, and analyzes his relation with other land artists such as Robert Smithson, Walter de Maria, Richard Long and David Nash, and his place in the contemporary British art scene.

The Art of Andy Goldsworthy discusses all of Goldsworthy's important and recent exhibitions and books, including the *Sheepfolds* project; the TV documentaries; *Wood* (1996); the New York Holocaust memorial (2003); and Goldsworthy's collaboration on a dance performance.

Illustrations: 70 b/w, 1 colour. 330 pages. New, special, 2nd edition. Publisher: Crescent Moon Publishing. Distributor: Gardners Books.

ISBN 1-86171-059-3 (9781861710598) (Paperback) £25.00 / $44.00

ISBN 1-86171-080-1 (9781861710802) (Hardback) £60.00 / $105.00

CRESCENT MOON PUBLISHING

ARTS, PAINTING, SCULPTURE

The Art of Andy Goldsworthy: Complete Works(Pbk)
The Art of Andy Goldsworthy: Complete Works (Hbk)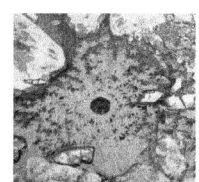
Andy Goldsworthy in Close-Up (Pbk)
Andy Goldsworthy in Close-Up (Hbk)
Land Art: A Complete Guide
Richard Long: The Art of Walking
The Art of Richard Long: Complete Works (Pbk)
The Art of Richard Long: Complete Works (Hbk)
Richard Long in Close-Up
Land Art In the UK
Land Art in Close-Up
Installation Art in Close-Up
Minimal Art and Artists In the 1960s and After
Colourfield Painting
Land Art DVD, TV documentary
Andy Goldsworthy DVD, TV documentary
The Erotic Object: Sexuality in Sculpture From Prehistory to the Present Day
Sex in Art: Pornography and Pleasure in Painting and Sculpture
Postwar Art
Sacred Gardens: The Garden in Myth, Religion and Art
Glorification: Religious Abstraction in Renaissance and 20th Century Art
Early Netherlandish Painting
Leonardo da Vinci
Piero della Francesca
Giovanni Bellini
Fra Angelico: Art and Religion in the Renaissance
Mark Rothko: The Art of Transcendence
Frank Stella: American Abstract Artist
Jasper Johns: Painting By Numbers
Brice Marden
Alison Wilding: The Embrace of Sculpture
Vincent van Gogh: Visionary Landscapes
Eric Gill: Nuptials of God
Constantin Brancusi: Sculpting the Essence of Things
Max Beckmann
Egon Schiele: Sex and Death In Purple Stockings
Delizioso Fotografico Fervore: Works In Process 1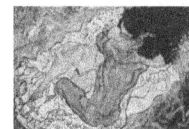
Sacro Cuore: Works In Process 2
The Light Eternal: J.M.W. Turner
The Madonna Glorified: Karen Arthurs

LITERATURE

J.R.R. Tolkien: The Books, The Films, The Whole Cultural Phenomenon
Harry Potter
Sexing Hardy: Thomas Hardy and Feminism
Thomas Hardy's *Tess of the d'Urbervilles*
Thomas Hardy's *Jude the Obscure*
Thomas Hardy: The Tragic Novels
Love and Tragedy: Thomas Hardy
The Poetry of Landscape in Hardy
Wessex Revisited: Thomas Hardy and John Cowper Powys
Wolfgang Iser: Essays
Petrarch, Dante and the Troubadours
Maurice Sendak and the Art of Children's Book Illustration
Andrea Dworkin
Cixous, Irigaray, Kristeva: The *Jouissance* of French Feminism
Julia Kristeva: Art, Love, Melancholy, Philosophy, Semiotics and Psychoanalysis
Hélene Cixous I Love You: The *Jouissance* of Writing
Luce Irigaray: Lips, Kissing, and the Politics of Sexual Difference
Peter Redgrove: Here Comes the Flood
Peter Redgrove: Sex-Magic-Poetry-Cornwall
Lawrence Durrell: Between Love and Death, East and West
Love, Culture & Poetry: Lawrence Durrell
Cavafy: Anatomy of a Soul
German Romantic Poetry: Goethe, Novalis, Heine, Hölderlin, Schlegel, Schiller
Feminism and Shakespeare
Shakespeare: Selected Sonnets
Shakespeare: Love, Poetry & Magic
The Passion of D.H. Lawrence
D.H. Lawrence: Symbolic Landscapes
D.H. Lawrence: Infinite Sensual Violence
Rimbaud: Arthur Rimbaud and the Magic of Poetry
The Ecstasies of John Cowper Powys
Sensualism and Mythology: The Wessex Novels of John Cowper Powys
Amorous Life: John Cowper Powys and the Manifestation of Affectivity (H.W. Fawkner)
Postmodern Powys: New Essays on John Cowper Powys (Joe Boulter)
Rethinking Powys: Critical Essays on John Cowper Powys
Paul Bowles & Bernardo Bertolucci
Rainer Maria Rilke
In the Dim Void: Samuel Beckett
Samuel Beckett Goes into the Silence
André Gide: Fiction and Fervour
Jackie Collins and the Blockbuster Novel
Blinded By Her Light: The Love-Poetry of Robert Graves
The Passion of Colours: Travels In Mediterranean Lands
Poetic Forms
The Dolphin-Boy

POETRY

The Best of Peter Redgrove's Poetry
Peter Redgrove: Here Comes The Flood
Peter Redgrove: Sex-Magic-Poetry-Cornwall
Ursula Le Guin: Walking In Cornwall
Dante: Selections From the Vita Nuova
Petrarch, Dante and the Troubadours
William Shakespeare: Selected Sonnets
Blinded By Her Light: The Love-Poetry of Robert Graves
Emily Dickinson: Selected Poems
Emily Brontë: Poems
Thomas Hardy: Selected Poems
Percy Bysshe Shelley: Poems
John Keats: Selected Poems
D.H. Lawrence: Selected Poems
Edmund Spenser: Poems
John Donne: Poems
Henry Vaughan: Poems
Sir Thomas Wyatt: Poems
Robert Herrick: Selected Poems
Rilke: Space, Essence and Angels in the Poetry of Rainer Maria Rilke
Rainer Maria Rilke: Selected Poems
Friedrich Hölderlin: Selected Poems
Arseny Tarkovsky: Selected Poems
Arthur Rimbaud: Selected Poems
Arthur Rimbaud: A Season in Hell
Arthur Rimbaud and the Magic of Poetry
D.J. Enright: By-Blows
Jeremy Reed: Brigitte's Blue Heart
Jeremy Reed: Claudia Schiffer's Red Shoes
Gorgeous Little Orpheus
Radiance: New Poems
Crescent Moon Book of Nature Poetry
Crescent Moon Book of Love Poetry
Crescent Moon Book of Mystical Poetry
Crescent Moon Book of Elizabethan Love Poetry
Crescent Moon Book of Metaphysical Poetry
Crescent Moon Book of Romantic Poetry
Pagan America: New American Poetry

MEDIA, CINEMA, FEMINISM and CULTURAL STUDIES

J.R.R. Tolkien: The Books, The Films, The Whole Cultural Phenomenon
Harry Potter
Cixous, Irigaray, Kristeva: The *Jouissance* of French Feminism
Julia Kristeva: Art, Love, Melancholy, Philosophy, Semiotics and   Psychoanalysis
Luce Irigaray: Lips, Kissing, and the Politics of Sexual Difference
Hélene Cixous I Love You: The *Jouissance* of Writing
Andrea Dworkin
'Cosmo Woman': The World of Women's Magazines
Women in Pop Music
Discovering the Goddess (Geoffrey Ashe)
The Poetry of Cinema
The Sacred Cinema of Andrei Tarkovsky (Pbk and Hbk)
Paul Bowles & Bernardo Bertolucci
Media Hell: Radio, TV and the Press
An Open Letter to the BBC
Detonation Britain: Nuclear War in the UK
Feminism and Shakespeare
Wild Zones: Pornography, Art and Feminism
Sex in Art: Pornography and Pleasure in Painting and Sculpture
Sexing Hardy: Thomas Hardy and Feminism

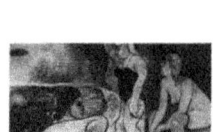

In my view *The Light Eternal* is among the very best of all the material I read on Turner. (Douglas Graham, director of the Turner Museum, Denver, Colorado)

The Light Eternal is a model monograph, an exemplary job. The subject matter of the book is beautifully organised and dead on beam. (Lawrence Durrell)

It is amazing for me to see my work treated with such passion and respect. (Andrea Dworkin)

Sex-Magic-Poetry-Cornwall is a very rich essay... It is like a brightly-lighted box. (Peter Redgrove)

CRESCENT MOON PUBLISHING
P.O. Box 393, Maidstone, Kent, ME14 5XU, United Kingdom.
01622-729593 (UK) 01144-1622-729593 (US) 0044-1622-729593 (other territories)
cresmopub@yahoo.co.uk   www.crescentmoon.org.uk